then there was you

Center Point
Large Print

Also by Kara Isaac and available from
Center Point Large Print:

Can't Help Falling

**This Large Print Book carries the
Seal of Approval of N.A.V.H.**

then there was you

KARA ISAAC

CENTER POINT LARGE PRINT
THORNDIKE, MAINE

This Center Point Large Print edition is published in the year 2019 by arrangement with the author. Published in association with MacGregor Literary, Inc.

Scripture quotation taken from the New International Version® Copyright ©1984 by Biblica Inc.® Used by permission. All rights reserved

The characters and events in this book are fictional, and any resemblance to actual characters or events is coincidental.

The text of this Large Print edition is unabridged. In other aspects, this book may vary from the original edition. Printed in the United States of America on permanent paper. Set in 16-point Times New Roman type.

ISBN: 978-1-64358-088-3

Library of Congress Cataloging-in-Publication Data

Names: Isaac, Kara, author.
Title: Then there was you / Kara Isaac.
Description: Point Large Print edition. | Thorndike, Maine : Center Point Large Print, 2019.
Identifiers: LCCN 2018052738 | ISBN 9781643580883 (hardcover : alk. paper)
Subjects: LCSH: Large type books. | GSAFD: Christian fiction. | Love stories.
Classification: LCC PR9639.4.I83 T48 2019 | DDC 823/.92—dc23
LC record available at https://lccn.loc.gov/2018052738

For the SisterChucks:

Jaime Jo Wright, Laurie Tomlinson,
Halee Matthews, Sarah Varland,
and Anne Love

There are no words that can ever express
how glad I am to be one of you!

ONE

Paige McAllister didn't think it was possible, but there was something worse than being single and thirty at your nineteen-year-old sister's wedding.

At least if you were single, you had hope that buried somewhere in the groom's collection of great-aunts, bucktoothed cousins, and inebriated, barely legal frat-boy friends, was the man of your dreams.

Instead, here she was, boyfriend AWOL, leaving her alone to face down the familial barbs about her aging ovaries.

"There you are, Paige." Right on time, the woman who could never pass up an opportunity to provide commentary on that very topic.

Paige attempted to turn around without the bustle on her bridesmaid dress taking out a small child. "Aunt Lillian. How are you?"

Her steely haired great-aunt offered a harrumph as she peered up at her niece. "Would be better if this was your wedding. Does Alex know that after thirty the risks of birth defects go up twenty percent every year?"

Apparently human biology had regressed in the

last six months. It had been thirty-five at the last family gathering. Paige kept her smile pasted on. "I'm sure Alex appreciates your concern. I'll be sure to let him know."

Another harrumph, followed by a jab to her side. "You haven't ruined yourself, have you? He'll never buy the cow if he's getting the milk for free."

Paige's already strained smile collapsed like a bad soufflé. "No, no milk." She was not having this conversation. Not with anyone, let alone an abrasive octogenarian. "If you'll excuse me, I think Sophie needs me for something."

She stepped around her great-aunt and worked through the crowd, scanning the buzzing ballroom for a glimpse of her boyfriend's trademark pinstripe suit. Nothing. She couldn't wait to hear what his excuse was this time. The one time she'd swallowed her pride and admitted she needed him, there was an empty pew space where he was supposed to be.

If only Ethan were here. Her brother could always make her laugh no matter what, and if there was ever an occasion where she needed a sense of humor, it was this one. He would've even been able to make the blue taffeta monstrosity she was trussed up in bearable.

No. Don't think about it. She blinked back tears. Searing grief had long since worn down to a dull ache. He was gone. But on days like this, it seemed like Ethan's absence took up more room than everyone present.

"Hey, Blondie. You look gorgeous." Alex's lips brushed her lobe, the whispered words tickling her ear. For a split second her body melted back into his.

No! "Where were you?" Paige spun around so fast he jumped back.

"What do you mean?" Alex's green eyes widened as he ran a hand through his tousled blond hair.

Wow. Even in her anger she couldn't help but appreciate how handsome he looked in his suit, shoulders made to appear even broader by the expert cut of the pinstripe fabric. No doubt it cost more than she earned in a month.

How was it possible to want to both kill and kiss someone in the same moment?

"You missed the wedding. Where were you?" She hissed the words, hyper aware of the various family members milling around them in the ballroom.

The ceremony, the photos, the dinner, the endless speeches, the mingling . . . all had conspired to keep her from hunting down her boyfriend. However, they had done nothing to cool her anger.

Alex threw her a crooked grin—the same grin that had captured her heart in the beginning and, despite everything, kept it ever since. The top two buttons of his white shirt were undone and his green tie hung loose. She battled the urge to strangle him with it.

"Oh, baby, I'm sorry. I got an urgent call from the office. I had to take it. You understand how it is." He rolled his eyes, but his expression revealed the pride he took in his apparent indispensability.

A searing jolt shot up her body, so strong she wouldn't have been surprised to see smoke coming out from underneath her poufy skirt. "Understand? Understand what? That your job is more important than me? Than my family?"

"Baby, don't be like that." He reached out for her hand but she snatched it away.

"Don't touch me."

"Paige." His tone was one normally used on preschoolers. "C'mon. So I missed the service? So what? It's not like it mattered. I'm here now." He stepped toward her, a mischievous smile on his face. "I've missed you." His fingers brushed the small of her back as he circled her waist, drawing her closer, lips moving toward hers.

She lurched back, thrusting one hand against his chest to keep him away. Her insides were melting, the way they always did when he used that smile on her. He was too much of a looker for her own good.

"Alex. You missed Sophie's wedding. All I

asked for was one day. And you couldn't even give me that. You knew how much I needed you. With Ethan gone and now Sophie . . ." She trailed off, self-preservation stopping her from uttering the next few words.

His eyes narrowed. "Oh. So that's what your little tantrum is about."

"Excuse me?"

"You're mad at me, all right. But not because I missed the service. You're mad because it wasn't you getting married. You're upset Sophie made it up the aisle first."

He knew her too well. Yet somehow not at all. She scanned the room, looking for an exit. They were so not having this discussion here. Grabbing his hand, she pulled him toward the nearest set of French doors.

"Paige." Nate's voice halted her mid-stride.

"What?" Paige swung around to face her friend.

Nate's steady supportive gaze tugged at her. "Sophie asked me to tell you they're having the first dance soon."

"Okay, great. Thanks." She summoned up an attempt at a breezy smile. Nate was the last person she wanted to know that she and Alex were having a fight.

Nate's blue eyes flickered from Paige to Alex and back again. "Is everything okay?"

"Fine. Great." The tremor in her voice betrayed her. Alex's accusation rang in her ears, his condescending tone compelling her to confront it. "Can you let Soph know I'll be there in a couple of minutes?"

Nate gave her a look that said he wasn't buying her assurances. "Sure."

Paige opened the French door, stepping onto the large terrace. Outdoor heaters had been set up to make outside more inviting but guests remained cloistered indoors. She and Alex were alone. Thank goodness.

"Is that what you think?" The words escaped before the latch had even clicked into place behind Alex. She kept her back to him, drawing a breath of the crisp evening air.

"That you're mad it's Sophie getting married and not you?"

She turned. Alex leaned against the balcony railing, arms propped up behind him, as if he hadn't a care in the world. Behind him, the lights of Chicago gave the appearance of a halo to match his angelic looks.

Paige walked across the terrace, away from him. She couldn't let him kiss her. If he did, she would relent and everything would return to the same old cycle. She turned back when there was a safe distance between them. "Yes."

Alex pushed himself up from the railing and walked toward her. "Well, it must be about more than me missing the service. That's hardly a big deal. It's not like I missed our wedding."

"And when exactly is that going to be?" Had she just—She gasped, her words enveloping the space between them. She had. She'd done it. Asked the question that'd haunted her for years. Her foot started, the nervous *tap tap tap* echoing from below.

"Excuse me?" He froze mid-stride.

She bit her lip, forcing herself not to take it back. Say it, say it again. "Our wedding. When is that going to be?" This time her words were slower, more measured. She forced herself to look him in the eye.

This was it. She was finally going to know where she stood. Would have been nice if it had been somewhere other than her sister's wedding, but beggars couldn't be choosers. And in this relationship, she was definitely the beggar.

Paige wrapped her arms around her waist and clutched her elbows, bracing herself. She'd suspected for a while she loved him more than he loved her, but recently she'd wondered if he loved her at all, or if he just managed to pull out some faux imitation of the real thing when required.

He looked at her, his gaze flickering. His face flashed with a multitude of emotions that she couldn't quite interpret. Fear? Disbelief? Shock?

"Baby, come on. We've discussed this. My career is rocketing ahead right now. It's not the time for me to settle down. Another year, and I should be established enough to think about it, but not now. It's not the right time."

Was he joking? Her toes were tapping so quickly her entire left leg jiggled.

"Another year?" Her voice rose as she tugged a piece of wayward hair behind her ear. "That's what you said five years ago, then three. That's what you said when you moved to Milan, then London."

She shoved down the poisonous accusations that bubbled up inside her. Ones that demanded to know what kind of guy went through with an international transfer when his girlfriend lay critically injured in hospital. She didn't need to ask what kind of girl let him. She knew. The kind who was too broken to fight. The kind who spent every second of every day wishing she hadn't been dealt the cruel hand of survival.

Alex pressed his lips together. "What do you want from me, babe? I'm here, aren't I? I'm with you now. Can't we just enjoy the time we have before I leave?"

What a waste. The words vibrated in her head as she saw for the first time what she knew her friends and family had seen for years. That her boyfriend's universe was only big enough for one star. That his life revolved around him and him alone. That she had put her life on hold waiting for someone who was never going to commit to her.

"You don't want to marry me." Her words were hushed. All her fight disappeared, replaced by surreal resignation.

"I what?" He stiffened.

"You don't want to marry me." His lack of denial sealed it. "I'm so stupid. All this time I've told myself you needed to get this out of your system. But I'm kidding myself. How could I have thought you loved me? After almost seven years together, it's too much to ask for you to live in the same country."

"Paige, don't . . ." He stepped toward her.

She shook her head. Stupid. So stupid. "Don't. I'm not mad at you." And she wasn't. She was furious with herself. "This is my own fault. I was the stupid wallflower girlfriend who let you take jobs all over the world. Who understood when you could only find time for me . . . what? Three, maybe four weeks a year? I should have made you choose a long time ago."

She rubbed her left arm, her fingers running along the familiar line of the scar that ran from wrist to elbow. The bones ached, signaling an upcoming change in the weather. A constant reminder of all she had lost.

"C'mon, baby. It's not like that. I love you. You know that. You're the only girl for me." He took one tentative step toward her, then another.

Paige flinched at the too-familiar words. She took a step back, then more, until the cool railing

15

pressed against her back. The same platitudes he rolled out so convincingly every time she dared press him for more than two separate lives lived thousands of miles apart.

"Do you? Want to marry me. Ever?" She didn't even know why she asked the question. Right now, she'd sooner hurl him off the balcony than pledge herself to him for better or worse.

He swallowed and searched her face. "Of course. One day. I just need more time."

She pushed herself away from the railing. *"Are you sure he's worth waiting for, Ping?"* Her brother's words echoed through her head. One of the few times he had ever questioned her decision.

She should have listened to Ethan, to everyone. To the disquiet on her parents' faces when yet another Christmas or birthday rolled around and he had another excuse not to be there. But no. Instead she allowed him to convince her that their relationship was *special*. Huh. The only thing special about it was that she was an especially good doormat.

Sure, there were his good looks and the undeniable chemistry they had when they were together—*when* being the key word.

It wasn't enough. She stared at him, standing only a body length away, and knew. She couldn't live anymore stuck in perpetual relationship limbo. She needed to end this tonight. While she had the courage and before he got back on his plane to London.

Tell him. Say it. She stepped back again, gripping the railing behind her. "Alex, I don't have any more time to give. It's been six years. If you don't want to marry me now, you're never going to." Her foot stilled as a wave of calm enveloped her.

Alex tugged at his cream cuffs, then further loosened his tie. "C'mon, baby. You don't mean that. I know it's not easy seeing Soph get married, but we're not them. We're different. We're special. Let's not ruin our last night together fighting. Let's go back inside, have fun, dance. I'll be back in July. We can talk then."

"We could, but we won't."

A sneer curled Alex's lip. "Oh, I get it."

"Get what?"

"Old puppy dog eyes in there has finally convinced you to give him a chance."

"Grow up, Alex. You know Nate and I are just friends. Stop trying to change the subject." No one else deserved to be dragged into this putrid conversation, let alone the one guy who had been nothing but good to her.

"Then let's both just take some time, talk this through in July. Tell you what, why don't I put some feelers out? See if there's space coming up in a US office."

She almost laughed. How many times had

he said those exact words when he sensed she was losing patience? She was tired of fighting. Exhausted from promises never kept. Of being made to feel like she was expecting too much. It was way past time for this to be over.

"Paige?" He snapped his fingers in the air.

She narrowed her eyes. Had he seriously snapped at her? "What?"

"Why can't we talk about this in July?"

"Because I won't be here." The words dropped out of her mouth before she'd even processed what she was going to say.

What was that? The flash of surprise on his face was no doubt matched by an identical one on hers.

"What do you mean?" Disbelief flickered across his features.

"I'm moving, Alex." Her mouth had bypassed her brain. Again. She was moving? Where?

"What? Where?" His tone was half incredulous, half suspicious.

"To . . . Sydney."

Sydney? Sure, Kat had been trying to convince her to get a work and holiday visa and spend a year on the other side of the planet, but as a joke!

He looked at her like she'd just said she was taking a spot on the next space shuttle. Then he let out a mocking laugh. "You realize that's in Australia, right? Which would require you getting on a p-l-a-n-e."

Like he was telling her anything she didn't already know. "I know where it is." She refused to even let herself think about the word he had just spelled out. "Kat loves it there. She already has a job lined up for me." That would be news to Kat. She hoped her cousin's comment that there were more jobs than water in Australia was accurate.

"No you're not." He said it decisively, as if he had inside knowledge. He tugged at his lapels then his cuffs again. "Good try, babe. You almost had me for a second, but c'mon. Your friends are here, your family, your job. We both know it's never going to happen."

He'd called her bluff. She had no plans to move. She was just having a temporary meltdown. His patronizing tone infuriated her. "Watch me."

For the first time in the conversation she saw a shadow of uncertainty cross his face.

"Paige!" Her sister's silhouette appeared in the doorway. "It's almost time for the first dance."

They didn't even turn, their eyes locked on each other. Neither willing, able, to give the other what they wanted.

"Is everything okay?" Sophie walked across the terrace, the cheesy lyrics of the latest hit love song following on her heels. She h _____
before she reached them. "Um, do _____
minute?"

Paige glanced at her. She was

grown-up in her princess wedding dress. "Every-thing's fine. Sorry, Soph." She turned back, her eyes meeting Alex's with finality. "We're finished."

She reached out for her sister's hand and walked toward the dance floor, where a teenage groomsman waited to mangle her feet.

Dear Lord. What had she just done?

Two

Three months later

Paige stared at the two boarding passes in her palm. O'Hare to LAX followed by flight QF12 direct to Sydney. She was actually doing this.

She, Paige Noreen McAllister, usually as impulsive as the average sloth, was moving to Australia.

For six years she'd existed, living in the shadows. Believing she didn't deserve better. Until she'd walked away from Alex and realized she couldn't live that life anymore.

All that remained was getting out of the bathroom, through security and onto the plane.

She sucked in a deep breath. She could leave the bathroom. That was a step forward, right?

"Are you okay, honey?" An African-American woman asked the question as she discarded her paper towel into the trash.

"Fine, thank you." Paige summoned up a tremulous smile as she shoved her boarding passes back into her purse and gathered up her carry-on. Her shoes echoed against the tiled floor as she navigated down the short hallway and back out into the noisy bustling departure terminal.

Making her way to the nearest set of screens, she triple-checked the gate number for her flight.

"Paige." The familiar voice bearing her name came from just behind her.

Oh, no. Please no. She cast a longing glance at the nearby doors, proclaiming "passengers only past this point." If only she'd waited until she was through security to find a bathroom.

She turned, searching for the face she knew she would find. "Nate."

"Hey." Her friend stopped in front of her.

"What are you doing here?" She ground the toe of her boot into the floor. She'd already navigated the emotional farewells last night. Which was why she'd decided to not tell anyone when her flight was cancelled. Nate, here, alone, was what she'd been trying to avoid.

"I was checking online and saw your flight got cancelled. Is everything okay?" His worried blue eyes stared into hers.

"Fine. My new flight leaves in a couple of hours and they got me on another one to Sydney so . . ." Paige trailed off, unsure of what to say next. She didn't want to ask what he was doing here. She knew the answer, and it wasn't one she wanted to hear.

The tightening in her temples signaled the impending arrival of a tension headache. The problem with a romantic declaration of love at an airport was that they were only romantic if the feelings went both ways.

She shifted on her feet then propped her violin case against the handle of her carry-on suitcase to give her a second to regroup. What now? Everyone thought she was oblivious to how Nate felt. At first, she was. By the time she'd realized that his feelings were more than platonic, it had seemed better to pretend she didn't know. Not to rock the boat.

Which had been the story of her life since Ethan died. The result? Over six years with a guy who never had to commit, a boss who never gave her the promotion she deserved, and allowing the shame of survival to turn her into a person that she no longer recognized and—if she was honest—didn't like a whole lot.

"Paige, there's something I have to say." Nate stepped closer, then reached out and took her hand.

She took a step back, only for something solid to slam straight into her shoulder and pitch her forward into Nate's arms.

"I'm so sorry. Are you okay?" A tall guy in a blue hoodie ran his hand through tousled dark hair, brow crinkled with concern.

"Fine. Totally my fault." She disentangled herself from Nate's hold.

"No, it was mine. I was distracted." The guy

had an accent that definitely wasn't American and nice grey eyes. He looked between the two of them, as if knowing he'd interrupted something. "Sorry about that, mate." With one last apologetic look he turned and merged back into the crowd.

Paige looked down to where Nate had grabbed her hand again, her stomach clenched. "I should get going too." She squeezed his hand, then attempted to untangle her fingers from his, but he held on tight. Oh, dear.

He took a deep breath, blue eyes smoldering, grasp now sweaty. Ugh. "Paige, I . . ."

She had to stop him. Stop him from saying the words he'd never be able to take back. They would ruin everything. It wasn't like she didn't love him. She did. Just not like that. "Nate, I know." She looked into his eyes, willing him to understand what she meant. *God, please let him get it.*

He searched her eyes, his brow furrowed.

"Nate." She squeezed his hand again. "You're an amazing friend. After Ethan died, I don't know what I would have done if you hadn't been there. I'm going to miss you so much. But I . . . I need to go. I need to work some things out for myself, and I can't do it here."

She saw the flash in his eyes. He got it. He sighed and mustered up a smile. "Well, you can't blame a guy for trying."

No, she couldn't. She blinked back tears. She

was going to miss him. But he was an amazing guy and deserved so much better than damaged goods. Maybe, with her out of the way, he might be able to find it.

"Hey. You're off on a big adventure. I'm so proud of you for doing this. Ethan would be too." Nate pulled her close and wrapped his arms around her.

The familiar scent of Hugo Boss enveloped her, his secure embrace easing her fears. Was she making a huge mistake? Was she going to find herself on the other side of the planet only to realize what she had been looking for was right in front of her? "Thank you."

He stepped back slowly and gave her hand a final squeeze. "Go, kiddo. The sooner you do, the sooner you'll come back to us."

His final words sucked the breath out of her. They'd been spoken before. By her mother. Standing in this very airport. Two weeks later, she'd come back broken beyond repair, and her brother had come back in a coffin.

THREE

"Ladies and gentlemen. The plane is now ready to board. Priority passengers are welcome to board now or at your leisure."

Josh Tyler took once last gulp of his lukewarm black coffee and shut his laptop. Not that there'd been any point opening it. Six weeks of bouncing around the US had caught up with him. He was so tired the screen was little more than a blur. Every movement was like fighting quicksand, his fast reflexes a distant memory.

He hoped he hadn't ruined that proposal in the terminal when he'd mowed over the blonde girl. He wasn't lying when he said he'd been distracted. He had been—by the look of adoration on the guy's face and the feeling he was about to drop down on one knee.

Then the woman had stepped back at the same time he'd swerved to miss an abandoned luggage cart, and . . .well, he hoped one day they'd be able to look back and laugh at the stupid foreigner who almost kiboshed their big moment.

Which reminded him, he needed to stop into David Jones when he got back to Sydney and

26

replenish his wedding gift stash. James and Evelyn's was this weekend. And he'd missed three others while he was away.

Shoving his laptop back into his carry-on, he stood. At least this time he was just a groomsman, not best man, so he didn't have to worry about a speech. Instead, he'd spend his energies trying to avoid slow dancing with any single girls and giving them the mistaken impression he was interested in something more. He'd had his chance at love and ruined it. Didn't deserve another. It was better, safer, that he lived the life of a nomad. Always soon to be on a plane to somewhere else, usually never to return to where he'd just been.

He grabbed his bags, tried to shake off the cloud hanging over him and headed toward the lounge exit. Home. He needed to be home. A few days of chilling out with the guys would get him back into sorts.

"Pastor Tyler?" The lounge attendant's interruption was so timid he almost missed it.

Mr. Tyler. Josh. He battled the instinct to correct her. Pastor Tyler was his father. If there was one thing he never wanted to be, it was a pastor. "Yes?"

"I hate to bother you but, well, my daughter is a big fan . . ." Her voice trailed off as she held out a copy of Due North's latest album.

"Sure. Of course." He reached into his pocket

for his ever-faithful companion, the black marker. It had been a long time since he'd signed a CD. The iPod generation preferred glossy photos and T-shirts. "What's your daughter's name?" He peeked at her nametag. "Christine."

"Zoe. No y."

He pulled the lid off the marker with his mouth and quickly scrawled, *To Zoe. Enjoy. And keep on going for God! Josh Tyler.* He winced at the cliché. It was his default when he was too tired, too busy, or too over-it to think of anything original. So-called talented songwriter he may be, but gifted autograph crafter he was not.

"There you go." He returned it with a smile. Always with a smile. It was the one thing his mother had drilled into his family. They had plenty of people wanting to take a swipe at them. Appearing arrogant or uninterested in public was a luxury they couldn't afford.

"Thank you so much. I can't begin to tell you how much this will mean to her." Her face flushed with gratitude, the CD case clutched to her chest.

His stiff smile relaxed into a genuine one. This was what it was about—real people who got up before dawn to go to work, trying to give their kids a better life than they'd had.

He grabbed his bag and got moving before melancholy could overtake him. A wife. Kids. He didn't deserve any of it. It was better to just not wish for things he'd proven himself unworthy of.

16E. Never did Paige think she'd be grateful for a middle seat but she was. If she was lucky, maybe she'd land a fellow flyer with bad body odor or an iPhone full of photos of grandchildren. She'd take anything that might serve as a distraction.

Her gate was just ahead. She passed a custodian buffing the floors, the loud hum of his machine filling her ears. The lights were bright, too bright for so early in the morning. She squinted against the glare, focused on getting to her destination.

The queue at her gate was short. Only one woman checking boarding passes. *FINAL CALL* flashed on the screen above. Paige had spent the last hour loitering in the magazine aisle of the bookshop, waiting until the last possible minute to come to the departure lounge. Now she was here she needed to get on board before her brain caught up with what her body was doing and she lost her nerve.

Smack. She hit something immovable. All she could see was a haze of navy.

She bounced back and stumbled, her hands so full of her carry-on that she couldn't even put her arms out when she started to fall.

"Careful." Fingers wrapped around her elbows while forearms locked under hers, holding her upright until she recovered her footing.

How humiliating. "Thanks." Paige looked up, straight into amused gray eyes. A day or two worth of stubble covered the guy's lower face and his brown hair stuck up like he had stumbled straight from bed to the airport without looking in a mirror. *Zing.* The current traveled up her arms, down her body to her feet, and she stumbled again.

"Whoa." His fingers gripped around her elbows even tighter.

"Sorry." Her cheeks were aflame.

"It's okay." He loosened his hold on her, as if checking that she could remain upright without his help.

"I'm fine. Really." Paige looked at him, defensive for no rational reason. He looked familiar but she couldn't place him.

"Okay." He stood there, just looking at her.

"What?" The word came out harsher than she'd intended. Her cheeks could heat a small building.

He cocked an eyebrow at her. "Um, you're standing on my foot." He moved his left foot enough for her to feel it under her boot.

If there was ever a good moment for the rapture, this was it. Her entire body was on fire with embarrassment. "Sorry. It's . . ." She quickly moved her foot and stepped back.

He gave her a slow smile. *Zap.* That one shot down her spine. "It's way too early to be awake, let alone here. Trust me, I get it."

How had she not registered his gorgeous Australian accent earlier? The sultry drawl almost took her out at the knees.

She'd heard it before. But when? The kaleidoscope in her mind finally clicked the pieces into place and she wanted to fall through the floor. The terminal. He was the guy she'd backed into during her awkward conversation with Nate. She was 99% sure of it.

"Sir?" They had reached the front of the line. The guy turned and handed the woman his boarding pass. She scanned it and handed it back. "Thank you, sir. Enjoy your flight."

"Thank you." He strolled into the jetway, not pausing to look back.

"Ma'am?" Paige handed her pass to the woman while watching the handsome stranger disappear. She felt an odd pang of disappointment that he hadn't waited for her. *Stop it! No more hot guys, remember?* As much as she hated to admit it, the physical attraction was one of the reasons she'd stayed with Alex so long. Too much physical attraction, not enough substance. She wasn't making that mistake again.

"Thank you, ma'am." The woman handed her boarding pass back. "We're boarding front and back today, so you need to turn left at the bottom."

Paige stared at the archway leading to the air bridge. The last time she'd flown out of O'Hare,

Obama had been in his first term as President and she'd been a fun loving twenty-four-year-old whose biggest concern was whether she'd packed enough books in her carry-on to keep her entertained between Chicago and New Zealand. Today that same bag was stuffed with medical records documenting why she would set off metal detectors at airports for the rest of her life.

"Ma'am? Are you all right?" The gate attendant was looking at her with something that bordered on concern.

"Yes, fine. Sorry." She tried to put one foot in front of the other, tried to pretend she did this all the time, but her feet refused to move. Her heart thumped at a speed usually reserved for a high intensity workout, and it felt like there was a plastic bag over her mouth cutting off her air supply. Alex was right. She couldn't get on a plane. She'd been kidding herself to think she could. She swung around, almost colliding with the two people behind her.

"Watch it!" The overweight businessman held up his hands, as if afraid of being contaminated. A combination of stale sweat and alcohol assaulted her. Both he and his companion smelled like they'd come straight from a bar.

"I'm sorry." She muttered the words as she walked back to the empty gate lounge.

Back to what? The question repeated in her mind as she watched the woman scan the boarding passes of the last remaining passengers.

Nothing. She had quit her job, leased her condo, and while Chicago was filled with people who loved her, they also treated her with kid gloves, fearful that one wrong move would cause her to break on them again. She had to get on that plane. No matter what it cost her. It couldn't be more than the last time.

FOUR

The seats were even more cramped than Paige remembered. Or the general population had gotten larger. Probably both.

Her lungs constricted, fighting her own building panic. Her attempts to suck in air felt like breathing through a straw.

Her fingers scrambled for her seatbelt. She had to get off. Before it was too late. What on earth had made her think she could do this? How could she have believed enough time had passed to banish the terror now crawling up her throat?

The plane picked up speed, taxiing down the runway, bouncing from side to side. They weren't even going to get off the ground. Or they would for a second, then would come plummeting back to earth, the plane shattering like it was made of Lego. She'd be spat out onto the tarmac like one of those poor girls on that Air Asiana flight that crashed at SFO in 2013. Because that was how her life worked.

The metal clasp finally gave way beneath her grasping hands and the belt of death fell away.

Grabbing the headrest in front of her, she tried to get to her feet, tried to open her mouth and scream whatever words she needed to make it stop. To get thrown off the flight, back to Nate, back to safety.

The forces of the speeding plane pushed her back into her seat. Her fingers scraped at the seat in front of her again. It wasn't too late. If only she could stand up, they'd have to abort takeoff. Let her out.

A vice against her waist pinned her to her seat. *Jesus, help me.* The thought ricocheted through her mind. Her vision cleared enough to see it was the muscular arm of the aisle passenger. His elbow rested on her left armrest, while his fingers gripped her right one.

Clear blue eyes bore down on hers with authority. "Ma'am, you need to stay in your seat."

It was a courtesy statement. She clearly had no choice in the matter. The plane let out a shudder as the front wheels lifted off the ground. As they left earth, the tendrils of terror only tightened. *Please let it be fast.* Some sort of explosion ripping them into eternity before they even knew it had happened.

She sagged against the seat, her energy gone. No point fighting the inevitable. She couldn't even find the words to protest as the stranger reached over and clipped her belt back together.

"Do you have anything you could take?" His words jolted her head left.

"Huh?"

He had salt and pepper hair and looked to be in his fifties. "A sleeping pill, maybe? Something that will knock you out for a few hours?"

Her mother had pressed a packet of something into her palm, "Just in case." She'd protested, but given up and slid the small cardboard box into her purse to placate her mom.

"I think so." She fumbled for her purse, eventually catching the straps and pulling it onto her lap. She dug through its contents, extracted the box and showed it to her seatmate.

"Good." Taking the box from her trembling fingers, he flicked open the end and withdrew the foil packet. "Hold out your hand." Popping a couple of pills, he tipped them into her open palm and nodded to the water bottle she had stashed in the seat pocket. "Booze usually works better, but that'll do. In half an hour, you'll be out like a light."

The two little white pills on her hand stared up at her like beacons. She was stronger than this. This was only the flight to L.A. Shouldn't she save pharmaceutically induced unconsciousness for the long haul to Sydney?

Her fingers closed over them. No. She could do this. It was only four hours. She didn't need— *Oh dear God.* The death capsule lurched and

36

dropped, engines screaming in a symphony of torturous high-pitched sound as they fought for air. Her body lifted from her seat as the belt tightened across her legs, straining to hold her down. Her mind screamed. Incoherent words, images, memories, in no particular order. Was this how Ethan had felt in his final moments?

No, her brother was brave. He'd gone to meet his Maker serenely among all the chaos that raged around them.

The plane stabilized, and everyone around her seemed to let out a collective rush of pent up breath.

The intercom crackled to life. "Ladies and gentlemen, please ensure you keep your seatbelts tightened. We anticipate more turbulence ahead."

Paige was going to lose her mind with one more bump. Loosening her grip, she peered at the small pills that promised oblivion. Opening her mouth, she knocked them back dry.

Her brother was the hero, not her.

Josh let out a sigh and paused the movie. It was the third he'd tried, after a couple of TV shows. None had been able to keep his attention for more than a few minutes. At least the early turbulence seemed to be over.

Stretching his legs out, he turned his screen off and attempted to distract himself with a sip of his pre-breakfast smoothie.

He hated smoothies.

Running his hand through his hair, he squashed the desire to give himself a good slap. He had to get a grip. With eighteen hours of flying still ahead of him before he was home, he would lose his mind by the time he reached Sydney if he didn't stop mentally replaying the scene at the gate. O'Hare was a huge airport. What were the odds of the two of them falling over each other twice?

There was something about the blonde that tugged at him. He didn't know why. He knew nothing about her. Besides, she was taken. If he'd had the presence of mind to check out her left hand there probably would have been a sparkling rock on it. What was he doing even thinking about her?

His life was not conducive to a relationship. It was better this way. He couldn't afford to lose control of his senses ever again. There was too much at stake.

He'd been away from home for too long. That was all. Once he got back, he could forget all about strangers in airports who made him wish for something more.

Pushing his footrest down, Josh stepped into the aisle. He needed the bathroom and a strong coffee, in that order. Then he'd spend some time reviewing the new song Amanda and Connor had been working on.

The business class cabin was almost full. Most of its inhabitants either tapped away at various electronic devices or had their eyes closed, allowing the soothing hum of the engines to lull them back into lost sleep.

The curtain behind him opened and a flight attendant tugged a drinks trolley through. He stepped back to give her space to move past him. The metal contraption slid through, dragging the blue material with it.

She gave it another tug, but the curtain stayed stuck. "I'm so sorry, sir. It'll just be a second."

"Let me help." He reached over the trolley, found where the material had snagged against a protruding tray, and eased it free. "That should do it."

In the economy cabin, a movement a few rows down caught his eye.

It was her. About eight rows down, easing her way into the aisle from a middle seat. Her hair was now pulled back in a messy ponytail and the jacket she'd been wearing had been discarded, leaving a green T-shirt.

She paused in the aisle, her hand on the seat back of the row in front of her. She probably hadn't seen him and had no reason to look his way. Economy bathrooms were in the back of the plane.

She took a step, then another, in his direction. Without warning, she lurched to one side, almost tumbling into the lap of an unsuspecting passenger. At the last possible second, she steadied herself and tried to walk forward, but instead wove side-to-side like a barney on a surfboard, despite the now-stable plane.

Her gaze bounced all over the place, like she couldn't focus. She staggered a couple more rows then stopped, her scattered focus landing on him. Her eyes caught his and he found himself pinned by her clear, unwavering, gaze. And a strong whiff of liquor.

Then as quickly as it was cast, the spell was broken, as she doubled over and vomited on her own feet.

Josh wrenched the curtain closed on the classy scene. He glanced at his watch. It wasn't even eight. Who started drinking before breakfast?

Whatever her reason, he hoped she got help. He'd loved a woman with a drinking problem once. It had almost destroyed them both.

FIVE

The second-worst twenty-one hours and fifty-five minutes of her existence were over. At last. Paige stopped in front of the sliding doors that would open to her new life. She should pause here, savor the moment, make some sort of meaningful observation, but the truth was her head was spinning like a pageant girl's baton and her tight grasp on the baggage cart was about all that was keeping her from the floor.

Whatever her mother had given her must've come from pharmaceutical purgatory. Never again. The last time she'd felt this sick she'd been a naïve twenty-year-old who'd believed a fresh-faced frat boy when he swore the punch was virgin.

She forced her feet forward, pushing her heavy cart through the sliding doors, and found herself at the top of a ramp leading into the deafening arrivals hall.

"Paige, over here!" Her cousin's voice cut through the noise. Paige followed the direction of the call to where Kat stood flailing her arms, even though her bright, retro-inspired top was a beacon on its own.

Paige navigated through the crowd toward her cousin. Everything hurt. Even trying to smile. "Hey. I said you didn't need to come get me. I was going to catch the train and then a cab." She'd had it all planned. Known exactly what she needed to take and to where. Although she'd failed to factor in managing everything with two hundred dollars of excess luggage in tow.

Kat enveloped her in a hug, her five-foot-seven frame mirroring Paige's.

"Not come get you? Don't be silly. My favorite cousin is moving Down Under. This is the most exciting thing that has happened all year." Kat's usual hybrid accent had taken a distinct swing into all-Australian. Her abilities as a linguistic chameleon came courtesy of an American father, Australian mother, and a childhood spent on diplomatic postings.

"Liar, pants on fire." Paige tried to squash the wave of insecurity that hit. Kat was a sought-after film and TV makeup artist who lived a jet-setting life. They might look like sisters but that was where the similarities ended. Kat was adventurous. Outspoken. Fearless. Everything Paige wasn't. The woman had even won an Oscar, for Pete's sake.

"Okay, fine. Second most exciting." Kat laughed as they navigated around plastic seats and walked toward another large set of sliding doors. She gestured to an older man in a navy suit standing near the exit. "Geoff, can you take Paige's luggage?"

He stepped forward, and there was a slight awkward pause as Paige hesitated, unwilling to relinquish her death grip on the solid cart.

"Geoff's our driver. I booked us a car."

Why? "Don't you have one?"

Her cousin shot her an embarrassed look. "It's in the shop."

"Again?"

Her cousin shrugged. "What can I say? I only got back a few days ago and it always takes me a while to get used to driving on the left again. A few prangs are inevitable."

A few? It felt like every time they Skyped Kat's poor car was getting repaired. "You're a road menace."

"Yeah, but you love me." Kat wrapped an arm around her shoulder as they maneuvered around a crowd of Japanese tourists and out the door.

A blast of hot air warmed her skin and welcomed her to her new home. Planes roared over the white terminal and the huge gray cement parking building rose in front of them. Between flights, the sounds of an espresso machine emanated from a nearby outdoor café, shielded by assorted trees that were a stark contrast to the ugly industrial structures. Kat marched along the pavement, cutting a swath through the crowd. Paige willed her lethargic legs to match her cousin's pace.

"This is us." Kat gestured to a late model BMW a few feet away.

The driver pulled out his keys and clicked a button. The car beeped to life, lights flashing, and trunk opening.

Turning in a full circle, Paige lifted her head and tried to absorb everything. She was back in the Southern Hemisphere. Where the seasons were inside out and even the water went down the drain in a different direction.

Ugh, spinning was a bad idea. Now everything moved in all sorts of directions, the concrete rolling like an outgoing tide underneath her feet. She centered her gaze on the back windshield of the car, sucking in slow breaths.

"I'm so glad you made it. I wasn't sure you would." Kat spoke softly, her words almost drowned out by the noise surrounding them.

Paige looked at the person who knew her best in the world. She wasn't just talking about the flights.

She swallowed down the hurricane of emotions that threatened. "Me neither."

They held each other's gaze for a moment. The wobble on her cousin's mouth hinted at suppressed emotion. Kat didn't do vulnerable. Paige could count the number of times she'd seen Kat cry on one finger.

"C'mon. Poor Geoff is waiting. We can catch up when we get home." Kat opened the back door, placing a pair of gorgeous designer-looking sunglasses over her eyes. On the other side, the driver stood next to the other back door—open, waiting for her.

She'd made it. She was jobless, boyfriendless, and only knew one person in the entire country. But, for the first time in a long time, Paige could breathe.

Home sweet home. Finally. Traffic on the M5 had been nose-to-tail, as it always was when he came back from the US, since the major airlines managed to time their arrivals to hit the worst of the morning peak.

Josh dropped his duffle bag and guitar case at the bottom of the stairs, and padded down the hallway, his footsteps muffled by the plush gray carpet.

His mother stood in the bright kitchen, her slim back to him as she dried dishes, Jenny Simmons playing from the speakers on the bay window in front of her.

He paused for a second, his eyes soaking up the familiar sight. His mother, oblivious to his presence, belted out a worship song, her enthusiasm almost making up for the fact that she couldn't carry a tune if it was handed to her in a bucket.

He snuck up behind her and popped his head over her white T-shirt clad shoulder, wincing as she chose that moment to hit a particularly high note with great enthusiasm. No wonder the poor dog was nowhere to be seen.

"Mum, if you wanted to audition for the band, all you had to do was say so."

"Eek!" Her blonde head jumped, almost hitting him in the chin, as she swung around and swiped at him with the blue dishtowel. "How many times have I told you? Don't do that. You're going to give me a heart attack one day."

"Well, stop making it so much fun."

His mum laughed, green eyes crinkling at the edges. "Careful or I might get a desire to make liver for your welcome home dinner. Where's my hug?"

She wrapped her arms around his waist as he reached down, bending to encompass her petite frame, almost lifting her off her feet as he enveloped her.

"We've missed you."

"I've missed you too."

"How was America?"

"How was South Africa?"

Their words mingled together, and they laughed.

"Okay, I'll put the jug on and we can have a

proper catch up. You just missed your father. He's had to go into the office."

"Really?" Monday was usually their day off, one they guarded fiercely when they weren't traveling. "Is everything okay?"

A shadow flickered in across her face. "Just a meeting with HR about a disgruntled ex-employee. He doesn't even need to be there, but you know your father. Always likes to be in the loop with everything that's going on." Her attempt at laughter seemed forced.

Josh's hands clenched. When would people stop going after his family? The last time there had been a situation with a disgruntled ex-employee it had spiraled into a major media beat-up. Caused his parents so much stress his mother's hair had started falling out. *God, whatever it is, help me to remember it's in Your hands.*

"Josh." His mother patted his elbow. "It'll be okay. It always is."

He took a deep breath and let it out long and slow. She was right. Even in the most impossible of situations, God always came through. Somehow.

"Go, sit down." His mother gave him a push towards the breakfast bar. "Are you hungry?"

"I'm good. I ate on the plane." He grabbed one of the wooden stools and sat down, watching as she filled the electric jug from the tap with one hand while putting away cutlery with the other.

47

"So how was the tour?" His mother flicked the kettle on and turned to open the fridge.

"It was great. Full on—a different city every other night was completely insane, so I'm not sure if we'll ever do that again. By the time we got to the end everyone was exhausted."

"I'm sure you loved every second of it." She busied herself assembling what she needed for the tea.

"Pretty much." His mother knew him well. He did love life on the road. Visiting new places. Meeting new people. Spending most nights with thousands of people worshipping. "Oh." That reminded him. "Has Kel dropped off my guitars?" On big tours, he traveled with three.

"Not that I've seen."

"Odd. She said she was going to." The rest of the band had headed home a few days before him, since they weren't needed for the Chicago conference.

"Maybe she's waiting for you to get back before she brings them over." His mother raised an eyebrow at him.

Not again. "Mum, c'mon. She's just spent weeks on the road with me. I'm probably the last person she wants to see anytime soon." He dodged the insinuation. He had long since given up trying to convince her that Kellie did not have a thing for him. She was like another sister.

"Hellooooo. Anyone home?" The front door

slammed as the familiar voice came from the hallway.

His mother tilted her head and offered a knowing smile.

Josh scowled at her. Talk about bad timing.

"In here, honey," his mother called out.

Kellie trudged into the dining room, slender frame weighed down by the two guitar cases she carried. "Whew, these things are heavy." She put them down next to the wall and looked up, brushing a strand of dark hair out of her eyes. She broke into a smile when she saw him. "Hey, great leader. I didn't think you got back until tonight."

Weird. They'd talked about which flight he was on. "Just landed. Was catching up with Mum since it's been such a *long* time since we've seen each other." Emphasis on the long, hoping she'd get the hint.

"I know. It's been ages." Kellie pulled out the stool next to Josh and plunked herself down on it. "How are you, Auntie Janine?"

Josh's mother managed to shoot him a sympathetic look, while smothering a grin at the same time. "I'm great thanks, honey. Josh was just telling me about the tour. Sounds like it was a long slog."

"It was." Kellie tilted her head, pressing it against Josh's shoulder. "But it was great. And Josh did such a great job. The new songs were a huge hit. You would have been proud."

"I have no doubt." Mum poured boiled water from the jug into a teapot. "Tea?"

"I'm good, thanks."

"Thanks for dropping them off." Josh nodded toward the guitars, moving enough to make her lift her head off his shoulder. "So what do you and Sarah have planned today?" No doubt all sorts of mischief, knowing his little sister.

"Nothing. Sarah's got a big exam next week so she's cramming and no fun at all." Kellie pouted up at him, her full bottom lip poking out.

"I'm sorry. We were totally out of your way. You should have said. I could've waited until tomorrow to get them back. Or picked them up from church."

"Oh, it was no problem. Since you're here, do you want to work on some new songs? I've got a couple of ideas."

Writing songs was the absolute last thing he wanted to do. Kellie the Energizer Bunny. She never seemed to need time off.

"Kel. Seriously. Take a break. For once. If only so the rest of us don't feel so bad about needing one. Go." He waved his hands. "Make the most of a day off. The songs can wait."

"Yes, boss." She slipped off her stool. "So how was Chicago? Meet any nice girls?"

A picture of the American flashed through his mind. He mentally kicked himself. Again. She kept invading his thoughts, even though girls who got drunk and puked on their own feet were about as far from his type as you could get.

"Josh?" He landed back in reality, where Kellie was looking at him with wide brown eyes.

"Kel, I was at a men's conference. It's not exactly a potential-wife-spotting Mecca."

"You'll find her." Kellie's tone was confident. "You never know. Maybe, in the end, she'll be right in front of your nose."

The image of the blonde, her nose almost touching his as she struggled to regain her balance, appeared as if right in front of him.

He needed to get a grip. And some sleep to reset his brain. Maybe then it would sink in that he'd never see the drunk American again.

"Here we are." Kat threw open the door with a dramatic flourish. "Home, sweet home."

Paige hauled two of her bags into the entryway and gasped as she found herself facing floor-to-ceiling windows overlooking the ocean and, beyond that, the city. She'd suspected Kat's place would be nice from the plush lobby, but this was jaw-dropping.

"Oh my gosh. This is, it's . . ." She left her bags where they stood to go and press her face up against a window. The harbor was the blue of postcards and she could just make out the curves of the world-famous Sydney Opera House in the distance.

"I know. It is, isn't it?" Kat walked up beside her. "I have to admit that for all his faults, my father does have good taste in real estate."

"This is his?" Kat's father was about as different from Paige's as two brothers could be. Paige's father was all about family, while, Kat's father had been a sporadic presence in her life ever since her parents' divorce, preferring to throw money at the hole his absence created.

"Yup. No way I could afford it, Sydney prices being what they are. I pay peppercorn rent and, in exchange, tolerate dinner and a lecture on how I'm not living up to my potential every time he's in town."

Paige didn't respond. She'd learned years ago that there were no words that could make up for an 80% absent, 100% critical, father.

"Speaking of potential, you said you have a couple of job interviews lined up already?" Kat pushed herself off the window and walked through a large archway.

Paige followed her into an open plan kitchen/dining/living area. "Two." HR from both firms had called within hours of her sending in her resume to talk about short-term opportunities they had going since her visa only allowed her to work for six months. Both positions came with decent money and okay hours as far as logistics management went. Though pretty much anything would be a step up from an incompetent boss who did no work but took all the credit for Paige's efforts.

"You're definite about not teaching?" Kat pulled a couple of plates out of a drawer in the kitchen and opened a white box sitting on the marble counter. A pile of glistening pastries sat inside. "Sydney's elite would pay big money for their kids to have lessons from someone like you."

Paige shook her head, shoving down the ache that the words evoked. "I can't."

Kat passed her a plate and pushed the box her way. "It just seems like such a waste of your talent."

All the talent in the world couldn't magically fix her wrist. "I like logistics. I'm good at it." Besides, music and logistics management had more in common than people might imagine. Both focused on details.

"If neither of them work out let me know and I can do some asking around."

"That would be great." Paige could only dream of having Kat's connections in film, TV, and theater. Paige picked up a croissant and took a big bite. "Wow. This is amazing." She managed the words around a mouthful of buttery bliss.

Kat helped herself to an apricot Danish. "What about the Alex situation? I know we've Skyped but it's just not the same." Her cousin had a habit of changing topics at whiplash speed.

Paige placed her croissant back on her plate, then moved a few crumbs around the ceramic surface with her fingers. "I can't believe I wasted a fifth of my life on him."

Kat leaned forward against the counter. "Look at the bright side. At least you didn't marry him. Though if you'd even tried, I suspect our whole family would have stood at the 'any objections?' part of the ceremony."

"I know." She'd always known her family hadn't been Alex's biggest fans but she hadn't realized just how much loathing they'd hidden from her. "After we broke up Sophie told me Ethan couldn't stand him." Just saying her brother's name sent shards slicing through her.

Her cousin tore the end off her Danish. "I doubt anyone was ever going to be good enough for his little sister. But when Alex took that job in Milan, man, Ethan was so mad."

"I didn't know." She knew he wasn't thrilled, but mad?

Something in Paige's tone caused Kat to pause her pastry inches from her mouth. "Oh, honey. Ethan was your biggest fan. I don't think he could understand how any guy could leave his baby sister for some job, no matter how impressive the title or how good the money."

A memory of Ethan standing on the sidelines at her first gymnastic meet flashed through Paige's mind. For three days, her fourteen-year-old brother had watched a platoon's worth of elementary school girls who hardly knew what end of the ribbon to hold, so he could cheer her on for every one of her performances.

Sobs choked her throat. "I miss him, Kat. I miss him so much."

"Of course you do. He was one in a million, your brother. And I know he's so proud of you right now. I can just see him up in heaven cheering you on."

Paige wasn't sure about that. Kat wouldn't be either if she knew the truth. That Paige had made Ethan a promise as he lay dying. And broken it every day since.

Six

This was not what Paige had been expecting when Kat said she had a lead on a job. Not even close.

She stood on a perfectly manicured lawn and stared at the words written across the huge glass front doors in curvy italics. *Harvest Central.*

Only the biggest, most renowned church in Australasia. Only everything she hated in a church. She'd thought Kat did too. Big, flashy, wealthy. It had its own college, day care and probably zip code. It wasn't a building. It was a campus. And not one campus but four—South, Central, Hills, and Yarra.

Thousands of people. Not to mention the albums, the DVDs, the band, the conferences. Their events filled the Sydney Events center for days on end, the influx of out-of-towners ensuring finding last minute accommodation was up there with getting a hotel bed in Bethlehem the night Jesus was born.

Paige sucked in a deep breath and checked her watch. Past experience with megachurches aside, the chance to be involved with the *Grace* conference would be any planner's dream. The event spanned two days and included over ten thousand women and a range of international speakers. It was a logistical nightmare waiting to happen. Someone who could pull off a conference of this magnitude could do anything. It was exactly the kind of thing she needed on her resume to propel her into being a serious contender for the next level of job opportunities when she went home.

In the two weeks she'd been in Australia she'd had six job interviews and been offered two jobs. Perfectly adequate jobs paying perfectly decent money. But she could have done both of them in her sleep. She wanted something that was going to challenge her. Push her beyond her comfort zone.

Paige eyed up a billboard plastered on the side of the building starring the smiling faces of the church's world-famous senior pastors. Well, there was no doubt this job would do that.

The sliding doors opened and a dark haired woman around her age exited with a purposeful stride.

"Do you need help finding somewhere?" The woman slowed when she saw Paige standing there.

"I'm here for a job interview. I'm supposed to go to the main office."

"Just through the door, then take the stairs on the left."

"Thanks." The automatic doors whooshed back open as Paige stepped forward.

"Hey." The woman touched her on the shoulder. "Good luck. It's a great place to work."

Paige laughed, her nervousness bubbling up. "Thanks. I think I'm going to need it."

The person tilted her head and studied Paige, the sun catching her caramel highlights. "You've never been here before, have you?"

"No. I just moved here from Chicago."

"Well, want to know a secret?" The woman dropped her voice.

"Sure."

"It may look all very impressive and intimidating but at the end of the day we're all regular people. There just happen to be lots of us."

"Thanks. I'm Paige, by the way."

"Kellie. Now go." She smiled as she motioned Paige forward. "We may be regular people, but turning up late for an interview is never a good look."

Thanks to Kellie's directions, Paige found the office without a problem. Subtle jasmine scented the air of the reception area, and soothing worship music crooned through hidden speakers. She shifted in the seat the receptionist had pointed her to with a perky smile, resisting the urge to open her resume and give it another scan.

Pressing the tips of her shoes into the carpet to keep them from tapping, she forced herself to take deep breaths. She could do this. She'd managed the Chicago Marathon, for crying out loud—tens of thousands of runners, road closures, and more red tape than you could shake a marker at. Especially after the Boston Marathon bombings.

"Paige?"

Her gaze turned upwards, and her breath stalled. She'd assumed she'd be meeting with some mid-level staffer with a fancy title like Associate Vice President of Outreach Support.

Paige hadn't even considered this possibility. The person whose image graced DVDs, conference posters, and books stood right in front of her. Her blonde hair fell in a perfect glossy curtain, touching the top of her shoulders. Her stylish yet modest wrap dress showed off her slim tanned arms to full advantage.

Lurching to her feet, she thrust out her hand, towering over her prospective boss. "Mrs. Tyler. I mean Pastor Tyler . . ." Her words petered out. Wow, way to impress.

Janine Tyler let out a soft laugh and gave her hand a gentle but firm shake. "Please, call me Janine. Kat has been a huge asset to our single mother's outreach program and we were thrilled to get her email saying that you might be able to help us out with *Grace*."

Might be able to help them out? That was like saying Ryan Gosling was sort of good looking.

"Let's have a chat in my office." Janine turned

and walked away, her high heels cutting a trail through the plush carpet.

Paige followed Janine past the front desk and into a hallway. Large windows flooded the space with natural light, the right side filled with people working in an open space and the left lined with doors, some open, some closed. Glass panels with blinds allowed a glimpse into each office.

"Maggie." Janine paused by a desk toward the end of the hallway. An older woman with a gray bob looked up. "This is Paige. Paige, this is my right-hand woman, Maggie."

Maggie rolled her eyes but a smile crinkled her face. "Lovely to meet you, Paige. Welcome." She turned to Janine. "On that note, you're due at Little Lights story time at quarter to. And don't forget you promised them the *Hungry Caterpillar* today."

"Yes, ma'am." A couple more steps and Janine opened a door at the end of the hallway. "Here we are." The glass panel beside this door was slightly larger than the others, giving Paige a glimpse of a chocolate brown love seat and a coffee table.

Opening the door, Janine waved her inside. "Can I get you anything? Tea, coffee, water?"

"A water would be great." She paused, waiting for Janine to tell her assistant.

"Great. Make yourself at home. I'll just be a couple of minutes."

Paige watched her head back down the hall. She wasn't getting them herself, was she?

"She always gets the drinks. The only time I've seen her come close to losing her temper was when someone asked Maggie to go fetch them a coffee."

Following the voice, Paige turned to discover a woman with auburn hair sitting on a second couch. A purple smock stretched across an impressive baby bump, black tights poking out from underneath.

"Hi, I'm Emily. I'd get up, but as you can see," she gestured at her enormous bump, "I'm not exactly amenable to easy movement."

Paige crossed the room and perched on the edge of the same couch as Emily. "I'm Paige. When are you due?"

Emily blew out a breath of air. "June."

Paige's jaw sagged. June? It was only April.

"I know, I know. I look like I'm ready to burst. To be fair, both my mother and Nonie warned me that all Johnston women expand like a puffer fish when they're pregnant. I just didn't realize we were talking Veruca Salt-like proportions." She gave her bump an affectionate pat. "Anyway, enough about me. What brings you to Sydney?"

Paige pulled out her rehearsed answer. "My cousin Kat is based here and loves it. When I realized I was eligible for a working holiday visa, it seemed like a great opportunity to experience living somewhere different."

Emily rubbed her stomach in a circular motion, quirked a smile. "That bad, huh?"

"What?"

"The breakup."

Good to know it was that obvious.

Emily waved a hand. "I went out with a guy for four years, then he announced he'd fallen in love with his flatmate. Felt like I couldn't turn around without seeing the two of them all over each other. So off to the big smoke I came."

"Well I didn't have to worry about that. Alex didn't even want to live in the same country when we were together." Where the words came from, Paige didn't even know. It was as though Emily invited openness with her honest face and maternal vibe.

"Bet he didn't think you had it in you to do the same, did he?" A grin covered Emily's face and Paige couldn't stop returning it.

"That would be an understatement." The last contact she'd had with Alex, he'd told her the joke had gotten old and it was time to give it up. When she'd told him it wasn't a joke he'd asked her to reimburse him for his July airfare since he'd been coming back to see her. What a charmer.

Emily's lips puckered. "Why do I get the sense there might be someone else in the picture?"

O'Hare appeared in her mind. Though, for some reason, it was the dark eyes of a disheveled stranger who took center stage rather than Nate, who she'd talked to an hour ago. She shook Mr. Dark and Disheveled out of her head. She hadn't thought of him since arriving in Sydney. Why now? "No . . . Yes . . . Maybe . . . I don't know."

Emily tilted her head. "Sounds complicated."

A sigh escaped her. "He's a good friend. I guess I'm hoping that a bit of distance will provide some clarity."

Paige tried to glance over her shoulder without making herself too obvious. How far away was the kitchen from here? Her nerves were pulled tighter than an eighteenth-century corset and, as easy as Emily was to talk to, she needed to get on with convincing Janine she had the skills and experience for this job.

"Well who knows? Maybe a nice Aussie guy will sweep you off your feet. Then one day you might even get to become a human bowling ball like me." Emily shifted uncomfortably on the couch, her tone wry.

"We could all only live in hope to be as gorgeous as you. Lord knows I was a washed-out wreck for all three of my pregnancies." Janine reentered the room, closing the door behind her. She passed chilled bottles of water to them both, took a seat on the opposite sofa, kicked off her heels, and perched the balls of her feet on the coffee table. "That's better."

This was officially that most disconcerting job interview Paige had ever been to. Her fingers tapped against the cover of her resume and she glanced at her watch. Twenty past. Hadn't Maggie said Janine needed to be somewhere by quarter to?

"Now Emily, have you enlightened Paige as to who you are?"

Her couch colleague held the icy bottle against her décolletage and cast Paige an apologetic look. "Sorry, you must be wondering why I'm here. I've been the logistics manager for *Grace* for the last four years."

Oh. And Paige wasted their time together talking about a nonexistent relationship when she could have been getting critical insights into the role.

"Okay." *Smooth. Real smooth, Paige.*

"Did Kat tell you much about the role?" Janine took a sip of water.

"Not a lot, to be honest, but I've read the job description on your website."

"Well, let me share some thoughts with you." As Janine explained how the conference had gone from fifty women in a small hall three decades ago to the huge event it had become, Paige found herself leaning forward, absorbing every word.

Janine's passion and heart for the event were

contagious. As she spoke, Paige could imagine the thousands of women from all over the world being challenged and spiritually nourished.

"So how does that sound?"

"Incredible."

Janine's smile engulfed her face. "It is. Are you keen?"

Keen?

Emily clarified. "She means are you interested."

Paige glanced between them. "Absolutely." She tried to form her mouth around the big question in her mind and work out how to say it without being offensive. "Um, is part of the job requirement that I have to go to church here?"

She held her breath. What would she do if they said yes? It wouldn't be unreasonable on their part—of course they would want to employ people who went to their church. Who tithed back to them.

Janine smiled, shook her head, blonde hair swishing. "Definitely not. We'd love it if you did, but we appreciate that Harvest isn't for everyone. It's more important to us that you find a community that works for you. I can get Maggie to give you a list of other great churches in the area, if you'd like."

Paige stared at her, bemused. They didn't care if she went here? Janine had even looked genuine when she said "other great churches in the area," like she didn't see them as competition.

"Is that okay?"

Paige shook herself out of her stupor. "Yes, great. I mean it's not that I don't want to go here, it's just—"

Janine waved her attempt at an explanation away. "All I care about is that you find where you fit. If there's anything we can do to help, let me know." She reached down, pulled a manila envelope from under the coffee table, and slipped a stack of papers out. "All the details of the role are here. Like the ad said, it's a six-month contract to cover Emily's maternity leave. That works with your visa requirements, right?"

"It's perfect." While her work and holiday visa was valid for twelve months, she wasn't allowed to work for the same employer for more than six.

"Great. It's not just *Grace*. We'll also have you involved with other things as you have capacity and I'm not sure what you were on in Chicago but the salary is . . ." She flicked through a few pages and named a figure.

Some rough currency conversion in her head gave Paige a figure that was about the same as she'd made back home. It would be a little tight since she had some upcoming bills on her condo to meet, but doable given the minimal rent Kat had insisted on charging her.

"I hope that's acceptable. I'm told the exchange rate is in our favor."

"Yes, that'll be fine." Paige's head spun. "But . . ."

Janine put the papers back and slid the envelope across the table to her. "Now, if everything is agreeable, any chance you can start Monday? That will give you a couple of weeks with Emily before she finishes on May fifth and your contract ending the week after *Grace*."

Paige finally managed to get the words out. "But you haven't even interviewed me." They hadn't asked her anything about herself or her experience or her beliefs. They hadn't even asked for a copy of her visa to check she could legally work for them.

Janine laughed. "Actually, Emily did before I walked in. You just didn't even know it."

"But, she only asked me about me."

"Exactly. But what you don't know is that your Senior Pastor in Chicago is an old friend. We gave Mike a call, and he highly recommended you. Said you had been a great contributing member of the church. Would hire you to be on his staff in a flash. And since we know him, we know we agree theologically and doctrinally on key things so it's all good. And, most importantly . . ."

Janine rose and walked to an internal door. Knocking, she opened it and stuck her head through the gap. "Hon, would you mind coming in here a sec?"

A few seconds later, the door opened wide and

Greg Tyler appeared. Paige didn't have time to absorb the surprise before Janine grabbed his hand and dragged him to the couch.

"Honey, this is Paige."

His face creased with a smile. "Paige, great to meet you. Janine was thrilled to get your application. Has she charmed you into coming on board yet?"

Paige stumbled to her feet. "Nice to meet you too, sir. She, well, your wife is very convincing. I'm—"

"Paige is a little confused because she thinks we've offered her the job without a proper interview. Why don't you tell her what you told me last year when you came back from Chicago?" She turned back to Paige. "Greg did the half marathon last year."

Paige struggled to understand what was happening here.

Pastor Tyler wrapped his arm around Janine's slim waist and gave it a squeeze. "When I came home from Chicago, I said to Janine, 'Honey, sometime soon Emily is going to leave us for a higher calling and when she does, we need to pray that the Lord sends us the logistics person for the Chicago Marathon because that is one well-oiled machine.' And hey presto, here you are."

Janine nodded at the envelope in Paige's hands. "You don't have to give us an answer right now.

Think it over tonight and let me know tomorrow. We'd love to have you on the team but we understand that with your impressive CV you've probably got other offers to consider."

The rational side of her wanted to say yes on the spot to Janine's hopeful expression. This was a professional no-brainer.

But the emotional side reminded her she'd been here before. Had seen behind the veil of the slick front people, promotional machinery, and adoring congregants. And it had almost cost her her faith.

SEVEN

Paige hit the ground by the side of her bed hard and fast. Someone was being murdered outside, the horrible high-pitched screams cutting through her slumber. She threw open her door, and ran down the hall and into the living area. Where did Kat keep the phone?

There it was, sitting in its cradle on the bench. Grabbing it up, her fingers fumbled, c'mon, c'mon. Nine, then a one—

"Where's the fire?"

Her cousin stood on the other side of the kitchen counter, eating a piece of toast, calm as could be.

"Someone's being murdered outside my bedroom. Listen!"

Kat tilted her head as another scream reached them. Paige's finger went for the second one. What was the address here?

Suddenly the handset was flying from her grip, hurtling across the room like a small rectangular missile.

"Ow!" The back of her hand stung from where Kat's slap had landed.

"Please tell me I got you before you hit the second one."

"I think so." Paige rubbed her hand. Had her cousin lost her mind? Was crime in Sydney so bad that Kat would just stand by while someone was being mutilated? Wait, was she *laughing?* Kat was doubled over, shoulders shaking. After a few seconds, she gasped and hauled herself upright.

"What is so funny?" Paige crossed her arms.

"It's a kookaburra."

"A what?"

"No one is being assaulted. That is the call of a kookaburra. It's a native bird. They're every-where."

"That was a bird?" As Paige said it, its screech ripped through the apartment again. This time, wide awake, she could tell it wasn't human.

Kat nodded, wiped the straggling tears off her cheeks. "It is. But just for future reference, in Australia the emergency number is triple zero."

"Then why did you slap me?"

"Just in case they reroute nine-one-one because of all the Americans who think it works everywhere."

She did know that it was a different number. In her half-asleep state, instinct had kicked in.

"But since you're up, want to come to church with me?"

"To Harvest." The previous two weeks, she'd

71

managed to dodge the question by sleeping in or going for a run.

Kat raised an eyebrow. "You are going to be working there as of tomorrow. Shouldn't you give it a chance?"

No. She may have decided to take a chance and work for a megachurch, but that didn't mean she was going to go to one. Ever again.

"It's nothing like your old one, I promise." Her cousin widened her perfectly made-up eyes. "Please. It would be nice not to go by myself for a change."

Paige sighed. "Fine. Just this once. If I don't like it, do you promise to leave me alone?"

Kat held up two fingers. "Scout's honor."

Why not? Might as well do some early recon on what she'd signed up for. But she wasn't going to like it. She was well-acquainted with megachurches and they were all the same. They waited until they sucked you in and then they hit you with the fine print, the guilt, the obligation. And then turned against you faster than an angry rattlesnake if you didn't toe the party line.

People approached the building for the nine a.m. service. Like ants returning to their hill, they came from the parking lots in every direction, streaming into the big open doors that dotted the sides of the building housing the main auditorium.

Paige scanned the crowd bustling around her and Kat. Old people, young people, families, snuggly couples. People dressed up in suits and dresses, others looking like they'd just rolled out of bed and grabbed whatever was on the floor.

"Let's go upstairs." Kat tugged at her hand as they entered the first set of doors, pulling her to the left toward the same stairs she'd climbed on Thursday. At the top, they turned left instead of right, into a hallway where more doors were flung open. Greeters stood in the doorways, handing out bulletins and directing families to the kids' programs.

Kat grabbed two sheets from a smiling woman, and they headed through the next set of doors.

They were standing in the second level of a huge auditorium with chairs spread in a semi-circle, oriented around the stage on the main floor. From what Paige could see of the ground floor, it was already packed. They were on a mezzanine, which was filling up as the seconds ticked by.

"Come on." Kat strode down a few steps giving Paige no choice but to follow her. "If we don't hurry up, we'll end up in the nosebleeds."

"Excuse me, excuse me." Kat squeezed through people as she headed down the aisle, pausing at a row of seats about halfway down.

"Hi, can we get in here?" She flashed a smile at some teenagers on the end of a row. They duly stood to allow access to a few empty seats near the middle.

The middle? No, Paige needed to be on an aisle. Somewhere offering a quick escape. "Kat!" A panicked whisper fell from her mouth, but it was too late, her cousin was gone and the boys stood, waiting for her to follow. "Excuse me, sorry, excuse me."

Dodging toes, trying not to hit anyone with her purse, she clambered after her cousin, who had already dropped into an empty spot right in the middle of the row.

The sense of being trapped built even as she eased herself into her seat.

Her cousin slid a hair band off her wrist and pulled her hair into a perfect tousled ponytail with a couple of twists. "Just relax. It's going to be fine." She flipped open her bulletin and scanned it. "Excellent. Josh is back."

Sighing, Paige played along. "Who's Josh?"

"One of the worship leaders. When he leads, it's amazing. But he's not here very often. He spends most of his time on the road with the band."

Of course he did. Even she'd heard of *Due North*. Harvest's worship band sold out concerts wherever they went. She'd owned one of their earlier albums before it had fallen victim to her megachurch merchandise purge. These days the band had to be raking in the money. Well, something had to pay for all this—the buildings, the stage set up, the professional lighting. It had to be worth millions.

The buzz in the room grew louder. Their tier was now full and she could hear, and feel, people moving overhead. There had to be three thousand people in here.

At exactly eight fifty-eight, the band walked on stage. She craned her neck to get a glimpse of all the components. A huge choir filled the back right, with musicians and vocalists taking up the rest of the space.

The buzz grew. Her hackles rose. What did people think this was? A rock concert? They were here to worship God, not be entertained. Finally, a lone figure walked into the stage, guitar slung across his torso.

Obviously the famous Josh. Of course he had to come on last, the star of the show. He paused next to a female vocalist. Her caramel-streaked hair glinted under the lights. Was it the girl from the day of her interview? Paige squinted, but was unable to make out any distinct features. Finally, Josh made it to his own mic and plugged a cord into the end of his guitar.

He stilled, bowing his head as if in prayer. What a showman. After a few seconds, he raised his head and surveyed the crowd. There was something familiar about his stance, his profile. A tingle ran down her spine. He reminded her of the guy at the airport. She shook his head. *Don't be stupid, Paige.* There had to be millions of tall Australian guys with dark hair.

"Let's worship." His voice echoed across the arena. The congregation stood as one as the opening bars to the first song boomed out.

Twenty minutes later, Paige still stood, confused. Beside her, her cousin stood, arms raised, singing her lungs out. All around her, other people did the same.

But none of the rest of it was as she expected. No flashy lighting, no dancers, no visuals on the big screens to keep people engaged. No shouting or people bounding around the stage, working the crowd into a frenzy. Just big black screens with the words to the songs. The room vibrated with an unbroken stream of worship. The arrangements clearly composed by people who understood music.

On the stage, the lead guy had stopped playing his guitar and had his arms raised as they entered into the second verse of *Great is Thy Faithfulness*. Around him, some musicians continued playing while others stopped and were just singing. As much as she wanted to think it was contrived to seem like they were being carried away in the moment, it seemed genuine.

As the song tapered off, Greg Tyler walked onto the stage and uttered a short prayer as the band and choir left the stage.

"Please, be seated." His powerful voice echoed across the room. "The ushers are just going to take up the offering." She braced herself. Here it came, the lecture on trusting God with your finances, giving generously to carry on the work of the kingdom, a task which required money. Lots and lots of money. Maybe even a heart-wrenching professional video of some worthy ministry that could do so much more with an extra few hundred grand.

They never saw fit to mention the pastor's new Mercedes or the five-star staff "retreats".

Paige blinked. Pastor Tyler had already moved on to a notice about a food bank drive and asking for prayer for a missionary family in Uganda. The guy next to her handed her the offering bag and she passed it on to Kat. She watched as the ushers at the end of the aisles gathered them all up and walked toward the back.

That was it? There must be some darkness hidden under this shiny exterior. Whatever it was, they covered it well.

She turned to see her cousin looking at her. *See. I told you,* Kat mouthed.

Paige returned to face the front, the feeling of disquiet growing stronger. A church couldn't be this big, this wealthy, without something being wrong with it. And she was going to find out what.

• • •

Josh had no idea how his father could stand behind that pulpit and preach the way he did when people were doing their best to destroy him behind the scenes.

He clicked the last clasps on his guitar case shut, watching from his crouched position on the stage as his parents talked with the mob of people who accosted them after every service. Every person was treated as if they were the only one wanting their attention. No quick and easy getaway out the back doors for the Tylers. For as long as he could remember, his parents had stayed behind at the end of every service to talk to anyone who approached them. Most weeks they didn't get a chance between services to get so much as a bathroom break before the next one started.

An attractive middle-aged blonde woman was talking to his father. Her fingers rested on his forearm and she leaned forward, intent on invading his personal space. Josh wasn't the only one watching her. His mother's gaze was assessing the situation every other second, even as she talked to the person in front of her. One of the associate pastors was also keeping a close eye from the side, ready to intervene if given the signal.

And there it was. His father reached up and tugged his ear. His mother extricated herself from her conversation and made her way over to her husband, a charming smile fixed on her face.

Greg and Janine Tyler always had each other's backs. That was the only reason they'd survived everything that had been thrown at them.

"How blatant was it?"

Josh looked up to see his little sister had snuck up on him. "Was what?"

Sarah tilted her dark head toward where his parents stood. "That woman hitting on Dad. Mum looks like she wants to rip her throat out."

She was right. To anyone her didn't know her well, Janine Tyler would appear to be having a perfectly convivial conversation. But her smile was a shade too bright and the way she had her arm around her husband's waist while positioning herself slightly in front of him signaled a woman marking her territory.

Whether they liked it or not, appearances mattered. Especially in Christian circles. A fact the Tyler family had learned the hard way. More than once.

"And what's the latest with the sexual harassment case?" Sarah dropped her volume a notch as Josh stood, guitar heavy in his hand.

Josh glanced around to make sure no one else was near them. "How do you know about that?" His parents were notorious at keeping stuff like that to themselves. The only reason he knew was because the latest accuser alleged one of the "incidents" had occurred in the recording studio. A place where Greg Tyler never went, didn't even have a key for, and on a date the logs showed the band had been using all day for an album rehearsal.

"I didn't. I just guessed. Thanks." His sister's nursing studies took up most of her time so she wasn't privy to a lot of what went on at the church. But she had always been a people watcher and could usually tell before he could when their parents were under unusual stress.

Josh hefted his satchel over his shoulder. "Don't worry. It's even more baseless than usual. She didn't work for Dad and, as far as anyone can work out, the only time they were even in a meeting together it was with about ten other people." He made his way toward the wings.

"Well, at least that's something. Let's go check with them where we're meeting for lunch. I'll ride with you." Sarah headed for the stairs leading down onto the auditorium floor.

"You go. I have a couple of things to finish here. I'll meet you by the back door."

His sister turned to face him, wearing a smirk. "C'mon, big bro. Don't be afraid. I'll protect you."

"Little sis, the day I need you to protect me, you'll be the first to know." He wasn't afraid. It was that the stage was his safe place. No one was allowed up here except the worship team and the stage crew, but the moment he stepped off it into the auditorium . . . well, he didn't have his own version of Janine Tyler to watch his back. So it was better not to leave it exposed.

"Who is it that you don't trust? Them or yourself?"

Her question stopped him in his tracks.

Sarah tilted her head at him. "What? You think no one notices that every time you play you duck out the back door rather than run the risk of maybe having to talk to a girl who hasn't passed your CIA level screening process? Heaven forbid you might actually meet someone you like."

"You don't get it, Sarah." He was glad she didn't. At least one of them was sheltered from some of what came with being a Tyler.

His sister touched his arm. "Maybe not. But she was a long time ago, Josh. You're not that guy anymore."

Maybe he was. Maybe he wasn't. He'd prefer not to find out for sure.

EIGHT

Monday. Paige approached the familiar double doors. The fall breeze ruffled the leaves of the gum trees that dotted the campus.

Her toes curled as she stared up at the glass. She worked here. She worked *here.*

She shifted on her feet, still feeling off-kilter from the service yesterday. She'd listened to the sermon with intense focus, trying to find murky theology, half expecting a rah-rah feel-good message that could have served as a generic life coaching pep talk. But no, Greg preached from the Bible. Sure, there were a few examples and anecdotes thrown in for illustration, but mostly he spent his forty minutes unpacking the first ten verses of James. Paige had spent the rest of the day rattled. Worst of all, she wanted to come back next week for the second part of the series.

The now-familiar cacophonic screech of the kookaburra pulled her eyes upwards to the exotic birds dotting the tree canopy above. It was so loud it drowned out the myriad of other bird calls. Stupid squat long-beaked brown bird.

"Looking for drop bears?" Emily moved with surprising stealth for someone carrying such a large load.

Paige blew out a sigh of relief at not having to go into the building alone. "Sorry, what?"

"Drop bears." Emily held her hands about fifteen inches apart. "Angry little creatures with super sharp claws. About yay big, look a bit like a koala but nastier. Occasionally drop out of gum trees onto people." She shook her head, auburn curls bouncing, "If you ever get attacked, hit the ground and roll. They get disorientated easily so that will usually buy you time to get free."

The hairs on the back of Paige's neck stood up as she scanned the tops of the trees closest by. Was one watching her right now?

"Don't worry," Emily said. "They mostly come out at night. And we haven't had an attack on campus in years. I'm sure you'll be fine as long as you don't go for long late-night strolls under gum trees."

Fantastic. Yet another thing to add to the list of what could kill her in this crazy country: spiders, snakes, lizards, jellyfish, and now a zombie bear. And she'd just reassured Mom this morning that Australia was perfectly safe.

"C'mon." Emily grabbed her arm. "I was planning to take you for a tour first thing so we had might as well do it now."

They wandered across the lawn in the direction of a small squat building.

"So how many people go here?"

"Just this campus or all of them?"

"Um. All?"

Emily crinkled her brow. "This one, I think about ten thousand across five services. Maybe another ten across all the others."

Paige stopped in her tracks. "Doesn't it all just seem a little bit . . . big? I mean look at this." She waved her arms around at the huge grounds and the buildings.

Emily laughed. "I can't believe you think this is big. Honey, I've been to America. You could bathe a small African village in your regular-sized Coke cups."

She couldn't deny that.

"C'mon." Emily waddled on ahead of her. "I want to show you the recording studio. I heard some of the crew are rehearsing today for the new album."

Interesting place to start. "Am I going to be working with the band at some point?"

Emily glanced over her shoulder. "Possibly. They have their own logistics people, but here if any team is ever caught short, anyone on staff who is able to help out does."

Paige had worked with a band once before in her professional life. It was the only job she'd quit after being handed a wad of cash and told to procure goods and services that were both illegal and immoral.

Due North could only be an improvement.

"Dude. What is wrong with you?" Connor winced as Josh hit a wrong note and messed up the lyrics. For the fourth time. "The way you're playing, it sounds like Jesus died and stayed that way."

Josh looked at Amanda as she took off her earphones and nodded. "Seriously little bro, that was pretty awful."

"Sorry, guys." Josh slipped his guitar strap over his head. "I think I'm having an off day." He stretched out his fingers. He'd been struggling ever since the three of them had started practicing at seven, trying to get a jump on some of the new songs before the rest of the team came in at nine-thirty.

Connor and Amanda exchanged glances.

"Dude, you are not having an off day. You are not even having an off week. If this keeps going, you're going to be having an off month." His brother-in-law took a swig of water.

"Oh c'mon. It hasn't been that bad." Josh leaned against the window that separated the studio from the production booth. But even he knew it was.

"Yes, it has." Amanda nudged her hip against his. "And you know it. Seriously, you haven't been on good form since you got back and that

85

was over two weeks ago. What's going on?"

"I don't know." He groaned. "It's like I left my mojo in the States."

"Oh my gosh." Connor slapped his palm against his forehead. "How could we have been so stupid?" He cast Amanda a meaningful glance, and her eyes widened.

"Amy?"

Connor nodded sagely. "Yup."

Amanda pursed her lips. "Of course. But we can't blame ourselves. It's been a long time."

"What are you talking about?" Josh glanced between them.

Amanda rounded on him. "The last time you lost your mojo was after Amy." Who he'd dated for six months four years ago before they'd mutually agreed to go their separate ways. Or so he'd thought until she popped up on the cover of a women's magazine with a tell-all pack of lies slandering his family, and a sob story about how he'd broken her heart.

"And the only other time was . . . well, her." Eight years, and his sister still couldn't bring herself to say Narelle's name.

"You can say her name, Amanda. I'm not going to start rocking in a corner." That should kill this stupid conversation. Any mention of the girl who was almost his undoing usually got the subject changed at warp speed.

"So tell, who is she?"

Apparently not today.

"Any new girls in the band?" Connor directed the question to Amanda, who thought for a second and then shook her head.

"No, although I'm planning auditions for a couple of new vocalists. Any new single girls on staff?"

"Seriously, you two. There's no one." This was ridiculous.

Amanda turned to Connor. "Where's he been recently without us?"

Connor ran his hand through his hair, ruffling as he thought. Then a slow smile crossed his face. "Chicago. That conference after we finished the tour!"

Amanda let out a squeal. "Oh, you met an American. What's her name? Is she Southern? I would totally love a sister-in-law who says 'y'all'. It's soooo cute!"

The next thing he knew, Connor had started tapping out *Love is in the Air* on the keys. This was getting way out of hand.

"You're both deluded. For your information, the only girl I met in Chicago worth mentioning was a total unco at the airport who almost broke my foot. And she was not my type. At all."

"Sounds like the perfect meet cute."

His sister had totally lost him. "Perfect what?"

"In the movies when the couple meets for the first time. It's called a meet cute."

"You've watched too many chick-flicks. It wasn't a meeting and she wasn't cute. Sorry to disappoint." *Liar.* His conscience scalded him.

Amanda rolled her eyes. "Well that's a shame, because without a sob story about meeting the girl of your dreams but being cruelly torn apart by fate, you're just being a grump and you need to get over it."

A cough diverted all eyes to the doorway. Emily stood there, her body half turned toward the hallway as if preparing to make a hasty departure. "Sorry for interrupting. We can come back later if now's a bad time."

"No, no, of course not." Amanda waved her in. "My little brother is just in a snit for some unknown reason."

Emily took a step through the doorway. "We'll be quick. I wanted to introduce you to Paige McAllister. She's me for the next six months. Paige, this is Amanda, Connor, and Josh."

Josh had totally missed the second person, half-hidden behind Emily's belly. As she stepped forward, his mouth went dry. It couldn't be. There was no way.

But it was. And judging by the look she was giving him, she'd heard every word.

Paige strode down the hallway. She wasn't his type 'at all', huh? Well that was perfect because good-looking jerks weren't hers either.

Almost broke his foot. Whatever. She was like one-forty sopping wet while he had to be close to having a two in front of his weight. And she'd barely touched his foot. Maybe, *maybe,* she'd overlapped with a few toes. At most.

How was it possible? How could airport guy and worship guy be one and the same? What a hypocrite—Sunday, all arms raised, singing hymns like he meant it. Monday, first class moron.

Not his type. He should be so lucky. She was fun and intelligent and witty and—

"Hey." Emily's puffing broke through her thoughts. "Not sure if you missed the memo but pregnant women aren't so good at sprinting. Especially short ones."

"Sorry." Paige slowed her stride.

"Closest bathrooms are just around the corner."

"Huh?"

"Well I assume that's why you're striding it out like some model on Project Runway. It's certainly the only thing that gets me moving with any speed these days."

Good idea. She needed a few minutes to cool down. "That would be great, thanks." A thought struck her. "Emily?"

"Yeah?"

"What does unco mean?"

"As in if I was to say 'You're a total unco'?"

Paige shrugged. "Sure."

"It's short for uncoordinated."

What! "I am not! I was on the varsity volley-ball team. And I played violin. Do you know how fast your fingers have to go to play the violin?"

"I'm going to guess pretty fast." Emily stopped and looked at her like she was worried about her mental welfare.

"Very fast!" A twinge trailed up her arm. What she wouldn't give for her fingers to be able to fly over the frets, the bow dancing across the strings, the way they used to.

"Well then I'm sure you never have to worry about being called unco." Emily gave her a bemused look. "Did I miss something? It's not like Josh was talking about you."

Paige scrambled to save herself from falling into the hole she had just dug. "I . . . I felt sorry for the poor girl he was talking about."

"I'm sure he didn't mean it. He was just blowing off steam. The poor guy can't even walk around campus without being propositioned by some girl gagging to take our most eligible bachelor off the market."

Paige shrugged her shoulders, tried to maintain a neutral facade. "Really? I can't say he's my type."

Emily turned left into a smaller side hallway, a sign denoting the women's bathrooms on a door at the end of the corridor. "Huh. I thought super cute, men of God who are incredible musicians would be everyone's type."

"I've generally found musicians to be arrogant." She wasn't going to bother denying the good-looking part. His looks were a matter of fact rather than opinion. She refused to acknowledge the tingle that ran up her spine at seeing him again. Tingles were bad. She'd wasted six years on a self-absorbed jerk who gave her tingles.

"Okay, I'll give you that he can put up a bit of a wall and he wasn't at his most charming. But once you get to know him, he's a super great guy."

As far as Paige was concerned, he could take a flying leap. "Then I'm sure he'll have no problem finding himself a super great girl."

It was a big campus. Huge. They could easily avoid each other. And from the look of horror on his face when he saw her, he felt exactly the same way.

NINE

Josh slammed the front door behind him, the resounding impact providing the smallest bit of satisfaction.

The day had been a wash. Okay, he'd been a wash. Not even a blistering run at lunchtime had managed to shake him out of his funk, and it showed. He'd ended up abandoning the team to Connor and Amanda mid-afternoon, after it had become obvious they'd all be better off without him and his sausage fingers messing up every line.

He'd go back late tonight and review whatever tracks they'd managed to lay down. Then attempt to make up for the lost time tomorrow.

He had to shake this off. The timeframe they'd set for the new album was tight enough without their leader becoming as unreliable as Sydney trains.

What was she doing here? His mother had a reputation for trying to rehabilitate waifs and strays but this was a professional organization. *Grace* was a huge event, requiring someone at the top of their game. Oh, and a Christian would be helpful too. Had his mother even bothered to do any reference checking, or had Paige fed her some big woe-is-me story?

Tossing his car keys into the bowl on the entryway table, he shuffled through a pile of mail and shoved two envelopes bearing his name into his back pocket. Paige. It was so much worse now she had a name. It was bad enough when she'd been the anonymous blonde. Now Paige McAllister was burned into his brain.

They'd crossed paths for all of ten seconds in an airport on the other side of the world. He met hundreds of people every week. Why had this woman stuck in his mind? Besides, she had a boyfriend and a drinking problem, so he had no business thinking about her at all. It was like he was the butt of a cosmic joke.

He wasn't a total dropkick. He did feel bad about what she'd overheard in the studio, but at least now she'd keep her distance. The last thing he could afford was to lose his head, his heart, over someone who wasn't right. Again.

Josh drew in a deep breath. His family were experts at reading people. He had to get it together before dinner. At least if they suspected something he could chalk it up to a bad day of rehearsals. If he was lucky, maybe he could find a subtle way to enquire exactly how she came to be hired.

He leaned his guitar case against the staircase

balustrade, dumped his satchel next to it, and strode down the white tiled hall toward the kitchen and laundry. Thanks to his unplanned run, he needed a bottle of cold water and a fresh T-shirt.

He wrenched the neck of his T-shirt over his head as he approached the kitchen, the chopping sound suggesting his mother had already started prep. The scent of frying onions and garlic sent his stomach grumbling.

"Hey. Need any help with dinner?" He headed for the fridge, head down, still working his arms through the sleeves.

A pause in the chopping. "You might want to think before you remove any more clothes." Definitely not his mother's voice.

An unbiblical word exploded through his mind. He froze, then attempted to wrench his shirt back over his head, only to find himself stuck and standing in his own kitchen, blinded by cotton, arms flailing in the air, torso exposed. Finally, he managed to grab hold of the hem and yank it down over his stomach.

And there Paige stood, like something out of his worst nightmare. She leaned against the kitchen counter, one hand resting on a curvy hip, the other holding his mother's largest chef's knife.

"What are you doing here?" Paige was impressed with how cool her voice was, especially considering her knees had about given out from a few seconds of staring at Mr. #1 Bachelor's toned torso.

Thank goodness she'd recognized him from a glimpse of his head as he walked in, so had a few seconds to compose herself while he wrestled with reclothing himself. Long enough for her to see a small tattoo reading *Hannah* across one shoulder blade. She did her best to extinguish the flicker of curiosity the name written in cursive evoked.

Josh gave his T-shirt one last tug, then lit into her. "This is my house. What are you doing here?"

She shook her head. "This is the Tylers' house." If only he'd showed up a few minutes earlier. Before she'd assured Janine she was totally happy to slice some vegetables while she got changed.

"And I'm Josh Tyler." He spoke the words slowly, as if she were stupid.

It all connected with the force of a comet. Great, just great. "You're their—"

"Son. Ten points for such brilliant deduction." Turning around, he opened the fridge and pulled out a bottle of water.

And here she'd been thinking getting asked to dinner at her boss's house on her first day was a good thing.

Choking down her dismay, she forced herself

to assess the situation. He was her boss's son, so she may have to have more to do with him than she'd anticipated. But he was still arrogant and still a jerk and—bonus!—he still lived with his parents.

There were no chiseled abs or brooding gazes or cute accents in the world that could compensate for someone who couldn't cut the apron strings.

He took a gulp of water, his eyes never leaving hers, as if he was worried she might steal the family silverware. What was his problem?

"Out with it. Did you have one of your girlfriends lined up for Emily's job? Or were you hoping your mom would hire someone more your type?" Her stomach dropped. Had she really said that?

His gaze flickered over her, face inscrutable. "Since you asked, I don't think you're of fit character to be on the team for *Grace*. Let alone have such a critical role."

She gaped at him. Of fit character? He didn't even know her. Her fingers gripped the knife. *Put the weapon down, Paige. He's not worth it.*

"Great, you're home." Janine breezed into the kitchen, bottles of soft drink in her arms, work attire swapped for a T-shirt and pair of jeans. "Paige, this is my son Josh."

Paige twisted her lips into a half smile. "We met this morning."

"Let me take those, Mum." Josh transformed

into a doting son as he took the bottles from Janine and placed them in the fridge. "If you'll excuse me, I'm just going to get changed before dinner." He offered Paige a curt nod, then strode from the room, T-shirt sculpted to his broad, muscular back.

Janine let out a low whistle as she tucked some hair behind her ear. "Amanda was right about him being fouler than spoiled milk in January." She turned to Paige. "Don't mind him. The band is about to start recording a new album, and I'm told rehearsal didn't go well today."

Paige was certain his bad mood had nothing to do with music and everything to do with her, but she wasn't about to tell her boss that.

She wasn't sure how she was going to get through dinner with the glowering gargoyle at the table, much less survive the next six months, never knowing what corner he might be lurking behind.

Now the life she'd been desperate to escape didn't seem so bad after all.

Well, he'd survived dinner. That was about the best that could be said. Josh walked down the hallway toward his bedroom, not even finding comfort in his usual ratty T-shirt and old boxers. He'd hoped a good pounding of hot water might loosen up the knots in his shoulders, but they were still as tight as before.

It rankled him—her, sitting at his table, laughing with his whole family. As if she belonged there. Luckily his two livewire nephews kept everyone on their toes and distracted from the fact that if looks could kill, both he and Paige would have been buried in the back garden before the food had even been served.

His mother approached from the other end of the hallway, carrying a basket of laundry. Not his. No doubt Paige would assume it was. He'd seen the look of smug judgment that crossed her face when she realized he still lived at home. Like he was some thirty-something freeloader whose mother washed his clothes and tucked him into bed with a good-night story.

He wasn't going to deny there were benefits to the arrangement—like he ate far better at home than he ever would in some sort of bachelor pad. But the main reason was that both he and his parents spent as much time on the road as in Sydney, so it didn't make sense for him to have his own place. Plus it made his parents feel better that Sarah was never home alone for long.

"These yours?" His mother paused in her approach and held up a pair of white athletic socks.

He had no idea. "Maybe. I'll take them if they're going."

She threw them with an underhanded toss and he caught them midair. "You want to talk about what was going on tonight?"

"What?"

She raised her eyebrows. "You know what. Why my thirty-two-year-old ordinarily civilized son morphed into a monosyllabic adolescent grunter. Is there some new house rule I don't know about? Am I supposed to consult with you now, check that you're up to being a decent human being, before I invite someone for dinner?"

He winced and ran a hand through his damp hair. "Sorry. Bad day."

She studied him with all-knowing maternal eyes. "You've had plenty of bad days in the studio before, but you've never been so rude when we've had a guest. Thank goodness Paige's parents managed to raise her with better manners than we did you."

He hadn't been that bad. It wasn't like he'd been rude to her. "What do you even know about her?" The words slipped out before he could stop them.

His mother tilted her head. "Paige?"

"Yes."

"I know she's a brilliant logistics manager and her pastor back in Chicago raved about her. I know she's an answer to prayer and if she hadn't shown up, we may have had to resort to asking

Emily if she would mind just crossing her legs until November. Why?"

Josh shifted on his feet. "I don't know. I got an odd vibe. Like maybe she isn't what she seems."

His mother pursed her lips. "People are rarely what we think at first glance. I'm sure whatever brought Paige here from Chicago is a good story. So you're right. I have no idea if she's made mistakes she's trying to leave behind, but whatever she has going on, God has her here for a reason." She shifted the wicker basket to her other hip. "Besides . . ." She shot him a warning look. "You, of all people, know what it's like to need a second chance. You might want to err on the generous side in giving people the benefit of the doubt."

Her truth hit him straight in the gut.

"I don't know what's going on here. Maybe you've just let a bad day get to you, maybe there's something you're not telling me. But . . ." She grasped his shoulder as she walked by and leaned in on her tiptoes to plant a kiss on his cheek. "If I hear you're making Paige's life difficult, my son, I will take you down."

TEN

Paige stood in Kat's kitchen, staring at the scorched lumps that were supposed to be her famous vanilla cupcakes.

She couldn't believe she'd been so stupid as to not click that Kat's high-end oven would be in Celsius not Fahrenheit. Instead, she'd been distracted by a call from Nate and now her usual light and fluffy cakes of vanilla awesomeness, cupcakes baked at 300°C came black on top, raw in the middle, and in haphazard shapes and sizes from being hacked apart as she tried to get them out of the tin.

She looked at her watch. Almost eight-fifteen. She was about to be officially late for Emily's surprise morning tea.

A survey of the contents of the pantry showed nothing had miraculously appeared since the last time she looked.

Half-eaten boxes of cereal, tins of tuna, and boxes of protein bars mocked her. Not a packet of chocolate Tim Tams or chips to be seen, and no time to stop at a grocery store on the way. Maggie's email had come with a DO NOT BE

LATE instruction in bold, red, and 48-point font. There was no way Paige was getting on the wrong side of Janine's EA if she could help it.

She was just going to have to drown them in frosting and hope to heaven no one lost a tooth biting into one.

Paige poured vanilla frosting over the rocks until it oozed over the sides and dripped down the edges, then she scattered the container of sprinkles haphazardly over the top.

The cupcakes looked like they'd been made by a third-grader. Excellent. Hopefully that would stop anyone from being tempted to try and eat one.

Culinary disaster in one hand, Paige grabbed her keys with the other and headed for the door. *Grace* would be all hers after today. The thought was both exhilarating and terrifying.

Half an hour later, she pulled into the parking lot. A trickle of sweat traveled between her shoulder blades. Even though she'd studied the Australian Road Users Handbook right down to the last footnote, driving on the left was still an exercise in palm-sweating-blood-pressure-rocketing terror, and leaving fifteen minutes later than usual had put her right in the middle of peak traffic. Apparently it didn't matter what continent you were on. People across the world were the same during rush hour. Especially when it was raining. The Australians even had a few hand gestures she hadn't encountered before.

The clock on her dashboard yelled eight forty-eight. She had seven minutes to get to the morning tea location.

Paige opened the car door, tugged her skirt down, slung her purse over her shoulder and grabbed the plate of deformed cupcakes off the passenger seat. A gust of wind broadsided her as she climbed out of the car, slammed her door and locked it. She'd chosen today to wear her favorite pair of heels. What an idiot.

Stepping up and over the curb, she tried to protect the cupcakes from the rain as the wind battered her back, her feet sinking into the squishy grass as she angled toward the closest concrete path. The back of one shoe slipped off and she balanced on the other foot to pull it back on before continuing. Wha—The other shoe was now wedged in the sodden soil, and, plate tipping, she was headed face-first for the cement.

One second, Josh had been striding along, minding his own business and on time for Emily's morning tea. The next, some grey-shrouded figure was hurtling across his path, one arm like a windmill. A hand slammed straight into his raspberry shortbread slice, tipping it out of his hand and onto the sodden pavement.

He stood there for a moment, staring at the cellophane packet sitting in the puddle, before realizing he'd somehow caught the destroyer under one armpit.

"You okay?"

A gust of wind blew the hood off her head and the American stared at him. After the dinner at his parents, he'd decided to call her that. Paige was too feminine a name for the little spitfire.

She glared at him, all big brown eyes and wild blonde hair, her face suggesting she couldn't be less thrilled that he was the one who'd caught her. Well, he wasn't exactly psyched about it either. They'd managed to go the two weeks since she'd come to dinner without seeing each other, which he was fine with. He'd been hoping the promising trend would continue until she boarded her plane home.

He'd also been looking forward to a piece of the raspberry slice since the night before and now it was probably ruined. All because the girl couldn't manage to stay on her feet. Again.

"I'm fine. Thanks." She shook off his arm and turned her attention to the ridiculous red shoe that stood wedged in the mud next to them. The bottom of her coat took a dip in a puddle as she crouched down and pulled her shoe out of the mire before shoving it back on her foot.

She was holding a plate of something in her other hand, but the angle she was at meant he couldn't see what it was.

He grabbed a corner of the packet of raspberry

slice, fished it out of its watery grave, and flipped it back over. He wiped the plastic with his sleeve and studied it. Some of the icing had smeared a bit, but it might still be okay. Thank goodness for watertight packaging.

He turned back to the American. "I'm guessing we're going to the same place."

"Probably." Her hood was back up, her face shielded.

"Let's go then. Maggie does not react well to lateness to a surprise function."

Without even answering, she started walking, striding ahead of him. It was going to be like that, was it?

He easily caught up in a couple of steps. His mother's warning rang in his ears. He was going to be civilized if it killed him. "So what did you bring?"

She turned slightly and revealed the contents of her plate with a huff. "These."

"You're joking." The words were out before he could filter them. He was no Master Chef but even he could tell the lopsided cupcakes were burned. Her attempt to hide it was even worse. White icing slid off the tops and dripped everywhere. The multi-colored sprinkles had bled so the colors swam together. What could she be thinking?

He grabbed her shoulder and she swung around to face him.

"What do you think you're doing?" She used her spare hand to push his from her shoulder.

"Have you been drinking?"

She stepped back as if he'd struck her, the hood falling of her head again. "Excuse me?"

"You heard me. You can't walk straight and your cupcakes look like a stoned blind man made them." He leaned in, tried to get a whiff of her breath, but the wind and the rain made it impossible. "Are you drunk?"

The heat in her glare was so fierce he suspected the recent wildfires had burned cooler. "No. I'm not drunk. Sorry to disappoint. I'm just a stupid blonde American who forgot that ovens here are in Celsius not Fahrenheit and can't manage high heels in mud."

The raw honesty in her expression would be hard to fake. She was either telling the truth or a world-class liar. "I apologize."

He waited for her to tell him exactly what he could do with his apology. Instead, Paige looked at the plate in her hands, as if seeing it for the first time and a wry smile formed on her lips. Then something that sounded like a cross between a snort and laugh erupted from her.

The plate shook and a huge glob of icing slid off the top of one of the sad little cakes and onto her thumb. She looked up at him with such undisguised mirth in her expression that he couldn't help but grin back. "You're right about one thing though. These do need to be put out of their misery." Then she turned and chucked the whole thing, plate and all, into a nearby rubbish bin.

She marched off, leaving him standing in the rain and staring after her. He shook his head. The American was getting under his skin.

He didn't like it.

Not at all.

He'd fallen for women who weren't what they seemed before. Twice before. It had almost cost him and his family everything. A third strike would put him out for life.

ELEVEN

Call her a nerd, but no one could deny there were few things more beautiful than an updated Microsoft Project Gantt chart. And not just any old Gantt chart, but one that showed everything tracking on schedule. Some things even tracking ahead.

Paige allowed herself to revel in the glory of her beautiful project plan for a few seconds. Not even the page sitting behind it, an electronic bloodbath tracking the budget, could dent her good mood.

After a month, she still missed Emily's good-humored company, but it was nice to have her own space, to be able to do things her own way.

Leaning back in her chair, she pushed back from her desk and cast her gaze up to the window to check on the weather. She wanted to get to the mall during lunch and pick up some picture frames so she could personalize her office. Blue sky and wispy clouds greeted her. So far winter in June felt remarkably similar to a Chicago summer.

A knock sounded on her office door, and Maggie stuck her head in. "Heya. You've got a delivery."

"Great. That should be the stickers we ordered to go on the gift bags. Can you just tell the delivery guy to put the boxes in the photocopy room?"

A wide smile slid across Maggie's face. "It's not stickers."

"Oh?" She couldn't think of anything else due to arrive today.

Maggie gestured to her. "C'mon. You need to sign for it personally. It's in reception."

This was getting weirder and weirder. Paige pushed back her chair and stood, tugging her skirt down. If nothing else, it provided a good excuse to stretch her legs. "Okay, coming."

Two of the admin girls crossed her path, their usual casual nods turned to broad smiles when they saw her. What was going on?

As she neared the front desk, Chloe, the receptionist, looked up and gave her an equally large grin.

"There's a delivery for me?"

"Sure is." Chloe was still grinning as she nodded to the waiting area, obscured from Paige's view. She paused, legs almost unwilling to take her around the corner. Everyone was way too excited. Something was up.

Peering around the corner, she was met by a

blur of color. Pinks, oranges, yellows, purples, all combined in the world's largest bouquet of flowers held by a set of burly arms.

"Looks like someone has an admirer." Chloe's words broke through her haze.

"What?" Paige's fingers curled around the wall corner for support. An admirer? That was ridiculous. She spent her entire day surrounded by women, and the only guy she'd felt a flicker of anything for had proven himself to be an arrogant jerk.

She hadn't seen Josh since the cupcake debacle. The band had been on the road some of the time, which suited her fine. It was inconvenient enough that the whole altercation kept intruding on her thoughts at the most inconvenient moments. She'd never wanted to slap someone so badly in her whole life as when he insinuated she was a drunk but then when he'd pulled out that grin . . . well, that had sent her pulse rocketing for a whole different reason.

She shook her head, forcing him from her mind. "Are you sure they're for me?" She directed her question to Chloe, saving the delivery guy from having to check. The bouquet was so large, it obscured his entire head.

Chloe flicked her ponytail over her shoulder. "Assuming you're still Paige McAllister, yes."

She turned toward the deliveryman. Why hadn't someone warned her to bring her wallet?

She didn't have money on her to give him a tip.

"Thanks." She took the blooms from the guy's arms.

The face of a blonde, freckled teenager popped out from behind them. "Don't thank me, thank the guy who dropped a bomb on these things. I just need you to sign here." He poked a small device at her.

"Hold on a sec." She placed the bouquet on the coffee table, took the stylus he held out and scrawled her initials across the screen.

"Awesome. Have a nice day."

Turning her attention back to the behemoth, the delivery guy's words rolled over her. *Thank the guy who dropped a bomb on these.*

"So? Who are they from?" Chloe poked her head up like a tortoise from behind her desk.

Paige wrangled with the staples for a second, trying not to tear the wrapping as she pulled the envelope free and pulled out a plain white card.

Congratulations on two months on your big adventure. Missing you. Nate.

A smile tipped up her lips. She missed him too, more than she'd imagined she would. Missed his stability, his sincerity, his friendship. They still talked most weeks.

The flowers drew her eyes downward as she hefted them into her arms and sucked in the floral fragrance. She didn't even want to guess how much they had cost.

"What did you do? A night raid on the botanic gardens?" Josh's voice drifted from behind her and she flinched, the rectangular card slipping from her fingers as she turned. He cast a scathing glance over the bouquet. "Maybe next time he might like to sponsor a starving African village as a demonstration of affection."

She pierced him with a glare, trapping the card under the tip of her shoe. "Maybe you should take some of that attitude and—" She cut herself off before she could say something that would be the highlight of her day but definitely career limiting.

He tilted his head. "And?"

"Go talk to Jesus about it."

His mouth wobbled as he fought to contain the laughter that she could see in his eyes. "I appreciate your concern for my spiritual welfare, Miss McAllister." With that, he brushed past her and strode away.

Patronizing sod. Oh, well, it could always be worse. At least she didn't work for him.

"You just rest up, okay? We'll manage." Josh dropped his mother's desk phone back into its cradle, then stood and stretched his back.

Great. He'd been back in the city less than forty-eight hours and his tour planner had come

112

down with glandular fever. She'd be off work for at least two months. Right when they were already having trouble nailing down the details of their next New Zealand and US tours.

He shook out his arms. Why had he decided to make the call from his mother's office? If he'd turned around and gone back to his office to make it when he remembered, he would've missed seeing the arrival of the American's ridiculous floral tribute.

Go talk to Jesus about it. Ha. Jesus definitely hadn't been the first destination she'd had in mind.

He looked at his watch. Ten past twelve. He checked the schedule on his mum's desk. Yes, there he was. *Midday, lunch with Josh.*

He craved something greasy and meaty before he tackled his latest staffing problem. No doubt his mum would want to go somewhere that served organic rabbit food. Speaking of, her familiar blonde head teetered into the office, a precarious stack of books perched under her chin.

"What are those for?" Josh walked around the desk, ready to grab the books before they crashed.

"I'm good." His mother dropped the books on the side table under the window. "We're doing the women's Bible study on mercy next term. I need to start prepping some of the material." She turned toward him, tilting her head. "What's wrong? Some of the gear get damaged in transit?"

"Marcy has glandular fever."

She stared at him blankly.

"Our tour planner."

"Marcy, Marcy." His mother tapped a finger to her lips. "Petite brown-haired girl?"

Considering Marcy was at least forty-five, "girl" was stretching it a little.

"She was only part-time, right? Like two or three days a week?" His mother turned back to her pile, placing the top half of the stack on the table.

What did he look like, payroll? All he knew was she got the job done. "I think she did a total of two days but usually as four half-days while the kids were in school."

His mother smiled the kind of smile that made him suspicious. "Excellent. In that case I have the perfect solution. Someone was just telling me this morning they have some capacity."

"Who?"

His words hit his mother's back. She was already heading back out the door.

He groaned. The last time he needed assistance, his mother had saddled him with a single mother who "needed some support to get back into the workforce." The woman hadn't worked since the nineties and had spent most of her time eyeing him up in the way Potiphar's wife must have looked at Joseph. He couldn't get back on the road fast enough.

He blew a breath out between clenched teeth. He loved his mother, but he didn't have time to train up one of her little projects. He needed someone who could hit the ground running.

His mother marched back into the room with a pleased expression as the American followed her. She looked the opposite, all pinched brows and pursed lips.

Oh no. She was not going near his tour. Or his team.

He opened his mouth to say that in the last ten seconds a solution had magically appeared and he didn't in fact need any help. None at all.

"Paige will do it," his mother announced. "She can give you up to two days a week."

He shoved his hands into his pockets. "Surely the A—Paige is busy with *Grace*." Surely they'd both rather bang their respective heads into a brick wall for sixteen hours a week than be forced to work together.

"Actually, she's so brilliant that we're two weeks ahead on all the big milestones. Which makes her exactly what you need." His mother stepped toward him, her expression daring him to argue.

"Do you know anything about organizing a tour?" He turned toward the American. He could stare her down.

She shook her head, leaned against the doorway, looking polished in her white shirt, wide belt, and fitted gray skirt. "Nope. But I'm a professional logistics planner and event manager. How hard can it be?"

How hard could it be? Was she serious? "For a start there will be twelve concerts in eight cities over four weeks in two countries. You have over thirty band members, some will be on one tour, some on both. You have to deal with flights, transport, hotels, and freighting instruments. Musicians with charming little quirks like only sleeping on even-numbered floors and losing their mind if their seat number has an F in it. Would you like me to go on?"

She crossed her arms and stared at him. "Do I need to arrange to have every trash can, every letterbox, every pothole within a one mile radius cleared for bombs?"

"Uh . . . no."

"Do I need to have sixteen contingency plans for a terrorist attack, ranging across magnitudes, types, and level of lockdown required?"

"Um, no."

"Do I need to know the details of every hospital within a fifty-mile radius, their specialties, services, and how many casualties they can take?"

He shook his head. "No."

"Will I need to have everyone who so much as breathes near the logistics of the event screened by the CIA, FBI, and NSA?"

Okay, she had to be making that up.

She took his silence as surrender. "Then I'm sure me and your little tour will be just fine."

His mother patted him on the shoulder and grinned. "And that, my son, is what we old people refer to as getting schooled."

He didn't see what was so funny.

"Now you two go work out the details." She flicked her hands at them.

Luckily, he already had plans. "We'll have to do it later." As in never, because he was going to spend the afternoon finding another solution no matter what it took. "We're supposed to be having lunch."

She glanced at her schedule. "So we are. Even better. I've got a Bible study to plan, so you can take Paige out. Work things out over food."

He'd been sewn up tighter than the game ball at the Bledisloe Cup.

He plastered a smile on his face for his mother's benefit. "Great, shall we?"

From the American's expression, she'd prefer a lobotomy. That made two of them.

He gestured her out of the room ahead of him, then turned. "Bye, Mum."

She looked up, a twinkle in her eye. "Bye, honey. Have fun."

He'd turn into an organic, wheat-free vegan before that happened.

He waited until the two of them were out of the office, out of earshot, then leaned down beside her, the apple-y scent of her hair distracting him. Focus, Tyler! "Just so you know, you may have fooled my mother, but you won't have it so easy with me."

She stopped mid-stride and pinned him with a scathing glare. "Darlin', my last boss was a lazy, incompetent alcoholic who only had a business because of her rich daddy's connections. So unless you have the mafia in one back pocket and Al-Qaeda in the other, I could organize this tour with one arm tied behind my back and both eyes shut."

Food court for lunch it was. At least when they both lost it, there would be limited damage they could do to each other with plastic forks.

TWELVE

The car ride to the mall had had all the warmth of North Dakota in January, and it stank of gym socks and sweat.

Paige had tried to back out not once, but six times, on the silent walk to the car park. The only terse words Josh had uttered were that the boss said they were going to lunch, and so that was exactly what they were doing.

She hadn't even had time to put Nate's bouquet in a vase before Janine had come flying in and hustled her to her office, throwing around something about Paige being the perfect solution. So right now, gorgeous flowers lay dying on her desk so she could have lunch with her boss's stupid son.

At least he'd brought her to a mall. The food court resembled all the others she'd visited—overcrowded with the lunchtime rush, reeking of grease, with infants wailing and generic mall music pumping so loudly it would be almost impossible to hold a conversation.

"What can I get you?" Josh reached into his pocket.

"I'm capable of getting my own food."

He shrugged, his blue T-shirt stretching across his broad shoulders. "Suit yourself. I'll meet you back here in ten."

He disappeared into the crowd, and she turned to survey her options. A burger. That's what she would get. If she had to have lunch with him, she was at least going to have something good. The biggest stack of meat and cheese she could find fit the bill.

She weaved her way through the crowd, bypassing the Golden Arches for a sandwich joint with a flashing burger icon.

The line moved quickly, and within minutes, she stood in front of a boy who looked like he should be in school, not serving fast food for minimum wage.

"What can I get you?"

She scanned the menu above his head. "I'd like the Double Stacker please, fries, and a bottle of Diet Coke."

He paused, eyed her up and down. "Are you sure? It's pretty big."

She flashed him a smile. "Perfect."

He gave her another doubtful look, but tapped her order into the register. "That'll be fifteen-sixty."

She barely managed to keep her face under control. Fifteen-sixty for a burger and fries? It had better be impressive.

Digging into her purse, she pulled out her wallet and flipped it open.

Her heart dropped as she stared into its gaping depths. Oh, no. No notes.

Australian coins were her nemesis. The notes were easy, being color-coded and all. Purple for five, blue for ten, orange for twenty. But the change was annoying. One dollar and two dollar coins. Coins! No quarters. Things with weird shapes. And even though she was great with numbers, for some reason she lost the ability to remember which was which when someone was standing there, waiting for her to pay them.

She unzipped her change compartment, and emptied the contents onto her hand. Gold and silver mingled together in her palm.

She stared at them. She could do this. The gold coins were ones and twos. The big silver weird shaped ones were like half dollars.

"Do you want some help?" Josh materialized beside her holding a kebab.

If she said no, he'd just stand there watching her flounder around like she hadn't passed first grade math. So she swallowed her pride. "That would be great. Thanks."

As she extended her hand toward him, the sleeve of her blouse rode up her wrist, exposing the puckered start of her scar.

"Bet that hurt." Josh nodded toward her arm as he made quick work of plucking an assortment of coins from her palm and handing them over.

"Yup. Compound fracture. Needed screws, surgery, the works." Over the years, Paige had learned that trying to hide the scar once it had been seen or dodge questions about it made people more interested. Providing a little bit of detail was usually enough to satiate their curiosity and give her the chance to divert the conversation.

Josh opened his mouth but she cut him off before he could ask any more questions. "So which ones are the ones and which are twos? I can never remember." She threw on her ditzy blonde voice for good measure. She'd rather have him think she was stupid than have him ask questions that would force her to either lie, or tell the truth and become an object of pity.

"The two-dollar coins are smaller." Josh handed a last couple of coins over and the counter guy gave her the ticket for her order, and a bottle of Diet Coke.

Pocketing her ticket, Paige tipped the remainder of the pile back into her purse with a cascade of clinks as they stepped back from the counter and joined the people waiting for their orders.

"Thanks for that." Her words were terse and her fingers gripped the neck of the bottle in a stranglehold. She checked that the cuff was back in place. Hopefully with Josh it would be a case out of sight, out of mind. It had been a long time since someone seeing it had left her feeling so vulnerable and exposed.

"No worries. What did you order?"

"A burger."

She could feel him eyeing her. So maybe her skirt had been a little tight when she put it on this morning. Kat cooked better than Nigella Lawson, and she didn't have the funds to buy a whole new wardrobe. And that was before even considering the downright depressing Australian sizing system that had deemed her to be in the double digits for the first time in her life.

"What?" Her words came out sharp, accusatory.

"I didn't say anything."

Okay, to be fair, he hadn't. She snuck a glance. His expression didn't seem to hold any hint of "the girl needs to start laying off the burgers" in it.

"Sorry."

"What for?"

"I—forget it." She shook her head.

"Is this how it's going to be?"

"What?"

"Us working together. If we're going to be thrown together like this, maybe we could declare a truce, just try to be civilized."

Paige studied him. He seemed genuine, and yet . . . "Are you going to take back what you said about me not being of fit character to work for your mom?"

His gaze hardened. "No."

"Then yes, that's how it's going to be."

"Number fifty-four."

That was her. She moved toward the counter. Oh.

The woman at the counter pushed forward a plate with a towering monstrosity—three thick beef patties, bacon, cheese, an egg, a slice of pineapple, what looked like a hash brown patty, lettuce, tomato and something purple. The bottom half of the bun was almost flattened under the weight, and the top half teetered on the leaning pile. Next to it sat an enormous pile of fat fries. She wasn't sure she could lift the meal, let alone eat it.

She handed over her ticket, added her bottle of soda to the brown plastic tray, and grasped both sides.

The woman dropped on a couple packets of ketchup. "Haven't made one of these in ages. Your boyfriend sure must be hungry."

"It's for me." The women's eyes widened as Paige hefted the tray. The burger tottered, then in slow motion, the top of the bun and the first patty slid off the top with a *slurp*.

She had a better chance of playing for the symphony again than she did of getting through this lunch with what remained of her dignity still intact.

Which was fine. She didn't care what Josh

thought he knew of her. All that mattered was that he didn't know the truth.

Josh smothered a grin. The thing was bigger than her head. Paige sat on the other side of the plastic table with such a defeated expression on her face, he almost felt sorry for her. Almost.

She craned her neck and studied the burger from all angles, like a demolition worker sizing up a building that needed to be destroyed. There was no chance she could fit that thing in her mouth, although it would be entertaining watching her try.

She picked up a chip, stabbed it into her mound of tomato sauce, and took a bite, still eyeing the burger like it might jump off the plate and attack her.

Either she was going to have to admit defeat and disassemble the thing into manageable pieces or the first bite would send the contents flying in all directions. That he had learned from experience.

He sighed. No matter how much she irritated him, he wasn't that mean. "You might want to take it apart."

She cast him with a withering glare. "I can eat a burger, thank you."

"I'm sure you can, but—"

"In America, we call this a snack."

He shrugged and picked up his own kebab,

hiding his smile behind it. She couldn't say he hadn't warned her.

Using both hands, she leaned down on the top of the bun, squashing the monster down. Tomato sauce oozed out the side, then the sticky yellow of broken egg yolk, followed by a stream of purple beetroot juice. Grabbing both sides, she hefted the thing up like a trophy until it was perched in front of her mouth.

He glanced over his shoulder. The table behind then was empty. Thank goodness. Because something was sure to come flying in his direction, and when it did, he'd be moving fast. He wasn't going to end up wearing half a grease factory just because Little Miss Professional Eater America had something to prove.

She opened her mouth, then opened it some more. Wow. It was like the girl could unhinge her jaw or something. He'd driven in tunnels that were smaller. Taking a deep breath, she bit down. He coiled, ready to dive left or right. Like he was a fighter pilot in World War II dodging flak above enemy territory.

The burger wobbled and bulged, a lone pickle escaping and dropping to her plate with a *plop*. Then she pulled it away from her face and sat there chewing, serenely. He stared at her, at the burger.

She chewed for a few seconds, then swallowed. "Not bad. Needs some barbeque sauce." Then, turning the burger a few centimeters, she went for her second bite. This time nothing dropped, spilled, *plopped*. It all held together, like she was eating nothing more substantial than a peanut butter sandwich.

A ripple of something traveled through him. Admiration. Begrudging, but admiration nonetheless. Who was this girl who handled a burger better than any guy he knew?

Her sleeves had slid down her arms. The pale scar ran from her wrist to the middle of her forearm, then disappeared back under the cuff. That must have been some break. And the way her gaze had flickered and her breath hitched when he asked about it indicated there was more to it than she liked people to know.

He didn't need to know what it was. Everyone had their story. All he needed to know about Paige was that she could do the job that had to be done.

Yet his gaze kept returning to the scar.

Setting her burger back down, Paige picked up a couple of chips and popped them into her mouth. "You not hungry?"

She nodded toward his kebab, which he'd been holding for who-knew-how-long while he watched her. Smooth, Josh, real smooth.

She wiped her mouth with a napkin. "You can keep staring at me while I eat if you want, but how about you tell me about his tour?"

• • •

Paige was going to be sick. Sixteen kinds of grease fought in her stomach. She'd spent the last ten minutes forcing down a few more bites of the meat monstrosity while Josh gave an overview of the tour she was going to help with. If she never saw another burger in her whole life, it would be too soon.

But it had been worth it for the look on Josh's face when she took that first bite. First shock, then awe. It had been all she could do to keep a straight face and chew. She'd been fully expecting the thing to explode like a cluster bomb, raining meat and condiments on them both. Her biggest hope had been that at least he would get pegged with the egg. Yolk was almost impossible to get out, and his T-shirt looked it didn't have much life left in it anyway. Unlike her brand-new shirt.

She abandoned her food and focused on draining her Diet Coke.

"Are you going to finish those?" Josh pointed at her fries.

She shook her head.

"Do you mind?"

She pushed her plate forward. "Be my guest."

She studied him as he emptied out the remains of her ketchup onto her fries. His dark hair poked in multiple directions, long dark lashes framing his gray eyes. His T-shirt stretched across his broad chest, highlighting well defined biceps exiting from each sleeve.

Licking the ketchup from his fingers, he caught her gaze and smiled. It transformed his face, from arrogant and smug to—she tried to ignore the mini-hurricane it unleashed in the pit of her stomach.

So he was good looking. So what? He was still a jerk. That was what mattered. There was a Bible verse about that somewhere. She clearly needed to find it, memorize it, and chant it to herself every time she was around this guy. Which, unfortunately, now looked like it would be often.

Taking a swig of his water, Josh wiped his mouth with a napkin. "I have to say, that was impressive." He seemed to be offering a tentative truce. She regarded it warily.

"Thanks."

He took another sip, his eyes focused on the tabletop. "Are you at least a Christian?"

First her character, now her faith? "Are you?"

He choked. "Excuse me."

"Are. You. A. Christian?" She said the words slowly.

"How could I not be?"

Um, because, as her daddy used to say, going to church made you a Christian about as much as going to McDonald's made you a hamburger. She was thinking that applied even if you happened to be the son of megachurch uber-pastors. "Pretty sure there's a verse in the Bible about how people are going to roll up to heaven, claiming they did all sorts of great things in Jesus's name, and he's going to shoot them down." That was the Paige McAllister paraphrased translation. Available soon at a Lifeway near you.

"Touché." He held up his grease and ketchup-coated hands. "Okay, I'm sorry. You're right. That was offensive."

She stared at him. "Very."

He slurped the ketchup from his fingers, then sighed. "I apologize if I upset you. It's just I'm protective of my family. My parents get a lot of grief just for being who they are. They've been burned before trusting the wrong people."

She could understand that. Fine. If they were going to have to work together, she'd meet him halfway. "I'm good at what I do, okay? I'm not going to pretend I'm a big fan of megachurches, because I'm not. And I certainly couldn't care less if you and your band are some sort of big deal in the circles that you run in. Your whole life is basically my worst nightmare. So don't expect any kind of star treatment from me. But if you just let me do my job, we'll be fine."

He regarded her for a few seconds, then nodded. "Deal."

Something in Josh's gaze tugged at her, cutting through her doubt and annoyance. Had her wanting to know what his deal was. What had happened in his charmed looking life to make him so cynical.

Questions that would all have to remain unanswered. Josh Tyler had probably broken more hearts over the years than she'd played recitals. Hers was not going to be one of them.

THIRTEEN

"Hey." Kellie gave a cursory tap on the door to Paige's office.

"Um, hi." Paige turned in her chair as Kellie walked in and sat on her couch. She put down the stack of invoices she'd been triple-checking and eyed her surprise visitor. Kellie twirled a piece of long glossy hair. Her jeans-clad legs were crossed, polished brown boot dangling above the floor.

They'd had occasional interactions since Kellie was the worship liaison for *Grace*, but this visit was a first.

"I hear you're coming to help us out with the tour." Kellie crossed her legs, placing her perfectly manicured fingers on her knee.

Paige tipped back in her chair, twirled her pen in her hands. "Just for a couple of days a week. Things with *Grace* are under control, so Janine asked if I could give you guys a hand with Marcy being sick and all."

"Well, I just wanted to drop by and say welcome to the team. If there's anything I can do to help you with getting your feet under the desk, let me know."

"Thanks, I appreciate it." Paige glanced down at the pile of papers on her desk. She had to get them done ASAP but Kellie seemed like a genuinely decent girl. "How long have you been at Harvest?"

Kellie settled back in the couch. "My parents joined right at the beginning, when it was fifty people in a school hall in Yarra. My sister and I grew up with Amanda, Josh, and Sarah. Went to school together. Youth group. My mum was the church's first official employee after Greg. Admin assistant. It's just so crazy to think that now it's turned into this." She waved her hands around her.

"And when did you join the band?"

Kellie squinted for a second. "Eight, no nine, years ago. They're like a second family. You spend so much time on the road together, and long hours in the studio."

"I can only imagine." It wasn't hard. That had almost been her life until it was ripped out from under her feet. Paige forced herself back to the present. "You have a beautiful voice."

"Thank you." Kellie shifted slightly. "You must be super stoked getting to work with Josh and all."

Interesting. "I'm happy to help out the band however I can."

"But you'll be mainly working with Josh."

Paige studied Kellie's face for a second,

forming her response. "Well, once I know what needs to be done, I imagine I'll be mainly working with hotels, airlines, and your promoters in New Zealand and the US. Those sorts of people." In fact, her plan was to have as little to do with the man himself as possible. That they'd survived lunch the week before without blood on the floor had been nothing short of a miracle. Since then, their only contact had been a few emails.

Something like relief glimmered on Kellie's face. The picture became crystal clear: this poor girl had dibs on the position of Mrs. Josh Tyler. And why shouldn't she? She'd make the perfect superstar Christian wife.

"So you don't think you'll be working with him much?"

The sweet girl had it bad if she thought Paige might be competition. Paige managed to rein in her amusement and maintain a neutral expression. "I honestly don't know. But I'd imagine he's a busy guy so I'll try to bug him the least amount possible. I'm a professional logistics manager for major events. I've worked with some big celebrities and the one thing they all have in common is being time poor."

"True." Kellie sounded doubtful. Clearly she couldn't imagine why any woman wouldn't be jumping at the opportunity to work with Josh for as many hours as the Lord gave.

Paige exhaled slowly. She should say more, assure Kellie she couldn't be less interested in her trophy husband. The last thing she needed was for the woman to get in the way because she felt compelled to protect her turf.

Kellie pointed to Nate's bouquet. "They're gorgeous flowers."

Perfect. Paige pasted a dreamy smile on her face. "Aren't they? They're from a good friend back home. He sent them for my first two months working here." She leaned in and took a deep whiff. Okay, maybe that was overkill. But when she turned, Kellie had a smile on her face and was uncrossing her leg as if preparing to stand. She'd take that as a sign that she'd managed to remove the bull's eye from her back.

"Hey, Paige." Josh stuck his head in her door.

Paige watched from the corner of her eye as Kellie sat up straighter, chest thrusting out and giving her hair a discreet fluff. Josh's gaze flickered to Kellie for a split second, then returned to Paige.

"I wanted to let you know that if you need to make any international calls for the tour, come do it over in our offices. That's the easiest way to get the cost coded to the band."

"Okay, thanks." Paige reached for her invoices.

"Well it's been great chatting." Kellie stood, straightening her jacket. "Josh, do you want to grab a coffee and go over the songs for Sunday?"

Josh glanced at his watch. "I'm on my way to a meeting. You're leading worship this week, so if you're happy with the selection, send the song list through to the team."

Oh, the poor girl. The guy was clueless. Paige hoped she had a decent wingman on her team.

"Thanks for dropping by."

She shook her head as Kellie scampered away down the corridor on Josh's heels like an over-enthusiastic terrier. Good luck to her. Kellie and Josh. Now, that match made perfect sense.

FOURTEEN

Standing in the pre-dawn dark, suited up in a gray and blue jumpsuit, head adorned with a snazzy headlamp, Paige rued her decision to start her birthday with a McMuffin. Even if it was tradition.

She still couldn't believe Nate had coordinated this with Kat, her cousin a more than willing co-conspirator.

Kat loved surprises. Especially surprises that involved scaring the pants off Paige by hauling her out of bed at four-thirty in the morning.

Paige jiggled the little black wheel attached to the belt around her waist. The wheel that would soon be clipped to a wire running up the Sydney Harbour Bridge.

Hints of daylight surfacing on the horizon. The climb was timed so the sun would be rising as they reached the top.

Paige swallowed hard, glad these people had given two safety lectures and checked and rechecked their equipment. The bridge got taller and scarier every time she looked up. Majestic, imposing, steel arms twisting and reaching into the sky.

Her cousin stood behind her in line, her lamp highlighting her face, which was glowing with excitement.

Paige ran through the directions in her head. There were fourteen of them in the group. They would start in the climb base, then walk on catwalks below the bridge until they reached the southeast pylon. Then they'd ascend four ladders to the start of the upper arch before continuing along the bridge's outer arch on the Opera House side until they hit the top, where they could enjoy the view, pose for pictures. After that, they would cross the spine of the bridge to the Darling Harbour side to make their descent back to the base.

One of the guides came down the line, triple-checking everyone's gear. They'd already been breath-tested. No chance of someone getting to climb after a big night out.

Their group was a combination of ages and nationalities, all lined up in identical jumpsuits, like a chain gang from a prison movie. All the same, yet so different. From the guy who kept patting the obvious ring-box-sized bulge in his jumpsuit pocket to the young woman with tattoos curling above her neckline.

Her headset crackled. "All right everyone, sunrise is at seven oh-one this morning, so it's time to get moving."

The line shifted forward, Paige spun the little

safety wheel in her hand, waiting her turn to be clipped on.

When she reached the base, a guide attached her to the safety wire and she started walking along the catwalk. The traffic roared above, the sound of cars, trucks, and heavy machinery splicing through the peeking dawn. Then came the ladders. She soon felt her muscles protesting as she climbed, listening as the metal clanged and creaked under the weight of the group.

Of all the fears she had, heights wasn't one of them. Thank goodness. She soaked in the changing view. Half listened to the guide telling stories about the history of the bridge through her headset. Glanced below to see Kat's enthralled face close on her heels.

Whew. Despite the cool winter air, sweat wound its way down her back. She focused the beam of her headlamp on the next step, arms and legs feeling the burn as they climbed higher, passing the first level with the traffic. The headlights below disappeared into a blur of orange and yellow motion. She looked up, her shoulders and quads straining. It would have been nice if Kat had conjured up a reason for a training regimen to prepare for this. She sucked in a deep breath. One ladder to go before they started walking up the spine of the arch.

After she reached the top of the final ladder, she paused while a guide swapped her safety gear over to the next line. Once given the all-clear, she stood from her crouched position and peered over the side of the safety railing.

Time disappeared as she followed the rest of the group up the bridge. The view took her breath away. The harbor spread out in front of her, the golden sun peeked over the far horizon, illuminating the lights and outlines of boats cruising across the calm water. Right below them, the creamy seashell shapes of the Sydney Opera House emerged in the dawning light.

Ethan would have loved this. The thought flickered through Paige's mind and before she knew it, tears were streaming down her cheeks.

Her brother had a long list of things he'd wanted to achieve. Activities on every continent. In Australia, he'd wanted to climb Ayers Rock, scuba dive the Great Barrier Reef, hold a koala, and do exactly what she was doing right now.

The list had been in his wallet. Folded into four and stashed between receipts and coffee cards. Wallet, watch, phone, and keys. The four items in the clear Ziploc bag returned with his body. The ordinary belongings of a man who had no idea when he pocketed them that it would be for the last time.

Red, blue, and green pen. Sometimes pencil. The list was a haphazard collection of things added as they occurred to him. Ethan had managed to check off maybe a quarter of the items. He'd thought he had decades ahead of him to get it all done. They all did. She'd folded the paper back up and stashed it in her violin case with all the other dreams that died that day. Forgotten about it. Until right now.

Her cousin tapped her on the shoulder, gesturing to Paige's face as she mouthed *you okay?*

Paige nodded. She was okay. And since she was here, she was going to experience it for Ethan too. She looked around, trying to imagine what he'd be doing if he were here.

No doubt he'd be chatting up the gorgeous South American girl toward the back of the group. Though the requirement to keep their headsets on may have hampered his impressive charms, he would have seen it as a challenge, not a setback. He'd definitely be the guy making a face in every photo. Asking the instructors what it took to get a job here. Plotting how he could add "bridge climbing guide" to his long list of adventuring skills.

Her soul ached as the wind wrapped a cocoon around her. After six years, she was managing to navigate through most days without being sucked into the abyss of his absence. It simply sat on her radar, the never-wavering blip of guilt, ready to pierce her in those increasingly rare moments where she wanted to tell him something or ask his advice.

Then in moments like these, it seemed

impossible that he wasn't still here, joking he'd take her wheelie thing off the safety line, threatening to climb over her if she didn't move faster.

She peered up into the heavens. She wasn't sure if she believed any of that "watching over us" talk. If heaven was as great as the Bible said, she was sure her brother had plenty to keep him occupied without keeping an eye on what was happening down here. But just in case, she blew him a kiss and waved. The haunting ache in her arm reminding her it was her fault he wasn't here to conquer the bridge himself.

FIFTEEN

The alarm wasn't set. Josh peered at the familiar gray box, double-checking the series of lights. Definitely disarmed. Odd. The cleaners were vigilant about making sure it was set when they left at night. Josh locked the front door behind him, and trod through the dim, silent hallways toward his office. Eight on a Saturday morning seemed to be the only time the building was quiet enough for him to get a decent amount of work done without interruption.

Turning left at an intersection of corridors, he took a sip of his double-shot flat white and hefted his satchel further onto his shoulder before rubbing his temple. Maybe it was time to give into the clamor from the band's governing board and hire his own assistant. Even with the band's admin assistant and two interns, the workload was becoming more and more impossible for him to manage.

Then he'd have to delegate, and anyone who'd ever had to work with him soon learned he was terrible at delegation. He'd thought Paige was going to strangle him with her bare hands earlier in the week when he'd second-guessed part of the travel itinerary she'd put together.

His chest tightened at the thought. The American was more than adequate at her job; he'd give her that. Great, even. Already she'd managed to save them a few grand on their cargo costs. The team loved her, with her attention to detail, the way she made sure she understood exactly what was needed. But having her spend time in his building, not knowing in any given moment when he might be about to walk into her . . . It was messing with his head. Especially when the more he saw of her, the harder it became to reconcile Paige-the-detail-obsessed-logistics-planner with Paige-the-messy-drunk-from-the-plane.

Light spilled from the open door of his office. He skidded to a halt, coffee sloshing in his cup. He was sure he'd closed the door and turned the lights off as he left last night.

Josh crept toward the open door and slipped his bag onto a nearby chair, setting his coffee cup beside it. If he found someone in there with sticky fingers, he couldn't guarantee he wouldn't swing first and love them like Jesus second. The cost of insuring all their gear was already ridiculous.

"Sean, I know you can do better than that. That's not even as good as the rate you give Triple A members and I'm offering you almost twenty rooms during the off-season." The familiar accent wafted out from his door.

What was the American doing here?

Peering around the door, he found Paige at the spare desk in his office, lounging in the chair with her sneaker-clad feet up on the wood, as if it had been her space for years.

It wasn't her space at all. He'd waved to it and mentioned Marcy occasionally sat there, but it hadn't been an invitation for her to use it. Especially not when there were spare desks down the hall with the interns.

He leaned against the doorframe, studying her profile. She was so fixated on her conversation and the spreadsheet in front of her, she hadn't noticed him.

Her long legs were clad in track pants which looked like they could use a wash, and an oversized white T-shirt enveloped her frame. Her hair was piled on top of her head, held in place by a hideous fluorescent yellow plastic clip. A pair of rectangular glasses perched on her nose.

She looked a bit undone. Compared to her usual perfectly made-up and attired self, he preferred this look. A lot.

A smile crept onto her face, but didn't make it to her voice. "Sean, you're killing me here. You know how much I love you guys and I so want the band to stay with you, but one-thirty is as high as I can go."

She listened for a few seconds, then grinned and punched her free hand in the air. "All right, I can make it work at one-forty if you include breakfast and the upgrade."

Josh did the math on the currency conversion and felt his jaw drop. If she was getting similar deals at all their hotels she'd be saving them thousands across the whole tour.

"Done. These are my details." She rattled off her email and phone number, then the details of the credit card they used for tour-related bookings. From memory.

"Can you give me the confirmation number?" She picked up a pen and started scribbling on the pad beside her. "Got it. Thanks, Sean. They'll be perfect angels, I promise. Make sure you give my love to Mary and the kids." She ended the call and leaned back in her chair, grinning.

He was about to step forward when her chair ricocheted back on its wheels and she was on her feet, doing what he could only assume was some kind of victory dance. He'd witnessed a lot of terrible dancing in his time, but this had to be the worst. It looked like a safety video he'd seen once, warning of what it would look like if someone was getting electrocuted.

It made her more human. It made her more likeable. It made the next month a hundred times harder. How was he supposed to keep a cool distance when he'd been witness to this?

Now her arms were up in a V and Paige was shaking her behind like she was auditioning for a Beyoncé video. To the computer, jump ninety degrees to the wall, ninety degrees to his computer.

Oh no. He needed to disappear n—too late. She'd jumped around to face the door, and froze, arms still in the air, with the huge brown eyes of a kangaroo caught in the headlights of a car on the open road.

In spite of his best effort, he couldn't contain the grin that took over his face.

Paige tugged her T-shirt down and tried to sweep her wild hair back into the ugly clip. "Just so you know, you've been getting totally robbed on your US hotel rates for years."

Josh nodded. "So I heard. Thanks."

He couldn't do it, couldn't keep a straight face. He held up a hand. "Can you excuse me? Just for a second."

Without waiting for an answer, he strode down the hall, only making it as far as his coffee before he lost it.

The last time she'd been this humiliated, Paige had been sixteen, at a movie with a date. And her father, sitting two rows behind them. Halfway through *Notting Hill*, Johnny Conroy, football player and bible club co-leader, started to execute the good old yawn-and-stretch maneuver. "Lay a hand on my daughter, and it's the last time you'll be using it" had cut across Hugh's bumbling words to Julia. Needless to say, Johnny Conroy had never called again. Neither had any other guy that year.

At least Josh had had the decency not to laugh right in front of her. Judging by the sound echoing down the hall, he'd taken it all of fifteen feet away. She peered out the door. He stood there, leaning against the wall, whole body shaking with laughter, tears streaming down his cheeks.

Okay, so she wasn't the world's greatest dancer. But she had just saved them like a grand on their Atlanta hotel bill. In this business, you had to claim your wins where you could.

Slumping back in her chair, she buried her head in her hands as she imagined what he must have witnessed. It wasn't like she'd just done a minor victory dance. No. She'd pulled out the extended version in all its fist-pumping—oh Lord—booty shaking glory.

And she was one hundred percent certain it was not the Shekinah kind of glory that dwelt in the tabernacle in the Old Testament.

Covering her eyes, she groaned.

"Okay, it wasn't that bad." His voice came from the doorway.

She splayed open her fingers and peered through the gaps. Josh leaned against the door frame still grinning, but no longer weeping.

"I'm pretty sure it was."

He offered one of those pained grimaces people gave when you were right, but they didn't want to be the one to tell you.

She dropped her hands from her eyes, wanting to find a reason to be angry at him. Like for being in on a Saturday morning when she should have had every right to do her absurd jig in peace. But the whole situation was so ridiculous, she just couldn't. "On the upside, at least now you know dance is not one of my spiritual gifts."

Walking into the room, he dropped his brown leather satchel on the floor and spun around his chair to face her before sinking into it. "Just quietly, it's not one of mine either."

They stared at each other as he lifted his takeout cup to his lips. "Sorry. If I'd known you were going to be here, I would've picked you one up. What are you doing here anyway?" He kicked his feet up on the side of his desk and tilted back in his chair.

She copied his posture, but without coffee in her hands, she settled for slipping them behind her head. Oh, she wasn't. She was. Yes, she was still wearing Kat's hideous yellow banana clip. Would there be no limit to her shame this morning? "It's Friday afternoon in the US, the best time to get the people I needed to talk to about negotiating some reasonable hotel prices for the tour."

"How many have you done so far?"

"Just Atlanta and Nashville."

"And did you break them in Nashville as well?"

She couldn't stop the smile the snuck onto her lips. "It would be fair to say the Regency won't be making a lot of money off you."

He shuffled his heels over to where the end of his desk met hers, his chair turning so he faced her directly. "Paige McAllister. We have a bit of a problem."

"What?"

His brow furrowed, and he chewed his bottom lip for a second. "Well you see, I've thought about it and I just can't see how . . ."

Seriously? He was going to fire her when she'd already saved them like five grand?

". . . after this morning, we can still hate each other."

What?

He kept going. ". . . maybe even find a way to be civil to each other."

Bad idea. Really bad idea. The only reason she managed to think straight around him was because he made her so mad she could spit. If he turned all nice to go with the accent and the looks . . . Her mind would wander into dangerous territory.

"I mean you can still be all mean and snooty if you like, that's fine." He shrugged. "But I can't hate on someone who is so great at her job but dances so badly." He grinned at her, all dark tousled hair and teasing gray eyes.

Her heart raced like she was a cyclist in the Tour de France. No, not friends. Not with the guy who represented so many things that she hated, but made her forget everything when he unfurled that smile. She had to keep her distance. Be professional. Anything more than that was just asking for trouble.

She gave him her best deadpan look. "I already have plenty of friends, thanks."

He laughed.

Great. He thought she was joking.

Sixteen

Paige knocked on her boss's doorframe then shifted her immaculately organized stack of papers so they balanced against her chest. Janine had been traveling the last couple of weeks, so they had a lot to catch up on.

Spending her week split between Grace and the tour had its benefits—Paige was never bored or short of things to do. Although there were a few distinct disadvantages. She now had a front-row seat to Team Josh. Everyone held him in high esteem, a fact made worse by the fact that it appeared well deserved. He worked hard, was first to do the worst jobs, and was always watching out for the interests of his team.

Now she was losing too much of her sleep and her mind. She couldn't afford to get emotionally entangled with another guy whose future was in a different direction to her own. She had no interest in putting down roots in Australia. These jobs with *Grace* and the band were just what she needed on her CV to make her a serious contender for the types of roles beckoning from back home.

She tapped on the door frame again and peered around the half-open door. This time Janine looked up, her phone pressed against her ear, and waved her in. "I see what you're saying, but—" She made a face as she was cut off by whoever was at the other end.

Paige carefully set her pile on the coffee table and wandered toward the large windows overlooking the campus. The late August winter sun was out in full force, giving everything a sparkly and fresh glow. Trees rustled in the breeze, laughter drifting up from the daycare center, along with the sound of people talking as they moved between buildings. She pressed her forehead against the open window and drank it all in for a moment.

Under the window sat a long, slim table, with a few study and reference books stacked randomly among rows of framed photographs. The front pictures were the Tyler family at various ages and stages, including Janine with the compulsory eighties poodle perm trying to corral toddler Amanda and baby Josh. Even then he had a huge thatch of dark hair and serious gray eyes.

Then there was a photo of the first Harvest church, a school hall with maybe a hundred people gathered outside, dressed in what could only be described as true commitment to late-eighties fashion.

From that to this. Paige's confusion had grown

over the last few weeks. She'd come with Kat to an early service every Sunday. Every week, she'd sat in her chair, waiting for something to happen that would give credence to her skepticism. And every Sunday they taught the Bible and took up the offering with little fanfare. Nothing even close to the long guilt-inducing lectures on giving she'd been subjected to every week for two years.

Maybe her suspicions were ill founded. Maybe things were different here. Maybe Australian megachurches had found a balance that some of her homeland counterparts missed, or lost.

Her gaze moved to the back rows—mainly photos of Greg and Janine with various friends and high-profile acquaintances in Christendom.

One photo leapt out, and her breath whooshed out of her lungs like it had physically assaulted her. It couldn't be. But it was. She reached out and lifted the image with two familiar faces. They stood with Greg and Janine, all with their arms around each other, grinning like the whole world was at their feet.

"I'm never quite sure what to do with that one." Janine had crept up behind her.

"Are they . . . close friends?" Please say no.

Janine sighed, running a hand through her bob. "I would have said they were at the time, but after what happened, part of me wonders if we ever really knew them."

Paige's stomach was leaping around like she

was riding a bucking bronco. Did she tell Janine? Just leave it alone? It wasn't like Janine was standing here defending them, unlike the way some other pastors had closed ranks around them.

"I used to go to Saints United." The confession slipped out, fell to the floor.

Janine surveyed her, her expression suggesting she knew there was more to the story. "Do you want to talk about it?"

"Not really, but you should probably know."

Janine crossed the room and closed the door, gesturing to the couch. "Come, sit."

Placing the photo back in its place, Paige perched on the edge of the couch, wishing she were closer to the door in case things went badly.

Janine settled back and kicked off her high heels, curling her feet underneath her. "Take your time."

Paige was shocked when the tears came, choking her throat and streaming down her face. Ugly, snotty sobs welled up from deep inside.

Her boss didn't say anything, just leaned forward and pushed the ever-present box of tissues across the coffee table toward her. And they weren't the cheap ones. Three-ply with aloe vera. Clearly a lot of people did a lot of serious weeping in here.

Paige plucked out a couple, trying to wipe up her face in between gulps of air. This was ridiculous. It had been years ago, before much worse things. Why was she losing it now, when it was all long done? She'd even been vindicated, not that hard, incontrovertible evidence had made any difference to the "true believers".

She blew her nose and crumpled the tissue in her hand. She could do this. Greg and Janine weren't like the others. They seemed to care more about people than the material trappings of so-called spiritual success.

She sucked in a deep breath. "I lived in New Jersey after college, got my first real job there. In 2008, I volunteered to help plan the annual church conference for Saints United. They'd just built the new worship center. Had plans for a whole campus. Mark and Jill were determined the conference would be bigger, better, bolder, than anything before. It almost felt like they wanted to make other churches jealous."

Janine just nodded.

Paige kicked off her shoes and hugged her knees, trying to order the sordid tale in her head. It had been so long since she'd talked about it. "After a few weeks, I realized things weren't right with the conference accounts. There were invoices for things we hadn't ordered, or for things that we had, but for more than they should have been. I didn't have any financial authority so I flagged it with the accountant. He said he'd take a look.

"It was like we were hemorrhaging money. I went to Mark and Jill, but they told me not to worry about it. That the money side of things wasn't my concern."

She rolled her head from side to side, attempting to loosen the growing tightness in her shoulders. "At the same time, the pressure was increasing on the congregation to give more. Every Sunday the sermons before the offering got longer, about trusting God with your finances, about giving more than felt comfortable to grow your faith. One Sunday they took up the offering three times, insisting that God had told them the service wasn't allowed to finish until a certain amount had been given. They were so charismatic, so persuasive . . . people just believed them. I had friends who lived on noodles for weeks after giving all their grocery money. Single moms who couldn't afford their insurance co-pays. And still the money from conference registrations just disappeared."

And in spite of her suspicions, she'd still been sucked in. Not able to acknowledge what was right in front of her in black and white.

Paige drew in a deep breath. She could do it. It had been over eight years. "Eventually I approached the head of the governing board. There was over two hundred grand of expenditure that didn't make sense. And that was just from the conference accounts.

"The next day, I got summoned to a meeting. Mark and Jill were there, the entire governing board. They fired me." She shrugged her shoulders. "Though I'm still not sure how you fire someone who wasn't getting paid in the first place." Weirdly enough, that was one of things that had hurt the most.

"I walked out, out the building, out of the church, never came back. Thought that was the end of it." She was blabbing, the words tumbling out on top of each other like an ugly five-car pile-up, but she couldn't stop.

"I had a friend who was still going to the church. A single mom. I tried to convince her to go somewhere else, but she was caught—believed everything they promised. One Sunday, when they put the pressure on, she gave so much that she couldn't make rent. She got kicked out of her house. When she went to the church for help, they said she hadn't had enough faith." That was what had tipped Paige over the edge—seeing the very people the Bible spoke the strongest words about, the poor, the marginalized, the oppressed—being denied help while Mark and Jill lived in a gated community and drove matching top-of-the-line Chryslers.

"I went to the police. I'd taken copies of some documents. Their financial crime team started looking into it. Word got back to the church. They told congregants I'd been fired for stealing, but they had decided to be forgiving and not do anything about it. That now I was a scorned woman, out for revenge, trying to destroy the church with lies and accusations." The bitterness flowed out of her like a poisonous river. She looked at everywhere except Janine. Afraid of what would be written across her face.

She extracted another tissue to mop up tears that wouldn't stop. The people she had volunteered under for months, had thought were friends, had done everything they could to destroy her. She'd heard all about it. How Mark and Jill had stood in front of the church on Sunday morning, looking all sorrowful. Saying how they'd followed the biblical instructions for confronting sin in their midst, but that Paige had refused to repent and had needed to be "removed" from the congregation.

"Next my car tires were slashed. Then I was getting death threats in the mail. Once I even got spat on in the street. Even when it was proved that there were hundreds of thousands of dollars missing, from accounts I had no access to, it wasn't enough to stop the threats."

Her stomach rolled at the memories of those days, when she never knew when she might pick up the phone to find someone spewing vitriol at the other end or walk out of work or a recital to find her car had been keyed or windows smashed.

"I moved back to Chicago to get away from it all. I didn't go to church, any church, for over a year. I was so betrayed, so broken, that I couldn't face walking in the doors, wondering if the worship leader was having an affair, or the pastors had their fingers in the offering plates, if they were preaching one thing and living another. I still believed in God, but I didn't want anything to do with the institution."

It had been her wilderness year, wandering around in the desert, unable to believe she would ever find her way back to a place she had once loved.

Paige paused for a moment. "That's why I have a bit of a problem with megachurches." She chanced a look at her boss. Tears streaked Janine's cheeks, no hint of judgment on her face.

"I'm so sorry you went through that." Janine pulled a tissue from the box and blew her nose.

Since she was here, she might as well be completely honest. "I'm the last person you should want working here. I'm so cynical. I've spent the last three months trying to find out what's wrong with Harvest."

Janine swiped her fingers underneath her eyes. "Good. We don't want people to just swallow everything that is said, everything that happens. We want them to ask questions, be discerning.

No one on leadership here is perfect. If anyone sees anything that doesn't seem right, we want to know."

Paige could feel her face collapsing as disbelief swept through her.

Janine sighed, uncurling her legs. "You're right. Large churches present a unique range of challenges, but they're the same problems as in smaller churches, only on a larger scale. People embezzle at any church where the opportunity exists, people have affairs at church of any size because they give in to temptation. It's just the bigger the church, the more far-reaching the impact, the damage, the consequences, and the fallout."

Janine paused, seemed to be pondering what to say next. "Greg and I are far from perfect. We're not superhuman, able to resist getting big heads and falling into the trap of believing that Harvest's success is about us. That's why we have ourselves surrounded with good people who hold us accountable. But at the end of the day, it comes down to our own hearts. If we neglect that, if we lose sight of our relationship with God, then this whole thing is a sham."

Paige shredded her latest tissue onto the coffee table.

"Can I ask you something?" Janine's words were soft.

"Sure."

"What good things came out of what happened?"

Paige didn't even need to think about it. "I moved home. Got to spend more time with my family." Because of what happened, she'd ended up back in Chicago, spending time with Ethan when they had no idea time would be so short. She wrenched a couple more tissues out of the box, attempted to stem the latest rising tide. "I eventually found a great church. One that was what a church should be. My experience with Saints United made me appreciate Chicago Hope so much more."

Janine smiled. "See, that's the thing. The church at its worst is ugly. It's corrupt and self-serving and destructive. But the church at its best? It changes the world. It defends the oppressed, cares for the poor, and walks alongside those who need it most."

Her boss's hands slashed the air in emphasis. "That's why I'm here. In a couple of months, we get to welcome thousands of women to Sydney for *Grace*. To help inspire and empower them to be the Church at its best."

She clapped her hands, then pointed at Paige's perfectly ordered and tabbed up folder. "That's what that is all about! Not what type of slices we serve for morning tea, or what color the ribbons on the bags are, or how many disabled carparks we need, though that's all important. It's

162

about women meeting with God. That's all that matters. If that doesn't happen, it's all a waste of time."

Paige pondered her folder, swiped away her remaining tears and smiled. "Do you think I should give Him His own line on the Gantt chart?"

SEVENTEEN

Paige dropped her purse on the plush hallway carpet on her way to the living area. Her head was pounding, shoulders knotted, eyes gritty. It was like the entire day had been a never-ending, theological gymnastics event. And not the pretty type with ribbons and balls and smiling faces and pert ponytails, but the ugly kind where people grunted and flung themselves between creaking bars or contorted their bodies into impossible positions.

She pulled her hair into a ponytail, and shuffled toward the kitchen in search of an ice-cold Diet Coke.

Her cynically constructed image of how all megachurches operated had been blown apart. The doubts had been knocking for weeks: when she'd seen Janine drove a ten-year-old hatchback. As she'd navigated a procurement process that required three levels of approval. When she'd found out neither Greg or Janine could buy so much as a bunch of flowers with church funds. She'd tried to keep the door shut on her doubts, but today it got blown off its hinges.

She opened the fridge, pulled out a can, and popped it open, gulping a sip before collapsing onto the couch. She kicked her shoes off, picked up the remote, and settled back for the last few minutes of one of Australia's longest-running soaps, *Neighbours*. Even after three months, trying to work out what on earth the characters were talking about proved to be never-ending entertainment. Which was just what she needed right now—some angsty, no-thinking-required terrible television.

The front door banged shut, and Paige tilted her head, peering up over the arm of the couch. Kat walked in, clad in a conservative skirt and a floral top, her hair in a French braid and her makeup flawless. That meant one thing: her father was in town.

Kat threw her Coach purse on the floor, and sagged into the love seat across from her.

Paige pushed a bag of mini Violet Crumbles across the coffee table. There was a woman in need of chocolate if there ever was one.

"Thanks." The word was a cross between a sigh and a groan. Kat reached into the bag and pulled out a fistful of candy. Tearing one open, she demolished it in a couple of bites. Reached for another.

Wow. A visit to her dad was usually a tumultuous experience, but this was a whole new level.

Paige took a sip of her soda, let her cousin work

her angst out on the candy. She'd talk when she was ready.

"My father thinks I should freeze my eggs."

Paige choked, snorted, bubbles filling her nose. She clamped her mouth shut, barely avoiding spraying brown fizz everywhere. Finally, she managed to swallow. "You're joking."

Her cousin yanked at the hair tie holding her hair in place and ran her hand through the end of the braid with vigor. "I wish I was."

"Do you want to have a baby?" Her cousin had never seemed like the maternal type.

An expression Paige couldn't decipher stole across Kat's face. "It's a bit more complicated than that." Another wrapper hit the floor.

"What exactly did he say?"

Kat bit her lip. "That I'm thirty-two and my eggs are getting more substandard by the minute."

Ouch. Though, to be fair, Kat's substandard eggs were probably still better than most other women's A-grade contenders.

"Anyway, my father entertaining half of Sydney's elite discussing my reproductive organs over lunch brings me to my real problem."

"What's that?"

"I think I should break up with Dan."

"Say what now?" Kat and Dan had been together for three years, not that they saw each other very often given her jet-setting lifestyle and the fact he worked six weeks on/six weeks off on an oil rig in the North Sea.

Paige wandered back to the kitchen and opened both the freezer and the pantry. "You want ice cream or more chocolate?"

"Bring both."

Paige snagged a spoon from the counter and handed Kat the container of vanilla fudge ripple and the block of Berry Biscuit chocolate. She had to give the Southern Hemisphere points for chocolate variety. She'd thought Dove was heaven. Then she met Whittaker's.

Kat ripped off the lid to the ice cream and dug her spoon in. "I realized as I was driving home that I can't see myself having kids with him. Even if I wanted to."

"Are you in love with him?" Paige asked the question cautiously. Her cousin was a bit of an enigma on the romance front. She played her cards close to her chest.

"He's a great guy. But . . ." Kat shrugged. "We hardly see each other which, to be honest, is not that hard. It should be harder, right? If I loved him, long distance should be torture. I should be counting the days until I see him again. Wasn't that how you were with Alex?"

Alex. With a start, Paige realized her ex-boyfriend hadn't crossed her mind in weeks. Not since J—She shook her head before the thought could even finish itself. "I guess. Sort of."

"See?' Kat dug her spoon into the ice cream and loaded it up.

"Are you sure that it's not just that with your job you're used to not being with the people you love all the time?" Paige took a last swallow of her soda. "So it's not that you don't love him. It's that you have good long-distance coping mechanisms."

It was a shot in the dark. The only other time she and Kat had lived in the same city was a brief blissful period in their teens. The last five months were the first time she'd seen Kat with a guy in real life. From what she'd seen, Kat and Dan had a good thing going.

"Maybe." Kat didn't seem to be buying it.

Paige put her can back down on the coffee table. "What do you think is missing?"

Kat shrugged. "I don't know. The X-factor. The magic. Butterflies. The thing that makes you sure it's meant to be your forever. I've never been giddy about Dan. It's just always been . . . nice. Easy."

"Maybe the real problem is that nice and easy is underrated." She'd been circling that thought lately. Pretty much every time she had a message from Nate, talked to him.

Kat licked the spoon. "Ha!"

"What?"

Her cousin pointed the spoon at her. "You're one to talk."

"About what?" Paige was so confused.

"You have a thing for Josh."

"What?" She tried to make her tone appropriately shocked.

Kat rolled her eyes. "Good try, but fail."

"What makes you think I have a thing for Josh?" This time she switched her tone to light-hearted, as if she were just humoring her cousin. Her cheeks betrayed her, though, as they filled with warmth.

"Are you saying you don't?"

"You know how I feel about megachurches." Even if Harvest was the exception to the general rule, she wasn't cut out for the scrutiny, the expectations, that would come with being associated with the Tylers.

"And yet you work at a megachurch and attend that same one every Sunday. And I saw you trying to sneak that tithe envelope into the offering bag last Sunday."

"I have no intention of staying here."

Kat lifted an eyebrow. "Because your coming was such a well thought through plan."

"He's a musician."

Her cousin dipped deeper into the carton. "So are you."

"I was."

"No, you still are. Just because you can't bring yourself to play at the moment doesn't make you any less a musician."

"But if I don't." Her arm twinged just thinking about playing. "The last thing I would want is to be with someone who reminds me every day of what I used to be."

"You're reminded every day anyway. In case you haven't noticed, everywhere you go there is music. Church, the mall, the car, in your own head. Why wouldn't you want to be with someone who loves music as much as you do?"

The answer was so complicated, she wasn't sure she understood. The truth was, she hadn't yet found a way to be the better person, to watch someone else pick up an instrument and do what they loved and be happy for them, instead of wondering what she'd done to deserve losing that privilege.

"Josh and I, we drive each other nuts. I spend more of my time wanting to smack him than anything else. And he has never taken back saying that he doesn't think I'm of fit character to work for his mom."

Kat raised an eyebrow. "I know. It's very *Ten Things I Hate About You.*"

Which would be fine if she was Julia Stiles. But her life wasn't a romcom and there was no wannabe Heath Ledger in sight. "Kat, I wasted six years on a guy who had a life where I was never going to fit. I can't do that again."

EIGHTEEN

You have a thing for Josh. A week later, her cousin's statement still vibrated in Paige's head.

Sure, close working quarters had forced them to find a way to coexist, which, at some point, had turned into having a grudging respect for him. But a *thing* she did not have. Couldn't have.

She'd simply glimpsed beneath his arrogant exterior and discovered he wasn't the insufferable Christian megastar she'd pegged him as. But it still drove her nuts how he couldn't let go of the smallest of details or delegate anything. At least today was Friday—his day off—so she'd be able to get some work done without him second-guessing everything.

Paige turned her attention back to the spreadsheet in front of her, tracing her color-coded columns that tracked what equipment was going where, when, and by what mode of transport.

"A latte for the lady." And in he strode, setting a takeout cup on her desk.

Josh hadn't shaved, his hair looked like he'd just rolled out of bed, and he was wearing a rumpled hoodie and old jeans. It reminded her of the first time they'd met.

She took a swig of the coffee. Ah. He even remembered the half a sugar. "What are you doing here?"

"Forgot to print out a couple of song sheets for Sunday. I'll only be a few minutes. Why?" He spun her chair around, towering over her with mischievous eyes. "Am I messing up your day? Destroying your Zen?"

She hid her smile behind her cup. "Something like that."

Josh grinned. "Sorry, princess. I'll be out of your hair superfast." He turned and slid into his chair, hit a few keys to log into his Mac. "By the way have you—"

Paige breathed in the earthy scent of her coffee. "If you ask me one more time if I've sorted out everyone's dietary requirements, I'm going to throw my shoe at you." She had a whole spread-sheet detailing everyone's allergies, intolerances, trendy diets—as the case may be.

He glanced back over his shoulder. "Spoken like someone who's never been stuck in a plane for fourteen hours with someone who didn't get their special meal."

Paige twirled her pen between her fingers. "People with real food allergies don't usually trust airlines to get their meals right."

"That's not very loving."

"I ran out of love in the twenty-seventh minute of my conversation with the airline representative about who was dairy-free, nut-free, gluten-free, vegetarian, vegan, carb-free, and legume-free."

Josh spun around, scooted his chair closer and leaned in, stormy-grey eyes fixed on her. "Paige." He said her name like a caress and took her hand.

Her breath caught. "Yes?"

"Would now be a good time to tell you I'm going paleo?"

She yanked her hand back and pointed to the door. "Out! Out! Out! Out!"

He grinned and shuffled back. "You can't kick a guy out of his own office."

"Watch me." She grabbed up her container of pens and started pelting his back with them as he shook with laughter.

Her missiles bounced off and clattered to the floor as she ran out of ammo far too quickly. She was off her chair, trying to gather some backup, when he spun around and started pelting her with marbles.

"Ouch!"

The hard spheres rained down around her. She scrambled under the desk, seeking a shield from the onslaught and grabbed whatever she could get her hands on to throw back from her disadvantaged position.

Bad move.

Ethan had taught her never to give up the high

ground when she was, like, seven. Now she was being pelted as though she'd gone for a run in a hail storm. She dove further into the corner of her desk, trying to sweep his spent ammunition out of his reach.

A resounding *rip* echoed through the room.

She froze. Oh no. Surely not. Maybe her jeans were a little on the snug side now, but surely not so much as to . . . her fingers reached back, searching along seams.

Yes, there it was. A brand-new air vent, about four inches long, running right up the back seam of her Levi's.

Her fingers felt the flimsy material now revealed to the world and she stifled a groan. She hadn't done laundry for awhile and her morning hunt for clean underwear had seen her resort to a pair of threadbare floral granny panties.

The onslaught had stopped. Josh's feet inched closer, stopping near the edge of her desk. His face appeared a second later.

"Did you just split something?" His mouth wobbled.

"I have no comment." Paige shrank back into the corner. How was it possible? Every time. Every time something embarrassing happened, he was there to witness it.

A hand appeared. "C'mon. I won't look. I promise." She stared up at him. He held up two fingers. "Scout's honor."

"It's three." The correction was out of her mouth before she could stop it.

"Three what?"

"It's three fingers for Scouts. Two for cub scouts." Why couldn't she just keep her mouth shut? Now she sounded like a pedantic priss.

Josh shook his head as he reached his hand back down to her. "You know this why?"

She shrugged. "I remember random things like that. Details are my job." She curled her fingers in his, letting him help her up as she kept her rear facing her computer screen.

The floor of the office was littered with marbles, pens, and assorted stationery. Paige reached for the sweater draped over the back of her chair, and made quick work of tying it around her waist.

"You okay?" Josh frowned, studied her face with a concerned expression.

She bit her lip, but it couldn't stop a laugh from escaping, followed by a more unrestrained one. "What is it with you?"

His eyebrows rose. "What?"

"How are you always here for my most humiliating moments? Can't count my change. You're there. Can't stay on my feet. You're there. Turn my cupcakes into carcinogenic rocks. You're there. Split my pants. You're there. It's like you jinx me."

His mouth angled into a slow smile that

threatened to melt her faster than the Wicked Witch of the West. He reached out and tucked a piece of hair behind her ear, sending tingles down the side of her face. "Or maybe I'm just lucky."

Wow, he was close. Too close. Her body hummed with awareness.

Space. Self-preservation demanded space. But she had nowhere to go. She was already backed up against her desk.

His grey eyes flickered as they studied her.

A cough sounded from the doorway, sending Josh jumping back.

Emotion surged through her, she just had no idea whether it was disappointment or relief. A whole continuum of feelings seemed tangled up inside her.

Connor stood there, leaning against the frame, arms crossed and a smirk on his face. "You about ready?"

Josh ran a hand through his hair, turned toward his computer, then turned back again. "Yup. Just got to grab the sheets off the printer and I'll be done."

Connor stepped aside as Josh hurtled out the door, his footsteps echoing down the hall. "I'm glad I caught you here too."

"Oh?" What had just happened?

"We were supposed to be going to this missions fundraising ball tonight, but one of the kids is sick so Amanda can't go. She's tasked me with

176

finding someone to take her ticket. You keen?"

"What? How much?" Her mind was struggling to process.

"No, just take it. We don't want the ticket to go to waste. There's a whole table of us going. About ten, I think."

"Um . . ." Did she have any plans tonight? She had no idea. "Sure, sounds great."

"Great." Connor reached into his pocket and pulled out a slim rectangular card, placing it on the corner of her desk.

Josh walked back into the room, shuffling pages, not even looking at her. He didn't even bother to shut down his computer, just stabbed the button on the monitor.

He turned around and cleared his throat. "Okay, well, have a good weekend. See you next week."

"You too." Everything was buzzing. She had to get a grip. She was not going to become another simpering Josh Tyler groupie. Not ever.

NINETEEN

Josh pulled at his bow tie and looked around the large ballroom. He hated these events. He couldn't believe he'd been roped into it again. Last year he'd sworn it was the last time. But his mother had come home with tickets for the entire family and that was it. No arguing. No already-made-other-plans. Team Tyler, all starched up and on parade.

He'd make a note of next year's date and ensure he was in a country far away. At least this year all the band had contributed was some signed merchandise.

Last year it had been access for four people to spend half a day in the studio as they recorded their album. Never, ever again. Some wealthy father had bought it as a sixteenth birth-day present for his daughter. She'd shown up with three giggly friends. There was nothing more off-putting than trying to record a wor-ship album while four teenage girls ogled you.

Oh, wait. Yes, there was—one of them screaming "Marry me, Josh!" as they left, her friend's iPhone videoing the moment, ensuring it was captured for all eternity.

Sarah sidled up beside him, looking as happy to be here as he was. She owned one black formal gown from her Year 12 ball. And every year she proclaimed it was timeless and dusted it off. Lucky girl. This penguin suit had cost him the better part of a hundred bucks to rent. He should just bite the bullet and go buy one.

"How early do you think we can escape without Mum getting annoyed?" Sarah gave the front of her strapless dress a tug.

He looked at his watch. Eight eighteen. How had he only been here for twenty minutes? "Ten. At the earliest."

All he wanted to do was go home, put his feet up, and play some mindless Xbox game. Preferably one involving a lot of guns. The moment with Paige had left him shaken all day. Connor had wiped the court with him at squash because he couldn't get his head in the game.

He had replayed the moment all day, trying to work out what he was thinking. Would he have kissed her if Connor hadn't showed up? He had no idea. At least his brother-in-law had been kind enough to leave him stewing in his own funk instead of bringing it up.

Speaking of, there he was, all tuxed up, looking completely at ease. "I'm hungry. What time is the food up?"

"I think the program has everyone seated at eight-thirty." Josh looked around for his older sister. The only one of the three of them who didn't mind these things. "Where's Amanda?"

"Not coming. Mason's sick."

"Two dinners for you then." Lucky guy. This fundraiser always served good steak.

"Nah, we gave her ticket away."

"To who?" Out of the ten seats at the table, his immediate family would have taken six. His Uncle Phil, Aunt Jenny, cousin Lucy, and her husband Colin filled the remaining four. Who had Connor decided would be able to manage the Tylers en masse?

Connor let out a low whistle and pointed. "To her."

Josh glanced over. Almost got whiplash looking again. So that was why his brother-in-law hadn't said anything all day. The joke was on him. "You didn't."

"What?" Connor looked at him with wide innocent eyes.

"Don't *what* me."

Connor clapped him on the shoulder. "Consider it my apology for whatever it was I interrupted this morning."

Paige cut through the last of the crowd that was between them. Approached the other side of their table. He couldn't breathe. She wore a strapless, green-blue dress that clung to her curves like a wetsuit. Her hair spilled in loose waves past her shoulders.

She looked . . . he couldn't find a word for it. His brain was buzzing like it had short circuited.

"Easy, buddy." Connor leaned in. "You look like you're about to swallow your own tongue."

He didn't know this girl. This ethereal luminescent creature. He tried to remind himself she was the same person he'd spent all week with. Who'd split her jeans this morning. Who got drunk and vomited on her own shoes.

She'd approached Sarah and they were chatting, laughing on the other side of the table. Pointing at Connor, she flashed him a smile. Her gaze flickered toward him for a second before moving away again.

Sarah gestured to a seat between her and Lucy, and Paige put her sparkly purse down between the sparkling silverware. He ignored the stab that went through him. It was a good seat for her. The last thing he wanted was her beside him, forcing them to make awkward conversation through two hours of dinner.

"Okay, time to stop staring. It's getting a little creepy." Connor tugged at his elbow, forcing him to look away.

"What?"

Connor sized him up with knowing eyes. "Dude, you have it bad. When did this happen?"

"When did what happen?" He grabbed a glass

of orange juice from a passing waiter and took a gulp.

Connor rolled his eyes. "When did you take a tumble for Paige?"

Josh flinched. His parents had just joined the table. Thank goodness the buzz of a couple of hundred other people talking meant that they didn't seem to hear the question. "I haven't done any such thing."

"Yeah, because that's exactly how you were looking at her."

"I just . . . I was just surprised. She scrubs up well." He tugged at his collar. For the love, would someone please open some windows and get some air in this room?

Connor rolled his eyes. "Just don't mess it up."

"There's nothing to mess up." His instincts when it came to women stank. Both his serious relationships had ended up putting his family through hell. He couldn't lose sight of that.

"Okay, I know that you still carry some relationship baggage, but seriously. It's been years. Paige is a great girl. And you can tell yourself whatever you like, but the rest of us can see the chemistry from here to the Blue Mountains." He glanced over Josh's shoulder. "Including at least one person who won't be happy about it."

Before he could ask Connor what he meant,

a screech echoed across the room. "Ladies and gentlemen, if you could please take your seats, it's time to get the evening underway."

Josh grabbed the nearest seat and found himself between Connor and his mother. Paige sat directly across from him, glittering.

It was going to be a long night.

Paige pushed the remains of her plate of chicken away, half-eaten. Kat's dress fit tighter than an Olympic gymnast's leotard, and she could almost feel the seams bursting with every move. Just like her traitorous jeans.

Sarah and Grace had made for entertaining seatmates, but she'd been off her game the entire evening. Every time she looked across the table, she'd found Josh staring at her, studying her, like he was a lab technician examining a strain of drug-resistant bacteria.

She'd spent half the night looking down, wondering if her dress had slipped, if she'd poured gravy down her front. But she never saw anything amiss. Maybe the tux was doing it. She'd seen him tug at his bowtie a few times like it was strangling him. She couldn't blame him. As good as he looked tonight, she preferred the more relaxed version, the look that had almost undone her this morning.

Paige stifled a yawn as the auctioneer's voice droned on in the background. She'd wasted half the day imagining what might have happened if Connor hadn't showed up. Would he have kissed her? Would she have kissed him back if he did? Then what? Which left her where, doomed to repeat her mistake with Alex and still falling for the guy who was all wrong for her?

"Ladies and gentlemen, we are now reaching the end of our auction this evening. And, as per usual, we have saved the best for last. The kinds of experiences that money can't usually buy. Remember, all funds raised in the auction tonight will go toward combating human trafficking in Southeast Asia, so be generous."

Thank goodness for Destiny Rescue there were a lot of people in the room with far healthier bank accounts than hers. She'd planned to bid for something since she hadn't had to pay for dinner but even the starting prices were beyond her means.

A plate with a piece of fancy-looking cheese-cake landed in front of her. Surely her dress would allow a few teeny-tiny bites.

The first item was up—some holiday on a coast somewhere. She settled back and reached for her glass of water. Paddles went up at tables and bidding progressed. At least it looked like this round would move a bit faster than the others. And sold.

"And now our next item. Highly anticipated, I'm advised. A date with one of Australia's most eligible bachelors—Josh Tyler, worship leader of Due North."

What? The rest of the auctioneer's spiel was wiped away by the surprise rocketing around in her head.

Across the table, liquid sprayed from Josh's mouth, and he doubled over, coughing, Connor whacking him on the back.

"Oh, she didn't." Sarah reached over and grabbed the program out of Paige's hands. She opened it up and started laughing. "Oh Lord, she did."

"Who?"

Sarah pointed across the table to where her mother wore an expression that was half pride, half fear. "Guess." Beside Janine, Greg was leaning in, whispering something and she offered a partial shrug in response.

The poor guy.

"Ladies, shall we start the bidding at a hundred?"

"Two hundred." A paddle shot up at a table nearby. Heads rotated to see who it was. From Paige's vantage point, it looked like a woman around forty, in a sparkling dress.

"Two-fifty!" That was from a table on the other side of the room, a redhead who looked all of twenty.

"Three hundred." The first woman stood, waving her paddle with gusto.

Josh's face had the wild-eyed look of impending road kill.

"Three-fifty." A new woman in a dress with a neckline that almost plunged to her navel entered the bidding.

Even Greg's usually serene face was beginning to wear concern.

Paige leaned into Sarah. "Has he never been in a charity auction before?"

Sarah shook her head, dangly earrings bouncing. "Not in years. He got roped into a few ages ago but then refused to do any more. They were always won by women who were quite forward, if you know what I mean."

Oh. Wow. "So why would your mum sign him up for this one?"

Sarah grimaced. "She doesn't know how bad they were. Josh forbid Amanda or I from saying anything. After the whole thing with N—" Sarah cut herself off, eyes wide. As if she'd said something she shouldn't.

"Four hundred." Redhead was back.

Josh's expression was set like concrete.

Without thinking, Paige grabbed her paddle from the middle of the table and waved. "Four-ten."

The auctioneer peered down at her from his wooden podium. "Welcome to our new entrant at four-ten."

"Four-twenty."

"Four-fifty."

The young one had dropped out. It was between sparkles and cleavage.

"Four-sixty." Paige was on her feet. What was she doing? She didn't have four hundred and sixty dollars.

The two bid up to five hundred.

She looked at Josh and shook her head as she sat down. She couldn't do it. She couldn't afford it. His eyes pleaded.

"Bidding is at five hundred dollars."

He scrawled something on a napkin and held it up. *I'll pay you back.*

"Going once at five hundred."

She locked eyes with him. He crossed his heart.

Well, in that case, it was to fight against human trafficking. She smiled at him and gave him a wink.

His face sagged with relief and gratitude.

"Going twice at five hundred."

She teetered back up and raised her paddle in the air. "A thousand dollars."

The room collectively sucked in its breath.

"Sorry, miss. Did I hear you right? Was that a thousand dollars?"

"That's right. One thousand."

Beside her Sarah was practically under the table in spasms of laughter. Josh's face still sagged, but now more with disbelief than gratitude.

"Going once at one thousand."

The room was silent.

"Twice at one thousand." He looked from cleavage to sparkles. "Ladies." They both shook their heads.

"Sold. A date with Josh Tyler, to the young lady in the green dress for a thousand dollars."

Josh honestly wasn't sure whether he wanted to kiss Paige or shake her. A thousand dollars. *A thousand dollars.* That had better be one awesome date he was getting. With himself, since he was paying for it. He took a swig of water. At least it was going to a great cause.

His mother had better be planning on stumping up with some of it. At least half. What was she thinking? He'd have to find out later, since she'd disappeared faster than a dingo on a scent when the auction finished.

He finished his dessert and swiped a large wedge of his mother's serving of cheesecake. The band had started, filling the room with some swinging jazz. Across the table, she with the open wallet sat taking delicate bites of her dessert.

Before he knew what he was doing, he was on his feet, walking around to her.

Paige looked up and smiled. "Just think of what good your generous support will do."

"You're hilarious."

Paige scooped up the last piece of her dessert.

"I am. I also really don't have a spare $1000."

"No worries. Email me your bank details when you get home and I'll transfer the money tomorrow." He held out his hand. "In the meantime, care to dance?"

Surprise flickered across her face. "You remember you've seen me dance, right?" She put down her spoon and dabbed her lips with her navy napkin.

He nodded, grinning. "Thankfully, I'm a lot better than you."

She eyed him up. "Thought you said it wasn't your spiritual gift either?"

"Okay, I may have exaggerated to make you feel a little better. Not to rub salt in the wound or anything, but I am pretty good."

"Have you even seen these? Do you really want your toes being mauled by them?" She poked out a glittering sandal from beneath her dress, with a heel that looked like it could double as a very effective weapon.

"I'll take my chances." He waved his hand. "You going to leave me standing here like this, when you've just paid a grand for a date with me?"

She shook her head, waves bouncing. "Fine. Can't say you weren't warned." Her fingers curled around his and she stood. He saw the scar on her exposed forearm that he'd first noticed at their lunch in the food court. It ran from wrist to elbow, slight puckers and ridges telling a tale of major trauma.

She always wore long sleeves in the office. Even though it had been a mild winter for the most part. He hadn't even thought about it until right then.

As if reading his mind, Paige removed her hand from his and dropped her arm to her side, a wary look entering her eyes.

Whatever the story was, it obviously was one she held close. He, of all people, could appreciate that. He gave her a grin to lighten the moment. "Okay, my toes are as prepared as they'll ever be." Cutting through the crowd, they reached the edge of the mahogany dance floor. In the middle, the pros swirled, showing off their flash spins and dips. His hand settled on the small of Paige's back. She stood as stiff as an ironing board.

"It's not that bad. Just relax. Have fun." Placing his right arm around her waist, he picked up her other hand with his left and tried not to think about what he was doing.

"Easy for you to say." She put her free hand on his shoulder, and he tucked her closer into his chest.

She smelled like apples and flowers. The fragrance embraced him, unbalanced him. His pulse thundered in his ears. *Focus, Tyler, focus. It's just a dance, one dance. Pretend she's Sarah.*

That was impossible. There was nothing

brotherly about what he was feeling. The way Paige curved into him perfectly, making him want to run his hands through her hair. Or bury his face into the curve of her neck. All highly inappropriate impulses since he wasn't the guy sending her bouquets bigger than the Garden of Eden.

They moved with the music. Slowly at first, then faster as Paige relaxed and started to follow his lead.

"I should say thank you for rescuing me."

She arched an eyebrow. "Even though it's going to cost you a grand."

"I'm pretty sure my mother is going to find herself footing at least half of that."

She laughed. "Fair enough."

He maneuvered them through the outer crowd as the music swirled around them. "I should also tell you, you look beautiful tonight."

"Thanks. Not bad for a few hours' notice."

"And . . ." He prompted.

"And what?"

"You look very dashing too, Josh."

She grinned. "Well since you've already been told, no need for me to say so."

"Fine." He dropped her into a deep dip. She squealed as he caught her not far from the floor and pulled her back up.

"How about now?"

She grinned and shook her head, so he dipped

her until her hair trailed along the wood beneath them and left her dangling. "Now."

She was laughing so hard she could barely get the words out.

"What was that?"

"Would you like me to split this too?"

Ah, no. He hauled her back up, his face tinged with heat. He kept her moving around the dance floor, trying to distract his mind from the thought.

Surely the song had to be over soon.

Her hand moved up his shoulder. Her fingers lingered on his neck, her body tucked close. Every thought shattered like atoms.

"Josh." Paige's eyes glowed in the low light.

"Mmm." He was completely incapable of anything more coherent than that.

"When I first started, you said I wasn't of fit character to work for your mom. Why?"

Were they going to have this conversation here? The truth was, he didn't know anymore. He'd doubted what he thought he'd seen on the plane. He'd been watching her all night. She hadn't touched anything other than water and juice.

What could he say? That the last girl he'd dated had sold his family out to a tabloid? That the only one he'd ever loved had decimated the life they were planning together with secrets that left him with more baggage than LAX handled in a year?

Her brown eyes probed his, waiting for him to answer.

The song ended. "I—"

"Do you mind if I cut in?"

It was Kellie, tottering under the weight of a hairdo that would make Dolly Parton proud. Paige stepped back. "Of course not. Be my guest."

Kellie stepped in, grasping his shoulder as the next song started. "Heard what happened at the auction. Sorry. I would have saved you but didn't realize. I'd stepped outside to get some air."

He watched the girl who had saved him walking away, cutting through the crowd without a backward glance.

His arms felt empty. What if he had been completely wrong about her? Were his mistakes from the past still haunting him, leaving him chasing shadows where none existed?

TWENTY

Three days later, Josh walked into his office to find Paige staring at her computer screen. He paused. Friday had changed things. He'd found himself looking for her in the crowd at church yesterday. Even contemplated leaving the safety of the stage after the service to see if he could find her. Spent his entire time in line at the cafe debating whether to buy her a coffee.

He cleared his throat. "Morning."

Paige picked up a pen, scrawled something on the pad beside her. "Morning." She barely gave him a glance before returning her attention to the screen, clicked on her mouse a couple of times. A takeout coffee cup sat near her keyboard.

Okay. Good call on going no coffee. He settled into his chair, pulled out his laptop and logged in.

"Hey, do you have a copy of your last US tour itinerary?"

"Sure, somewhere. Want me to email it to you?" He clicked through a few files before he found it.

"Yes, argh! No. My email keeps freezing up.

Can you just tell me how you got from Nashville to Atlanta?"

He opened the file, squinted at the tiny print on the program. "Some of us flew via DCA and others via CLT. What are they?"

"Washington National and Charlotte. Let me see."

Suddenly he found his chair being nudged over as she wheeled herself up next to him and peered at the screen.

"What's your criteria for price versus transit time?" She tapped the screen pointing at the two departure and arrival times. "I can get a more direct route that will be 90 minutes faster but tickets are fifty dollars more per person. I was wondering if you had that option last time but chose to go for the routes you did to save money. Do you remember?"

He couldn't think about anything beyond the fact that her hair always smelled like apples. Why couldn't they just make shampoo that smelled like nothing? And he wasn't even going to let himself think about the way that her shoulder was brushing his or that her breath smelled like peppermint.

He cleared his throat. "Don't forget that Sam and Alana can't sit together on the long-haul flights."

Paige's brow crinkled. "What are you talking about? Why not?"

"Because they're dating."

"I know that. That usually means people want to sit together."

"It's in the touring rules. Did I not give you a copy?" Leaning forward, he navigated into a folder and opened a document. "Here. It applies to everyone who travels on tour with us. I'll email it to you."

Paige started reading the table of contents. "Accommodation. Couples. Days off. Dress code. Entertainment. Flights. Ground transport." She stopped speaking and started scrolling through the fifty-odd pages. "Closed toed shoes only. Dark or neutral tones are preferred. Women's heels on stage must be less than two inches." She swung to look at him. "Seriously?"

Of course she didn't get it. He would think it was ridiculous too if it wasn't for the "constructive feedback" he received every other day. "Every single one of those rules has come out of complaints we've received. Appearances matter. Every person associated with *Due North* has to be above reproach in every way."

Paige swung back to face the screen and kept scrolling. "I'm not disagreeing with you but has it ever occurred to you that some people will always find something to be offended by, no matter how many rules you have?"

"Trust me. I know. I hear from them often." He moved his chair a couple of centimeters to the right to give her a bit more space. Paige didn't even notice, her gaze fixed on the screen.

"You mean emails like that?"

"Like what?" He turned his attention back to the computer.

"Like that." She pointed to where the notification of a new email had popped up in the bottom right hand corner, containing the subject and the opening sentence. All of which indicated it was the kind of email that would force him to breathe deeply and sit on his hands.

"A few." A week. But they weren't her problem.

She nibbled her thumb for a second. "Do you mind if I read it?"

Did he mind? Not really. Would he prefer that she didn't get polluted by his hate mail? Yes. He shrugged. "Go for it."

She reached over to the keyboard and clicked on the rectangular box. He leaned back in his chair, staring at a spot above the computer. He didn't need to read it. After so many years, he'd already read every possible variation of that email.

His personal favorites were the ones that called him the anti-Christ and somehow managed to derive a 666 from everything that he wore, said, or played.

He heard a sharp intake of breath.

He cringed. "What'd that part say?"

Silence.

"C'mon, Paige. It's nothing I haven't gotten before."

"It's horrible." Her voice wobbled. "I'm not saying it."

He tilted his head back down. The email was gone from the screen, and Paige was blinking furiously, bottom lip looking shaky.

"Hey. It's okay. It comes with the territory."

"But why would someone say something like that?"

He shrugged. "Why do people do a lot of things? Because they're hurting, because they're lost, because they're in such a dark place they can't imagine that everyone else doesn't dwell there too." Those were the things he'd had to constantly tell himself to stop from hitting the reply key and raining down righteous indignation. Which, no doubt, would then get plastered on the person's social media pages and go viral.

"How do you deal with it?" Her foot tapped on the floor. He'd noticed she did that whenever she was nervous or agitated.

He thought for a second. "I don't answer to them. I answer to God and those closest to me. I pray every time that I walk on that stage that I am doing it for the right reasons, to bring glory to Him. That's all that matters. If I, or any of us in the band, spent our time trying to please everyone, trying to make our lyrics so inoffensive that they become meaningless, worrying about if someone thinks jeans are blasphemous, then we'd never do anything."

He ran his hands through his hair, tried to find the right words. "At its core, the gospel is offensive. We are all sinners. We all fall short of God. No matter how good a person we are, how nice a life we lead, we all need Jesus to bridge the gap for us. No exceptions. I'd be more worried if we weren't offending anyone. Then we'd have a real problem."

She was silent. He chanced a glance to his side. Paige had pulled one knee up onto her chair, wrapped her arms around it. Her brows were pinched, full bottom lip caught under top teeth. Had he gone too far? Been too forceful? The seconds ticked by, his discomfort growing with each one. She was probably drawing up a list of his many character flaws, comparing them to what he'd just said and judging him to fall desperately short of his own rhetoric.

Finally, she puffed out a little breath. "You're not what I thought."

That was not what he had been expecting. "Is that a good or a bad thing?"

She looked at him with uncertain eyes. "I don't know."

TWENTY-ONE

"All right, everyone. That's a wrap for tonight." The studio sound guy flicked his hand across his throat, resulting in muted cheers from the band.

Paige looked up from where she was working on her laptop. Never again would she think cutting an album was glamorous work. She'd wanted to bang her head against a wall a few times, and she wasn't the one being forced to sing the same worship lyrics over and over in the pursuit of harmonic perfection. And she'd only been here for forty-five minutes. The band had been in here for days.

"So, what did you think?" Kellie had materialized beside her, her hand twisting the top off a water bottle.

Paige hit *save* on her spreadsheet. Checked it was also saving to the backup location. "You guys sound great."

"I was thinking *Worthy* might be a good opener for the first night. Once we pull it together, it could be something special."

"You guys are the musicians. I trust your instincts on this." Although Kellie was right.

Worthy was a good song. They all were. A couple of them just needed a few tweaks.

She was only here because she needed to talk to Josh to tie off a few loose ends about the tour. She hadn't seen him since the day she'd read his hate mail. He hadn't replied to her emails, so she had resorted to stalking him in his studio while trying to work out the logistics of getting thousands of women at *Grace* in and out of eighteen bathrooms in a twenty-minute window.

"Okay, great." Kellie swung her leather bag over her shoulder and gave her a smile. "I should have the tentative song list and timings in a few days. We can have a coffee to discuss them."

"Sure, that would be great." Having coffee with the wannabe future wife of the guy she'd developed an irritating crush on was just what she wanted.

She turned her attention back to her screen. Just don't think about it. Don't think about him.

"So what did you think?" Josh leaned against the wall beside her, and the hair on the back of her neck rose.

"It's sounding great."

"I'm not sure about *Almighty*. It feels like something's missing. Do you reckon?"

That was one she remembered clearly because he was right. It was missing something, and she knew what. It had bugged her since she'd first heard it. The song was good, but it could be great.

It had the potential to be the next *Indescribable* or *Oceans*.

"I think you're right." Hopefully that would encourage him to work it out for himself. Telling him would only dredge up things she'd rather not think about it. Or reveal more than she wanted to share.

He burrowed his hands through his hair. "I knew it. Are we doing too much? Should we strip it back? Go more acoustic?" He was talking more to himself than to her. "Maybe Kellie should take the vocal lead. Or switch Amanda to the grand."

"Strings." The word was out of her mouth before she could stop it.

"Sorry, I missed that."

Oh, well, no backing out now. "It needs strings. Especially in the bridge. It's a haunting kind of song. Strings will add depth to the arrangement. Like this." She pulled up an old Planetshakers song that had always resonated with something deep inside of her. Clicked play on the sample.

Within a few seconds of the opening measures, they started—violins, a beautiful cello, pulling the listener into the song. She leaned back and closed her eyes, letting the perfect harmony roll over her.

When she opened her eyes, Josh was staring at her. "You're completely right. That's exactly what it needs. How did you know?"

Play it cool, Paige. Plenty of people learned

an instrument as a child and had a rudimentary knowledge of music. She shrugged. "I used to play the violin a little."

Her heart clenched as she spoke so lightly of what was once an intrinsic part of her life, back when she'd had big dreams.

Her fingers ran up her arm, fingers tracing the now familiar puckered ridges. Even though the surgeons swore it wasn't possible, sometimes she was sure she could feel the remaining pins under the surface, holding her bones together.

"Do you have any ideas for how it could work?"

More than an idea. The bars had been dancing in her head for days, ever since she'd first heard it and realized what the song was missing.

"Aren't you the professional musician?"

"True." He held both palms up. "But I've never played a violin. Look at these fingers." He held up his hands, spreading out fingers that were definitely on the thick side. "Imagine those trying to play a delicate instrument."

She shook her head, smiling.

"Puh-lease. I know you have something. It's written across your face." He reached out and spun her chair to face him. "Would you like me to beg, is that it? Because I will." He clasped his hands together. "Please, Paige, oh most wise strings guru. Please enlighten your humble servant—"

"Stop!"

"Not until you tell me what you're thinking, oh magical fairy of the classical shire."

"Okay, okay!"

He grinned with the glee of a little boy who had just been given a bag of candy.

She took a breath. "I was thinking maybe something a bit like this . . ." She pressed her lips together, and hummed a few bars.

He didn't move, eyes closed, his face focused in concentration.

She added a couple more. What was she doing? She'd reconciled herself to this part of her life being lost. She didn't need a glimpse of the joy that could no longer be hers. She stopped.

"It's amazing." Josh opened his eyes, capturing hers. "Could you do it? Play it against what we've got laid down so we can see how it works? I could source a violin for you."

Could she? She hadn't played her violin in over a year. Not since it got too hard to keep going, knowing she would never be as good as she was. Her skill from years of training had vanished in the instant it took to break her arm in two places, tearing tendons from bone and pulling apart nerves.

It wasn't a complex melody. Nothing technically difficult. But her reticence wasn't about a few measures of music, as much as it was about the loss that vibrated through her soul when she played. Every note could dredge up memories she spent her days trying to forget. She shook her head. "I . . . I don't know."

He opened his mouth, then closed it.

"You must have people you use for this stuff. Some of your songs have string arrangements. I could write it down for your people. They'd pick it up."

He studied her face and nodded. "Okay, but if you change your mind, just let me know. We're going to keep working on some of the other songs this week. There's time."

Her phone trilled on the desk beside her. Thank goodness. She glanced at the screen and picked up. "Hey. What's up?"

"Hi." Her cousin's voice lacked its usual verve.

"What's up?" She looked up. Josh had moved away to pack up some gear.

"I thought I'd let you know that Dan is on his way over. So . . ." A throat clear. "You might want to work late tonight."

"Why?"

A sigh. "I'm going to do it. Break up with him. I'm not sure how he'll handle it or how long it will take."

"Oh." Paige absorbed what her cousin was trying to tell her. "Are you sure?"

"A hundred per cent. And I need to do it before I leave for Chile."

"Okay, well good luck." *Good luck?* Paige cringed at her choice of words.

"Thanks. See you in the morning."

Paige set down her phone. Poor Dan was about to get his heart broken. He was going to cry. She just knew it. Guys fell for Kat hard. Yet Kat never seemed to make the leap from a-lot-of-like to love.

Paige sneaked another peek at Josh. His long lashes cast shadows across his cheekbones as he wound up some cords. He was humming the melody she'd suggested for *Almighty*, his rich tenor giving the notes extra depth.

Why couldn't she bring herself to do this for him? It would take half an hour, tops. Just enough time to see if her idea worked, and lay down a demo for the strings players if it did.

No. It wasn't her responsibility. She was here to be a logistics manager, not a musician.

She turned her attention back to her spreadsheet, staring at the cells as if they could magically re-arrange themselves and solve the logistics problems created by new health and safety regulations.

"What are you working on?"

She waved her hand at her laptop. "Feeding, watering, and bathrooming a gazillion women at the same time. I feel like I'm planning the church equivalent of the Normandy invasion."

Josh pulled the chair out from the desk beside

her, spun it around and sat down. Paige shifted her chair over as he leaned forward and peered at the screen.

"What am I looking at?"

His arm brushed hers as he leaned forward, his minty breath wafting across her face.

"Um." She forced her attention back to her screen. Just pretend it's Emily. Or Janine. Anyone except him. "Well, this is the layout of the main arena." She pulled up the next image. "This is the layout of how everything is looking around the exterior. I'm trying to work out how to get Section B through to coffee and the bathrooms without having to funnel them through merchandizing area C."

"We don't want them to go through merchandizing?"

"It's debatable, but my experience has been that forcing people to go through something like that ends up being counter-productive. Some people will want to buy stuff, but most of them will be fighting to get somewhere else, and they'll be swimming against the people who want to get in."

"Hmm," Josh peered at the screen. "What if—nope." He cut himself off. "That won't work. Maybe, if we—nope." Leaning back in his chair he stretched his arms out and looked at the screen again. "I've got it!"

"You have?" Paige wasn't sure if it would

be great or humiliating if Josh could solve in minutes the problem she'd been wrestling with for days.

"Yup." His hand reached out, and he slapped the laptop closed. "It's time to go home. This doesn't need to be solved tonight, unlike my need for dinner."

Was he about to—

"Besides, my mother would have my hide if she knew I'd left a woman alone here this late at night. I'll walk you out."

Paige felt her hopes deflate. No, he wasn't. Which was fine. She could run over to the super-market, pick up a few things, and come back. There were always things going on here until late at night, so she wouldn't have any problem getting back into the main office.

Standing, she made a show of gathering her stuff and shrugging on her jacket. Some takeout and a few snacks would do it. She had plenty of work to occupy her for the next few hours.

They walked in silence down the dim hallway toward the main doors. "After you," Josh held one of the doors open for her to slip through. "I'll just be a couple of seconds—need to set the alarm." He stepped back and a few seconds later a series of electronic beeps sounded.

Outside, evening was well and truly upon them. She'd completely lost track of time in the studio. It wasn't pitch black, but had darkened enough that the lamps lining the paths shed welcome light.

Staring across the campus, she realized the main building was also shrouded in uncommon darkness. Great, of all nights, tonight had to be the night there was nothing scheduled. And she didn't have the alarm codes.

Josh stepped through the door beside her, then turned around, using his master key to lock it. He looked at her, then paused. "You okay? You look a little . . . lost."

She peered up at him. His gray eyes glittered under the lamps that lined the main path. "Kat's breaking up with her boyfriend."

His face stayed blank.

"My cousin, who's my roommate. She's breaking up with her boyfriend. He's a nice guy who probably wants to marry her. But she . . . It's going to be . . ." She did a weird gesture with both hands.

Josh winced. "Ouch. Poor guy."

"That was her on the phone. Suggesting I might not want to come home for a few hours. I was going to get some snacks from the supermarket and come back and do some more work, but . . ." She waved a hand toward the main auditorium. "Tonight is the one night there's nothing going on."

Josh grinned at her. "So I get to rescue a damsel in distress?"

"I wouldn't go that far."

"Come back to our place for some dinner. There's always heaps of food. I have to go do a songwriting session a bit later but even if no one else is home . . ." He gestured toward her laptop. "You're welcome to take a corner of a couch and do more work or watch some TV, find a book, whatever, until it's safe to return home."

She looked at him. There was no hint of mocking in his gaze, just earnestness.

"Please. My mother will shoot me if she was to ever find out I abandoned you to go solo dine at Hungry Jacks or something equally tragic."

"I would hate to have the death of Christendom's most illustrious worship leader on my head. In that case, thanks."

His gaze flickered for a second, then stilled. "Where are you parked?"

"Oh." She waved her hand across the campus. "In the lot behind the community center."

"Seriously? We must be able to get you a better park than that."

"It's fine. I enjoy the walk." During the day, that was. Not right now, as she tried to match his pace under the canopy of shadowed gum trees. It would be just her luck to be attacked by a drop bear in front of Josh. She cast her gaze up into the branches.

"Do you think we should—"

"So, how did you enjoy your flight to Australia?"

"What?" She hadn't seen that coming.

"You know." He shrugged. "It's a long flight. People cope in different ways. A lot of the time, they drink too much."

This was one truly weird conversational shift, but whatever. She'd go with it. "Can't say I noticed." She'd been so busy breathing into a paper bag for most of the thirteen hours that the entire cast of Riverdance could have busted out a tap dancing, leg-flinging storm in the aisles and she wouldn't have seen it.

"I see."

She couldn't see his face, but there was edge to his tone that compelled her to continue. "I hate flying. On the Chicago-LA leg, I took something that was supposed to put me out of my misery but instead turned me into a woozy disaster. I basically survived the next leg by blowing in and out of a paper bag for thirteen hours with my knees up to my chin. So, no, unless you count the guy next to me spilling half his bourbon and coke on me, I wasn't paying any attention to what other people were drinking."

Josh had stopped dead in his tracks. "You took something?"

The way he asked the question made her defensive. Apparently for him, flying was as natural as breathing. Well, good for him.

"Yes, Mr. Professional Flier, I took a sedative my mother gave me in case I needed something because I hadn't flown since—" She caught herself in time and clamped her mouth shut.

"Watch out!"

She heard the yell a split second before something slammed into her shoulder.

"Argh! Get off me!" Throwing herself on the ground, she rolled over and over, her face smashing into leaves as she tumbled. She had not come half way around the world to be killed by a freaking tree bear.

"Paige? Paige!"

"Is it gone?" Her shoulder hurt but there didn't seem to be anything on her.

"Is what gone?"

She peered up at Josh who was standing above her looking confused but not concerned. "The drop bear!"

"The drop bear?"

"That just attacked me." She sat up.

He crouched down, looking at her. "Seriously?"

"What?"

His lips twitched. "You got hit by a remote-control helicopter." He held up a small, mangled device. "Or rather it was."

A boy who looked to be elementary-age and a woman ran up to them. "Oh my gosh, we are so sorry. It just got away on us. I knew it had gotten too dark to do this. Are you okay?"

Josh stood up, offered her a hand, and pulled her to her feet. "She's all good. Just got a fright." He handed the helicopter back to the boy. "Sorry, I can't say the same for your toy, buddy."

The kid took a look at his broken toy, then straightened his shoulders. "That's all right. I'm glad she's okay. From the way she dropped, I thought we'd really hurt her."

Josh's lips started twitching again. Paige didn't get what was so funny. Sure, it was just a toy. But if it had been a drop bear she could have been mangled, even killed.

"Okay, well then, if you're sure." The mom still looked doubtful.

"I'm sure." Paige managed to conjure up a smile. "It's fine."

She waited until they were about twenty feet away before she turned on Josh. "What is so funny?" She hissed the words between clenched teeth.

Josh was laughing so hard, he was doubled over. "Emily . . . Emily . . ."

She gave him a shove. "What about Emily?"

"Emily is going to be devastated she missed this."

"Missed what?"

He finally managed to pull himself together enough to stand up. "Drop bears."

"What about them?"

"There's no such thing. They're a joke people play on tourists."

"They're . . ." She struggled to understand what he was saying. "There's no drop bears?"

He shook his head. "No."

"I've been walking around staring up at gum trees for months for no reason?"

"I wouldn't say that. We still have some spectacular native flora and fauna for your admiration."

"I just rolled on the ground like a . . . a lunatic, for no reason." In front of him. Again. Always him! Even in the ever-increasing darkness she could see his wide smile.

"So it would seem."

New mom or not, Emily had some serious revenge coming her way.

Josh could almost see the cogs turning in Paige's mind as she stared at him.

Top teeth pinched her bottom lip, her lashes fluttering. She was going to cry. Oh, Lord, she was going to cry. Why? It was only a joke. And one that lots of people got pulled on them. Though, he had to admit, she was the first he'd met who had taken the drop bear threat so seriously.

He pressed his lips together to suppress laughter as the image of her tumbling across the ground replayed in his mind.

She drew in a shuddering breath, and he clenched his arms at his side to stop himself from giving her a hug. He was a heel for finding it funny. Obviously, it had scared the living daylights out of her. Paige was in a different country—one that did have some dangerous wildlife. How was she supposed to suspect Emily was pulling her leg?

"Look . . ." He stretched out a hand, which landed on her shoulder with all the finesses of a teenage boy taking a girl to their first dance. "You weren't—"

He stopped talking as she bent almost double with the force of her shoulders shaking.

He couldn't take it anymore. Dropping to his knees beside her, he peered up. The growing darkness made it almost impossible to see her face. "Look, I'm sorry, I know Emily didn't mean to upset you."

"Oh, my gosh." She swiped both hands across her cheeks. "I must have looked ridiculous."

"You're . . . laughing?"

She pulled herself upright. "Of course I'm laughing! How are you not?"

He stood. His smile came more from relief than anything else. "Well, you know, I thought you might be upset. You were pretty mad."

"Because I've spent months craning my neck at weird angles looking for nasty little bears that don't even exist." The nearest lamp cast a glow over her upturned face, giving her a halo and revealing a wide grin.

His breath stalled. When had everything about her stopped being annoying and become beguiling? He met plenty of pretty girls, including ones with cute accents like hers. What made her different from them? But there was something about her that captured him and refused to let go.

She ran a hand through her hair. "Ow!" She pulled a twig out.

"Hold on. There's a few more." He untangled one from her ponytail, then another.

"Thanks." Her whispered words caused him to still, and she caught his gaze. *She has a boyfriend. She has a boyfriend. Seriously Tyler, she has a boyfriend.*

"No worries." He tried to tell his feet to step back but they stayed. "Hold on, just a couple more."

His fingers betrayed him as they took their sweet time brushing across her hair to find a couple more leaves, their eyes locked the entire time.

It was Paige who broke the spell, pulling her gaze away to turn and point. "That's my car just in the second row. Thanks for walking me."

"No worries." Hadn't he just said that?

She took a few steps away, then turned around and paused for a second. "Thanks, Josh."

"See you soon." He gestured down the row. "My car's just down there. I'll follow you."

It was only as she unlocked her car and he

walked toward his that he remembered the other revelation of the night. She hadn't been drunk on the plane. He'd been an arrogant tosspot for no reason.

He reached his car and leaned his head against the cool driver's side window. She didn't have a drinking problem. Half of him was thrilled he was wrong, but the other half wished he'd been right. He was already in enough trouble. She wasn't available, and he had a sense Paige McAllister could cause him a lot of heartache if he let her any closer.

In his car, he revved the engine and pulled behind Paige to follow her back to his house. She drove incredibly slowly, hesitating at every corner, and he could've boiled an egg in the time she took navigating roundabouts. Admittedly, it took some getting used to driving on the other side of the road on the other side of the car, but he hated to think what time she must leave home to make it to work on time. Hopefully before all those prone to road rage got moving. Sydney drivers were not known for their loving embrace of unconfident drivers.

Finally, taking half an hour to complete what would ordinarily be a twelve-minute drive, she indicated and parked along the curb by his driveway.

Josh hit the garage door opener and pulled his SUV into his space beside his mother's hatchback. His father's slot was empty, but his sister's car sat at the curb in front of Paige's.

He hadn't thought this through. Mum and Sarah would leap to all sorts of wrong conclusions if he didn't explain before they saw Paige. He strode inside to find the two women of the house with bowls of ice cream in the family room.

Now he had about ten seconds before Paige was at the door.

His mother raised her head. "Hey—"

"I've brought Paige home for a few hours. Don't go reading anything into it. I'll explain later." He headed toward the front door, but not before he caught the beginnings of a grin climbing his mother's face.

He strode down the hall and threw open the front door just as Paige stepped onto the doormat. "Come on in."

Where was his mother? She was the quintessential hostess. Like his thoughts had conjured her, she appeared. "Well, isn't this a nice surprise."

Paige stepped over the threshold, then hesitated. "I don't want to intrude. Josh didn't think there would be anyone home."

His mother shot him a sideways look.

Paige caught the glance and flushed to her hairline. Her ponytail was smooth again. She must have taken a few seconds in the car to redo it. "I mean. Kat and her boyfriend . . ." She floundered there.

Man, she was cute, bright pink and stuck for words. *Stop it, Tyler.*

His mum just looked between them, bemused.

"Paige's cousin is breaking up with her boyfriend tonight, so she suggested Paige might want to work late. And I know you would have tarred and feathered me if I'd left Paige alone at work so I said she was welcome to borrow a couch here until it was safe to go home."

Understanding crossed his mum's face. Finally.

Josh glanced at his watch. "And on that note, I'm starving and am due to meet the guys at eight-thirty. I'm going to grab a sandwich. You want one?"

Paige smiled at him. The kind of smile that could make a guy believe he could conquer mountains. "That would be great."

Thank goodness he did have something on tonight, otherwise it would have been tempting to make up an excuse, any excuse, to get back out of the house.

TWENTY-TWO

"Oh, that was so good." Paige stretched out her legs in front of her and rubbed her stomach, the grateful recipient of one amazing chicken salad sandwich.

She placed the empty plate on the wide arm of the couch beside her and reached for the tall glass of juice that she'd placed on an end table. Taking a long sip, she relaxed into the cushions.

Sarah sat curled up at the other end of the couch in an oversized sweater and yoga pants, a dessert bowl cradled in her hands. Janine had disappeared somewhere after telling Paige to make herself at home, and Josh had left as soon as he'd wolfed down his own skyscraper-sized creation.

"Do you fancy my brother?"

Juice went everywhere—up her nose, down her airway, dribbling out her mouth. Paige hacked and spluttered, seeking oxygen. "I'm sorry." The words wheezed out of her as she grabbed a napkin and dabbed at the orange stain on her shirt.

"Here." Sarah handed her another napkin, a

grin on her face. She was a feminine version of her father and brother, with her dark hair and gray eyes. "So was that a 'yes' or a 'no'?" The girl was merciless.

"Um . . . no."

"You bought him at the ball." Sarah plunged her spoon into her bowl of ice cream.

"With his own money. It's not like we're going on a date." Paige dabbed at the stain but just managed to get little pieces of napkin stuck to it.

"Why not? He's a great catch. Do you already have a boyfriend?"

No, but saying that might only encourage her. "It's kind of complicated." She still caught up with Nate most weeks. Part of her sometimes wondering if maybe she'd get back home at the end of the year and realize he was exactly what she wanted.

"Hmm." Sarah didn't look convinced. "I know Josh can be a bit of a prat sometimes, but deep down he's a good guy. He's been burned in the past and doesn't meet many girls who are interested in him for him, if you know what I mean." She leaned forward, batting her dark eyelashes. "They're all like, 'Oooh Josh. You're sooo amazing. Your songs just touch me like, in places I've never been touched before. Let me just wave my left hand around so you can see how bare it is.' "

The girl did a perfect imitation of what Paige

had mocked herself when she'd seen Josh surrounded by a gaggle of groupies. "How do you know I'm not like that? I could be reining it in in front of your mom and you."

Sarah blew out a breath of air and pointed at Paige's shirt. "Well, for a start, you'd have at least another two buttons undone. And you probably would have found a way to pour an entire jug of water down your front while making your sandwich. Not to mention you actually managed to make your sandwich without finding some reason to drape yourself all over him." She started batting her eyelashes again. "Oh Josh, can you swirl the mayonnaise on my sandwich like that? That's so amaaaaazing. And oh, I can't get the lid off the pickles. Can you do it with your strong, manly arms?"

Paige snorted. "C'mon, they're not that bad."

"They're shameless!" Sarah widened her eyes. "Go watch them at a potluck sometime. It's incredible how many girls manage to drop cutlery in front of my brother and take so long picking it up you wonder if they've been snap-frozen down there."

"Now, Sarah, that's not very gracious." Janine walked back into the room, but her attempt to smother her smile betrayed her.

"You know it's true, Mum."

"Well, for better or worse, they're your sisters in Christ. And between your defensive tackles and your brother's paranoia, it's far more likely you'll never have a sister-in-law than that it will be one of them." Janine handed Paige a sweatshirt and a pair of athletic pants. "I thought you might want something more comfortable and you look about the same size as Little Miss Over Protective. And I've made up the guest room for you."

Guest room? "No, really, I . . ." For the third time in the evening, her vocabulary failed her. Not to mention that the idea of sleeping in the same house as Josh had turned her insides into a tumble dryer. Bad idea. Bad, bad idea.

"I insist. Greg is away for a few days and Josh crashes at Brad's place when they do a late-night songwriting session. We can have a nice girls' night and I'm sure we can find a shirt or top of Sarah's that will work fine with your suit for tomorrow. Besides . . ." She sighed. "From the little I've seen, Dan has got it bad for Kat. I suspect whatever they need to work through is going to take awhile."

That was true. Paige ignored the feeling of disappointment that seeped through her when she heard she wouldn't be seeing Josh again tonight. What was wrong with her? She saw him almost every day. "If you're sure it's not any trouble."

"Guest room is upstairs and third door on the right if you want to get changed. Bathroom is just beside it."

Paige looked at the sweats in her hands, then back up at Sarah and Janine.

Sarah smiled. "Do you happen to be a *Bachelor* fan? Mum and I were about to settle in for the latest episode."

"Only if you never tell anyone!" Janine said.

Paige hadn't felt like she'd belonged in this country since she'd set foot in it. Now, for the first time in months, she felt maybe she was going to be okay.

"I'm in." It was exactly what she needed to distract her from a real-life bachelor who had her mind wandering down foolish paths it had no business going.

Josh pulled his car back into the driveway. The songwriting session had lasted all of forty minutes with no progress before his cowriter confessed he was planning to propose to his girlfriend on the weekend and so was good for nothing more than sappy lyrics and talking through the proposal plan. From every possible angle.

At least now Josh knew to avoid the Botanic Gardens on Saturday afternoon. Though he couldn't figure out why Brad didn't pick somewhere inside when the late-winter weather was so unpredictable. Still, no doubt it wouldn't matter once Brad got down on one knee with his grandmother's ring—one of the ugliest things Josh had ever seen, something he couldn't imagine Gretchen wearing. That was love for you.

Paige's car still sat by the curb. His stomach did a strange flip. Must be indigestion from his massive sandwich and the two glasses of Coke.

Muffled sounds reached him as he stepped into the house.

Oh, don't tell me. Crossing the hallway, he peered into the formal lounge where three familiar heads lined up along the main couch, all entranced as they watched some wreck of a reality TV show.

A brown-haired guy with a sad yet resigned expression was spouting an awful line about life being a journey and he didn't think they were the right life companions. Across from him, a blonde girl struggled to keep herself in her dress as she leaned across the table and pleaded for more time.

"It's about time. He should've cut her loose, like, two episodes ago." His sister was never one to hold back. "I don't get it. He loves the great outdoors, and her idea of roughing it is four-star. How can she not see they'd be a disaster?"

"Sometimes people are so caught up in what they want to see, they can't accept reality when it's right in front of them." Paige spoke. "People convince themselves they can make all sorts of things work because they're blinded by physical attraction and refuse to see all the other things that make them completely incompatible."

Huh. The American made a lot of sense.

And that was exactly what he needed to remember. The fact that she was cute and her smile unwound him like a clock was irrelevant. The reality was that even if she didn't have a guy back home, they'd still be all wrong for each other.

He stepped back from the doorway, leaving the women to their trashy TV. He lived in reality, where things were a lot more complicated than spewing platitudes about being on a "journey" and working out which TV camera was best to stare mournfully into while supposedly agonizing over the final rose.

TWENTY-THREE

"Seriously, Sarah. You have been in there forever. Get out!" Josh hammered against the upstairs bathroom door. He'd overslept and would be late if his sister didn't get moving.

He had no idea what she did in there every morning, but as far as he could tell, it made no difference at all. She went in looking like Sarah, and came out a cleaner version. That should only require five minutes, not fifty.

The hairdryer switched off. Thank goodness. Then the water started. What was she doing? He gave the door another pounding. "If you are not out here in thirty seconds, I'm coming in. I kid you not. I can't be late this morning."

The tap kept running.

"Ten, nine, eight, sev—" The door flew open. "Fina—"

His words jammed in his throat at the sight of Paige, in glossy-haired glory, guest bathrobe on, hands on her hips, and one monster glare on her face.

"First, it's not your sister's fault if you slept in. Second, I have a killer right hook, and if you

227

so much as set a toe in this bathroom, you'll be meeting it." Slam. The doorframe rocked on impact, then the hairdryer blasted back on.

A low whistle came from behind him. "That was awesome. Can you please marry her?"

Great. Sarah stood behind him, leaning against the railing at the top of the stairs, a half-eaten piece of toast in her hand. Fully dressed, she had the bright, chipper look of someone who had been up for hours.

"She hates megachurches." Josh forced the words out, mind still stuck on the image of Paige in a bathrobe.

"So says the guy who had a full-on conniption when Mum and Dad talked about opening the satellite in Yarra because he didn't want to be *that* church." Sarah threw air quotes around the word.

"She's terrified of flying." While he could probably circumnavigate the globe on his air miles.

"And yet here she is, on the other side of the world. I'm assuming she didn't paddle a canoe." Sarah took another bite of her toast.

"She thinks I'm a jerk."

"And clearly you've just shown her the error of your ways." In the bathroom, the hairdryer ratcheted up another notch as if to underscore her words. "Is that it? Is that all you've got?"

Fine. "She has a boyfriend."

His sister paused, the last bite of toast halfway to her mouth. "You sure about that?"

"What do you mean?"

"Well, when I asked her last night, she didn't say she had one. She said it was complicated."

"Sarah." He imbued the word with warning and quashed the hope that welled within him for a split-second. "What do we say about going near someone who explains their relationship with *it's complicated?*"

"Don't." Sarah mumbled, staring at the floor. No doubt reminded that the last time a guy had used that line with her, it had translated into *I have three kids with two women and the tax office are after me for dodging paying child support.*

"Exactly."

The bathroom door opened behind him, and he turned to see Paige emerge fully dressed.

She gestured to the bathroom with a slight bow. "All yours." Then she grinned, causing the air to dance in his chest. "See you at the planning meeting?"

"Um, yeah. See you then." He strode past her, pushing the door closed behind him. He rested his forehead against the cool bathroom wall. A whiff of apples hit him. Blasted apples. What did she do? Carry perfume and spray every room she entered? Wherever he went, the fruit haunted him.

The image of her in a bathrobe in *his* bathroom

returned, trying to lure his mind to places it had no business going. Whether he wanted it to or not, everything became more complicated the moment she opened his bathroom door.

Paige stared at the wall of her office. It was lined with project plans, so if anyone looked in they'd have no reason to suspect she wasn't meditating on her Gantt chart.

She had to get a grip. It was almost lunchtime and she had achieved nothing. Well, nothing beyond trying to get the searing image of rumpled, just-got-out-of-bed Josh Tyler out of her head. All tousled hair, with an old gray T-shirt, and baggy shorts that only highlighted a pair of well-toned legs. He looked like he'd rolled out of a Calvin Klein ad.

Thank goodness his yelling had surprised her. She'd smacked herself in the face with the hairdryer, which had her react like an angry fire ant. If she hadn't done that, she probably would have drooled. Or worse.

Retreating into the bathroom to regather her tumbling emotions had been the only option. Plus, she'd seen Sarah over his shoulder, watching the whole exchange with glee. The last thing she wanted to do was fan any ideas.

Paige blew out a breath of air. This was pointless. Since she wasn't getting anything done on *Grace*, she had might as well try to get some tour stuff sorted. She looked for the folder on her desk. Not there. Of course. She'd left it in Josh's office last night.

She shoved her chair back and grabbed her coat. She'd go get it and bring it back here. Josh had meetings most Thursday mornings, so she could be in and out without him even knowing.

At least she didn't have to put her neck out looking for drop bears anymore. A quick search on Wikipedia this morning confirmed what Josh said: she'd been had.

Paige crossed the campus and soon reached Josh's office. The door was open, but the office was empty. Excellent. She grabbed the blue tabbed folder and was one foot away from being out the door when the phone on her desk started its shrill song.

Leaning over, she peered at the screen. A US number. Probably one of the hotels she'd been waiting to lock down. She picked up the receiver before the diversion she had in place to reroute calls to her office kicked in. "Paige speaking."

Her guess was right. She shrugged her coat off and sat down, then glanced up at the clock. After twelve. Surely after his meeting, Josh would go grab some lunch.

She leaned forward and turned on her computer. After dealing with that call, she handled a couple more and input the new details into the spreadsheet. More money saved. Shame she wasn't getting commission.

Digging in her drawer for a snack, she opened a packet of bagel chips and extracted a handful before opening her web browser to do some personal research. She'd retrieved Ethan's bucket list from her violin case after the bridge climb. Most of the things on the Australia list were way out of her budget, but she could manage to hold a koala for him.

She was doing a search for the Sydney Zoo as Josh walked in. He paused when he saw her.

"You always that feisty in the morning?"

She looked up at him, trying to ignore the way his T-shirt clung to his athletic torso. "You always that grumpy?"

He opened his mouth, then closed it. Smiling, he shook his head and proceeded to his own desk.

Paige tried to return her focus to her search, pushing her mind toward anything other than seeing Josh Tyler first thing in the morning.

She reached the zoo's website, clicked on directions and found herself lost trying to navigate the world of Sydney public transport. Taking her car wasn't an option. She doubted her blood pressure would be able to withstand left-hand driving in the city proper—driving around the suburbs was stressful enough. Well, when all else failed, ask a local.

She spun her chair. "Can I ask you a question?"

Josh swung around. "Sure."

"What would be the best way to take public transport to get to the zoo?"

"Taronga Zoo?"

She glanced back at her screen to confirm. "Yep."

"Probably take a bus into the central city which would take about an hour, then I'm pretty sure you can catch a ferry from Circular Quay to the zoo. That takes about fifteen minutes."

She nodded. "Okay. Thanks." Or not. He'd clearly used public transport about as much as she had. Catch a bus from where? Get off it where?

"When are you going?"

"Probably when you guys head off on your tour."

"Why?"

"I need to hug a koala."

He blinked. "Come again?"

She clicked her pen. "I need to hug a koala for someone."

The look on his face said he'd rather eat his own feet. "You really don't want to hold a koala. I know they're our national icon but I'm going to be honest. They're stinky and grumpy."

Huh. Wonder if her brother knew that. "Well, your tourism board has done a masterful job of convincing the world otherwise."

"Is that your main reason for going to the zoo?"

She nodded. "Pretty much."

"Well, I have a better idea. It would take you hours and a decent chunk of change to do it at the zoo, or you could just go to the sanctuary that's fifteen minutes from here and cheaper."

She blinked. "And they let you near koalas?"

"Yup." He checked his watch. "In fact, if we left now, we could get there for the one o'clock feeding. Assuming they're still on the same schedule as when I took my nephews last year."

She glanced back at her desk with the perfectly aligned, tabbed papers lined up like a battalion. She'd already wasted half a day.

"We could be back in, like, an hour and a half. That would give us plenty of time to make the planning meeting."

Paige nibbled her bottom lip. If his estimate was right, she could work late, finish up things once she got back.

"Or you and Kat could go together."

Her cousin was leaving for South America in the morning. Paige threw down her pen. "You know what? Let's do it."

He looked a little startled at her decision. "You sure?"

She smiled. "No time like the present." She turned around to log out of her computer before sanity struck. What was she doing? In her eagerness to fulfill Ethan's wish, she hadn't thought this through. The two of them would be alone.

On something that could be said to resemble a date. She could barely get the guy out of her mind as it was.

He was already gathering up his keys and jacket. Too late now.

Josh hadn't been able to think with her sitting so close. She hadn't even been talking. Or humming. Or clicking her pen. Or doing anything else that could be deemed distracting. Just breathing, and occasionally muttering something to herself.

He, meanwhile, might as well have stayed in bed. He'd been next to useless at his morning meetings, fighting his conscience insisting that he needed to 'fess up. Tell her what he'd seen on the plane. Apologize for making assumptions and being a world-class moron.

But apparently, for his penance, his conscience had decided that he should take her to go see koalas instead.

He hated koalas.

Ten minutes after his brain explosion, they were in his car, cruising familiar suburban streets on their way to Pennant Hills. Hints of spring hung in the air, green buds appearing on stripped back trees, warmth tinting the breeze.

He could do this. This time next week, he'd be winging his way to New Zealand. She'd be back to working solely on *Grace*. They wouldn't see each other for at least a month. He just had to stay on the emotional tightrope for another seven days. He refused to allow himself to tumble off. Something told him there would be no safety net if he fell for Paige McAllister.

"I saw you on the plane." His words just splattered out, bursting open in the silence like a ripe melon hitting the pavement.

Paige turned toward him, her brow furrowed. "What?"

No turning back now. "I was a jerk to you at the beginning because I saw you on the flight from Chicago to LA. You were stumbling up the aisle, you smelled like liquor, and then you . . ." He trailed off, unable to finish the sentence.

She'd closed her eyes. "Puked. All over my own shoes."

"Yeah."

"And you thought I was just another classless girl who got drunk on planes."

"I'm really sorry."

He could feel her looking across at him. "No wonder you didn't think I was of fit character to work at Harvest." She was silent for a few seconds. "Oh, wow. That crack at me the day of Emily's morning tea. You thought I had a drinking problem, didn't you? All your rudeness was because some guy spilled his bourbon on me?"

Josh chanced a glance at her. Her mouth was in a thin line, brows pinched. He returned his gaze to the road. There was no way he could admit the truth—that even when he thought the worst of her, there was still something that wedged her into his heart and his mind that he couldn't shake. The last time that had happened, he'd found himself in places he'd said he'd never go.

He turned into the sanctuary car park and scored a parking space close to the entrance.

"I'm sorry. I've been a real jerk to you. I've just . . . With Mum and Dad, the church, the band, everything, I've learned that trusting the wrong people gets you burned. So I'm a bit paranoid."

"A *bit* paranoid? That's the understatement of the decade." Paige pulled the latch on her door as she unclicked her seatbelt. She slipped out her door, her feet crunching on the gravel.

They strode to the bright yellow signposted entrance and paid their entrance fee. It was a quiet day, and there were no lines, which was good since they only had ten minutes until feeding time. Paige didn't so much as look his way the entire time, let alone speak to him.

The easy camaraderie they'd just established was gone. And he had only himself to blame.

Josh led the way to the main koala enclosure where they joined the small crowd that had gathered—mainly tourists, cameras slung around their necks, guide books and maps held close.

He looked to his side to see if they needed to try to get closer, but Paige was tall enough to see over most of the crowd. She had her gaze on the trees, where four koalas sat eating gum leaves and looking entirely unbothered at being the center of attention.

In an hour, they'd be back at work. Once the planning meeting was done, he'd find a reason to be out of the office for the rest of the afternoon. "I don't want to ruin this for you. Would you rather I just go wait in the car?"

Finally, she looked at him. "No. It's okay. I'm mad at you but I'm not that mad."

He'd take that.

A couple of keepers came to the front of the enclosure with a pair of koalas and started droning on about feeding and habitat. He focused on the talk with such ardent attention someone might mistakenly suspect he was a koala aficionado rather than a guy desperate to think about anything other than the girl standing beside him.

After about fifteen minutes, a line formed and slowly moved forward as people had their turn getting up close and personal with the bears. But there was no chance he was touching the grubby little things. Not that he would ever say that to Paige who bounced on her feet in anticipation as the line moved forward, like a hyperactive five-year-old.

When it was their turn, Paige reached for some gum leaves and said hello to the keeper before reaching a tentative hand out to touch the bear.

"So who are you doing this for? Someone back home?" Maybe if he made small talk it would distract her from how ticked off she was with him.

Paige stilled, only moving her hand, running it along the koala's back. "My brother, Ethan."

They'd shared an office for weeks and he didn't even know how many siblings she had. He only recalled references to a sister, but that was it.

He held up his phone. "Want me to take a photo?"

"Sure." She managed a strained smile as he snapped a couple of shots. So much for small talk distracting her.

"Is he back in Chicago? Is this your way of tormenting him, by ticking off his bucket list?"

She pulled in a breath. Her hand slid off the bear as she turned to face him. "He died. Six years ago."

Oh. "I'm sorry." And this was why he was never going to be a real pastor. In moments like this, he struggled to come up with the right thing to say.

She turned back to the bear. "I found a list of things he wanted to do in life in his stuff. I'd forgotten about it. Then Kat took me climbing the Harbour Bridge for my birthday. That was on his list for Australia. So was holding a koala. Figured since I was here, I should do a couple for him." She swallowed, attempted a shaky smile. "Though when I see him next, I'm going to tell him how bad they stink. No one tells you that in all the promo material."

"And do ourselves out of millions of tourist dollars?"

She looked around. "So what else is there to see here?"

"Honestly? Not a lot. Mostly birds, a few kangaroos, some wombats. Maybe a dingo or two."

She managed a half smile. "Not quite the zoo then."

"No, but not quite zoo prices either."

"Fair enough."

They walked away from the koala pen, wandering around a few other exhibits in silence. What should he do now? He felt bad that he'd made the trip even worse by asking about her brother, and didn't want to put his foot in it again. Which left him in no-man's-land since everything he'd done today had made things worse.

Paige saved him from his predicament. "Okay, don't take this as a get out of jail free pass, but there is an upside to you being a total jerk."

An upside? "How?"

"After Ethan died, I kind of sleepwalked through life. Stayed with the wrong guy, in the wrong job, lost. Coming here, having to stand on my own feet where people didn't know me, it's forced me to work out who I am. Not Paige, Ethan's sister. Or Paige, Alex's girlfriend. Just me, on my own."

She shoved her hands in the pockets of her jeans and focused her gaze on the path in front of them as she continued.

"Everyone at home had tiptoed around me, worried that if they said or did the wrong thing, I might break. It was refreshing to have someone to spar with. Be mad at." She looked up at him. The sight of an unexpected grin turned his heart inside out. "It's been awhile since anyone made me as angry as you did."

"And have you worked out what you want?" The wind blew unrestrained pieces of hair around her face and he fought the urge to capture it and tuck if behind her ear.

"I think so."

He couldn't stop from hoping it was him.

TWENTY-FOUR

Paige reached under her bed, slipped out the familiar black case, and placed it on the top of her comforter. She ran her fingers across the rough surface, then flipped the three clasps and lifted the lid.

The red velvet lining peered up at her, as if saying "finally." Positioned in the top of the lid were four bows. All in perfect condition. She may not play much anymore, but she still made sure her most treasured possession stayed tuned and well cared for.

At the bottom, nestled in its plush home, sat her baby. Paige ran her fingers along the polished maple, lingering over its mahogany hue. Even though she'd given up on playing again, she hadn't been able to bear leaving it behind.

She shuddered out a breath. Ever since her conversation with Josh in the studio, she hadn't been able to get the melody she'd composed out of her head. It appeared on her lips, in her head, in her dreams—a symphony of violins, violas, and cellos forming a perfect complement to the rest of the score.

Visiting the sanctuary that afternoon had strengthened her resolve. Ethan would be furious if he knew she was busy checking items off his bucket list while leaving her own great passion to molder away under a bed.

After two years of multiple surgeries and endless rehab, she would never forget the day she sat in the plush office of America's foremost hand and wrist specialist. The sixteenth specialist she'd seen. He'd confirmed what the others had all said: that her recovery was remarkable, almost miraculous, but this was good as it was going to get. Her arm and hand were never going to be capable of playing the way she once had. Too much had been broken, damaged, or crushed.

She'd gone home and put her violin in its case, storing it in the attic with everything else that no longer had a use. If she wasn't ever going to be a concert violinist again, what was the point of playing at all? Of being reminded with every pull of the bow of what she would never have?

"You can still play better than ninety-nine percent of the population," people had said, trying to comfort her. Or worse, "You can still teach."

She hadn't trained for twenty years to teach. She'd trained to earn a place in one of the world's best symphony orchestras, to play the most incredible pieces—Pag's Caprices 5 and 11, Locatelli's Labyrinth, the Beethoven Concerti, the Bartok Solo Sonata. Works of genius that brought people to their feet and required greater hand-brain synchronization than a neurosurgeon.

A sigh escaped Paige's lips. She hadn't played for a year and the ache never went away. She'd thought not playing would make her loss easier to bear, but she'd been wrong. While she would never be as good as she once was, maybe it was time to find out if she could find joy in playing again. In what she could do, rather than what she couldn't.

Reaching with both hands, Paige curled her fingers around the chin rest and the neck, lifting the instrument out of its home. "I'm sorry." She whispered the words to her old friend, whom she'd once spent hours with every day. She knew her Cavalli better than she knew her own family.

Resting it on her left shoulder, she reached down and selected a bow. Her fingers rested on the fingerboard and her body smoothly shifted into the straight spine, straight neck, relaxed shoulders posture that was as natural as breathing.

Closing her eyes, she sought to banish everything except the song, the simple notes, from her head. She pushed away thoughts of how or where she used to play, of fingers flying across the fingerboard like they were dancing on hot coals, of an orchestra swelling, ebbing, flowing in perfect harmony, of stages and standing ovations, evening gowns and encores. She shoved back those memories, focusing on this one song, this one tune.

She rolled the melody around in her head, her fingers moving over the strings, bow hovering just above, playing the air. Shifting, she moved the violin a fraction to the right and adjusted her hand position, seeking the perfect balance, where everything connected.

She tried again, her bow soaring through the air, her fingers finding the right positions. Finally satisfied, she pulled the bow straight across, listening to the timbre, and turned a couple of pegs before trying again.

Much better.

She pulled the bow back across the strings, testing the first few notes. Good. Closing her eyes, she let her hands take flight, giving sound to the music in her head. Repeating the notes over and over until they felt as much a part of her as breathing.

The music soared around her, haunting and longing and wistful. Paige couldn't hear anything else, couldn't think of anything else beyond the singing of crystal pure notes. She tweaked a few notes, tested a few variations of the tune, searched for perfection.

Finally, she opened her eyes to find Kat standing in the door, rivulets of tears running down her cheeks. Her cousin quivered a smile. "You're back."

• • •

Josh leaned back in his chair, scrutinizing the latest set of ticket sales on his Mac screen. New Zealand was almost sold out, with US sales going strong. By the time everything had been paid for, there should be enough for some reasonable Christmas bonuses. Not that money could make up missed time for those who left young families behind every time they were on the road.

Familiar footsteps echoed up the corridor. Paige. It was her second-to-last day in here. With everything pretty much wrapped up, it was time for her to permanently move back into the main building. He was trying to pretend he was looking forward to having his office to himself again, but he was failing. Miserably.

He didn't even turn as she walked into the room and set something on her desk with a clunk. "Morning." It was easier not to look at her. Every time he did, he almost choked on his own recrimination. For being such an idiot. For not telling her the whole truth.

"Hi." A pause. No sound of her chair being pulled out, of her computer being turned on. "Josh?"

"Yeah." He tilted his chair back and looked over his shoulder. Her hair was pulled back, her face uncertain. "What's up?"

"I want to help."

He was lost. Both in her dark eyes and what she was trying to tell him.

She shifted on her feet, brushing a wisp of hair away from her face. "With the strings thing. I can lay down a demo track if you still want me to."

He spun around and saw the black violin case sitting on her desk. "Really?"

She smiled. "Really. One condition. You don't tell anyone it was me."

Odd, but whatever. "Deal." He clicked on his calendar. Nothing until eleven. Perfect. "Let's go, then."

"Right now?"

"Sorry." He hadn't even checked if she had more important things to do. "When would work for you?"

She tapped the screen on her phone. "Actually, now is fine. I don't have anything until ten-thirty."

That gave them a good hour and a half—not that it should take that long. "Cool." He grabbed the studio keys and stood.

She lifted her violin case, easing it off the desk.

As they headed down the hallway, he tried to assess her demeanor. Had she forgiven him for thinking she was a drunk? Was she still mad, but doing him a favor anyway? "Thanks for doing this. You don't have to."

Something flickered across her face. "I know. But I want to."

He unlocked the studio door, and ran his fingers across the wall panel of light switches. Bulbs flickered to life, highlighting the two halves of the room. Soundproof studio on one side, and technical-lounging-everything-else side.

At the sound desk, he flicked on the inputs they would need. "Do you want to go in and warm up while I get set up?"

"I practiced this morning so I should be okay. I just need to hear the track a couple of times. First with the vocals, then without."

"Sure thing." Josh tapped a couple of screens, bringing up the tracks.

She placed her violin case on a desk in front of the window into the studio and unclasped the lid. Opening the case, she used both hands to lift out her violin.

Wow. Even from where he was standing, he could tell this was no ordinary instrument. It almost glowed, the light dancing across the subtle nuances of its surface. Craftsmanship like that did not come cheap.

She shifted it to one arm, cradling it like a baby while she selected a bow from the four tucked into the red velvet case. Her braid fell across her shoulder, her face a study in concentration as she studied one bow, then another, finding differences between what appeared to be identical.

He'd shared an office with her for two months and had no idea she was a musician. Add it to the list. Fear of flying. Dead brother. Violinist. Mysterious scar. What else had he missed in his blind judgment?

With every layer she got more remarkable, more irresistible. She reached out, long lean fingers removing the chosen bow.

Josh turned his attention back to his screens, making sure he had the tracks lined up correctly.

"Where do you want me to stand?"

"Either of the mics will be fine. Do you want some headphones?"

She bit her lip, her forehead creasing. "Do I?"

"They bring clarity, so you can try with, and then if you don't like them, take them off."

She nodded. "Okay."

"You pick a mic, I'll turn it on, and then you can just talk to me. Don't need to press a button or do anything."

"Got it."

She looked so worried he couldn't help himself from tugging at the end of her braid. "You'll do great."

She smiled. "Thanks. Okay, in I go."

Paige strode to the door, her blue wrap top clinging to her curves in all the right places. In the studio, she set down her violin and bow and placed a pair of headphones over her ears. He depressed a button on his control panel. "Can you hear me?"

She gave him a thumbs-up then picked up her

instrument, tucked it under her chin and raised the bow. "Can you play it with the vocals?"

He pressed a few buttons, listened to the opening bars, then his own voice filled the room. She closed her eyes and tapped her foot, holding her bow above the strings, unmoving for the whole song. When it finished, she didn't even open her eyes. "Again, please."

He restarted the song. This time, her bow played the air just above the strings. His ears reached for the notes that only angels could hear. At the end, she moved one ear of her headphones away from her ear and lifted her eyes to his. "Can I do it like this?"

"Go for it."

She took a breath, rolled her shoulders, then repositioned her violin. "Okay I'm ready. No vocals."

He pressed a couple of buttons, stripped the vocal track back, cued up the rest, and then set them rolling.

Eyes closed, violin up, she tapped her foot to the opening bars and lifted her bow. When the first notes came, they almost sent him into the wall. Pure and clear, the melody picked up the arrangement and set it free. Her bow and fingers moved, note after perfect note unfolding, building, releasing. As the song progressed, her face moved from concentration to serenity to joy.

He had never heard anything like it. In all his years as a musician, in the many songs that included strings in the arrangements, he had never heard anything like this. He felt the music from the tip of his toes to the longest hair on his head.

He closed his eyes and let the music sweep him away. Notes that picked up every nuance of the song. Regret. Redemption. Painful endings. New beginnings. It didn't need the words. It was all there, raw, haunting, ethereal. The final notes lingered, settling around him like a shroud. He grasped at the past, wanting to return to four minutes ago, and start it all over again.

"Who is that?"

He hadn't even felt Connor join him. Josh opened his eyes. "It's Paige."

His brother-in-law didn't even give him a glance, his attention focused inside the studio. "I know who it is, but *who* is she?" He pointed at the glass. "That is not just some girl who took a few lessons once."

On the other side of the glass, she lifted her chin, removed her violin and lowered her arm so the instrument rested against her forearm.

Lifting her eyes, she pinned him across the room. This was the point where he should be leaning on his speaker, telling her it was amazing. But there were no words. He'd been leading a worship band for a decade, helped create over a hundred songs but he'd never felt one echo in his soul like this.

He smiled, shook his head, and leaned on the button. "Who are you? A Juilliard prodigy in witness protection or something?"

She smiled and shook her head. "Not quite."

"Not quite about sums it up," Connor muttered, shoving his phone toward him. He glanced down to the web page Connor had opened. *Paige McAllister Named Youngest Ever Violinist to Join Chicago Symphony* ran across the screen. Underneath the headline sat a promo picture of her—evening gown, hair loose, Mona Lisa smile, holding the very same violin that was mere meters away. The date was December 2010.

His chest constricted. What happened to her? How had a violinist for the Chicago Symphony Orchestra ended up in Sydney planning his tour?

His gut told him the answer had everything to do with her brother and the scar she didn't talk about.

The problem was, women and their secrets had never worked out well for him.

TWENTY-FIVE

Josh shuffled through a stack of papers on his desk, searching for the agenda for their final tour planning meeting. It started in fifteen minutes and for the life of him, he couldn't remember what he was supposed to be covering. What was wrong with him? He played in front of thousands of people every week. How could the idea of having to be in the same room with one feisty blonde American have him so off-key?

Her violin performance had left him unable to stop thinking about her. Wondering about the secrets she carried. With all but the smallest details of the tour locked down, she'd moved back to her office. He hated walking into his and not finding her there. Hated that every time a new email popped up, he hoped it was from her. He had it bad. And he needed to shake it.

There. He found the piece of paper he needed, added it to his pile and headed out the door. Six days. He just had to manage six more days. Then they'd be back on tour. He'd be gone for a month. Paige would go back to working full-time on *Grace*, and they'd hardly need to cross paths.

Logic dictated she was all wrong for him. Logic. That was what he had to follow. Not his heart. What was the verse in Jeremiah about the heart being deceitful? He'd already learned that lesson the hard way. It had almost cost his parents everything they'd worked so hard for.

Plus the words that he'd spoken to Sarah kept coming back to him: people with a relationship status of "it's complicated" were a no-go zone.

He strode up the path leading to the main office. Even the gum trees reminded him of Paige, of the night of the not-drop bear. He just needed to be friendly, but professional. Nothing more. Avoid being alone with her and her cute accent and fiery eyes that made him want to dip her in his arms and kiss her breathless.

Why couldn't he make the smart choice? Someone like Kellie. She didn't send his pulse hammering like a construction site, but she was smart, loved God, and got the pressures that came with being a Tyler. They'd make a great team.

The main doors slid open in front of him and he trudged toward the stairs.

"Excuse me?" A guy in a green polo shirt approached, holding an enormous bouquet of flowers. "Can you tell me how I find the main reception?"

"Sure, it's just up here." He gestured toward the stairs. "I'm heading there myself."

"Thanks."

Josh turned to him as they strode up the stairs. "Who are you looking for?"

The guy checked the envelope pinned to the bright purple wrapping. "Paige McAllister."

Josh almost found himself eating wood as he tripped over a stair. He caught himself just in time. They reached the landing and Josh willed his feet to continue across the walkway to the office. "Sure, I know Paige. Follow me."

He bypassed reception, and led the way to Paige's office. She sat with her back to him, staring at the project plans pinned to her wall.

It was good these flowers had shown up. They provided reinforcement right when he needed it, reminding him about the guy at the airport who clearly adored her with every atom of his being. So why did everything in him want to sag under the weight of disappointment? He fought the urge to grab the flowers from the guy, rip the envelope off, and give them to her himself.

He tapped the doorframe.

Paige spun around, a smile creasing her face when she saw him. "Hey."

"Hey." He kept his voice cool. "There's someone here for you."

She stood, her brow wrinkled. "Who?"

Josh turned and beckoned to the flower guy, leaving him to make his delivery from her boyfriend aka Mr. It's Complicated. Whichever it was.

Time to put some distance between himself and the woman who could undo him with her smile and probably ruin him with her secrets.

More flowers from Nate. Another bunch so large, you would've thought she won the Nobel Prize or something. Paige's mind whirled like a roulette ball as she tried to focus on the agenda in front of her. She had to give him points for perseverance.

"What do you think, Paige?" Josh's eyes probed hers across the white-walled meeting room. "Do we let them release the tickets to the upper tier even though we know the acoustics aren't as good up there?"

"Only if they're at a discount and we say something to that effect. People should know they're buying inferior seats."

Josh nodded. "I agree. Did you get that, Matt? Let's do a twenty percent discount on those tickets." He directed his words to the conference phone connecting them to the New Zealand promoter.

What was he thinking about her latest delivery? She ground her teeth together at the urge to suddenly tell him the flowers sitting in her office weren't from her boyfriend. That she hadn't flirted with him while someone waited for her back home. Though, from what Sarah said, given how obvious the girls chasing him were, he probably hadn't even noticed her unwise flirtatious moments.

"Flights are all booked?" Josh stabbed his phone, looked at the time.

"Yes. All locked in. Itineraries will be emailed out tomorrow once we've confirmed a few other details." She needed to get it together. There were only three of them in the room. It was obvious if a third of the attendees were present in body only.

Her fingers drummed on the grey tabletop. Even though she remained a little irritated about the drinking thing, she'd still spent the last couple of days having to avoid him for fear that one more smile or one more teasing joke might pull the pin from the grenade and send her launching herself at him.

She didn't know what had possessed her to tell him about Ethan. But his response had only made her fall harder. He hadn't pried, hadn't tried to find out the details of what happened. Just let her say what she needed. Same with the violin. She could see in his eyes that he knew there was a story, but he didn't try to extract what she wasn't yet ready to give.

She forced herself back to the conversation. Connor was looking at her like he was waiting for her to respond.

Connor leaned back in his chair. "Accommodation is all confirmed?"

Paige checked her tabbed-up notes, not that she needed to. "Everywhere except Christchurch." Her stomach clenched. *Focus, breathe. You're okay.* "I'm waiting to hear back from the Heritage about some room changes. They should be back to me by the end of today."

Josh closed his notebook. "Well then, I think we're done. You have anything else, Matt?"

It crackled. "Nope. All good here. I'll get the discounted tickets released and send another update through on numbers at the end of the week."

"Great, thanks. We'll talk again soon." Josh pushed his chair back as he disconnected the call.

Paige gathered up her papers and water bottle.

"Con, can I grab you for a second?" Josh's question filled her with relief. Being alone with Josh Tyler was about as good for her emotional stability as a bottle of tequila was for an AA member.

"I'll see you guys later." Paige picked up her folder and headed for the door, leaving behind the guy who was everything she didn't want, yet was finagling his way into her heart, to return to flowers from the perfect guy who was everything she should want, yet didn't.

TWENTY-SIX

"Paige, come on in."

Janine looked up and smiled from her position on the couch in her office. It was only when Paige walked through the door that she saw Josh seated opposite. He was leaning forward, elbows on his knees, with his fingers tented and his face somber.

Paige glanced between the two of them. What was this about? Her feet led her forward, and she found herself perched on the edge of the same couch as Janine.

"Is everything okay?" She directed the question to her boss. Paige racked her brain for something, anything. Nothing. Since she'd played in the studio the week before, she and Josh had been professional, cordial, but nothing more. She had no clue why she'd been called to an unscheduled meeting with the two of them.

"We have a bit of a problem." Josh's voice turned Paige around in her seat to face him.

"What now?" Paige ran her hands through her hair. The last few days had been nothing but problems—accommodation mix-ups, cancelled flights, you name it. If she didn't know better, she'd be wondering if the band's tour was jinxed. Now she was just praying they all made it to Auckland in time for Friday's gig.

"Annie's broken her leg skiing. She's going to be in a cast for up to six weeks."

Paige groaned. She'd just spent the last three days briefing the logistics assistant who was traveling with the band on the New Zealand leg of the tour. "Oh, the poor girl. How is she doing?"

Josh shifted back into the couch cushions. "Well, right now she's fly high on some pretty strong meds."

Paige knew all about those. For years she'd knocked back morphine, tramadol, meperidine, and oxycodone like normal people took Tylenol. "So do you need me to brief Malcolm?" He was their second logistics guy, managing the US leg of the tour.

Josh shook his head. "Malcolm has a previous conviction issue. Nothing serious and usually not a problem, but it means he needs a visa to get into New Zealand and there's not enough time. It takes about a month."

They had three days.

Paige blew out a breath. It wasn't fair to ask someone in the band to do it. She didn't even think there was someone who could. They were musicians, not bill hagglers, transport bookers, or expense managers.

Janine leaned forward. "Paige, we know it's over and above the call of duty, but we were wondering if there was any chance you might be able to go."

Fear crept up her throat, threatening to choke her. "To New Zealand?"

No, not there, anywhere but there.

Janine nodded. "You're the only one we could think of who could do the job. And with a US passport, you don't need a visa for only two weeks."

She glanced at Josh. He stared at a spot slightly above her head, offering no hint as to what he thought of the idea.

"But what about *Grace*?" She choked the words out. With the band gone, she was meant to be returning fulltime to the conference. It was barely a month away.

"We've talked to Emily. She's going a little stir crazy at home. Turns out, unlike the rest of us who wandered around in a zombie-like daze for the first few months, she's got this first-time motherhood thing down pat. She's happy to come in a couple of days a week to keep things ticking over while you're away and we'll find an admin assistant to support her."

Paige felt like she was being crushed under the weight of expectation. They had no idea what they were asking. She couldn't go back there. Couldn't. Getting on a plane again was bad enough, but it was nothing compared to what she'd have to face at the other end. "Can I think about it overnight?"

Josh and Janine exchanged a glance, then Janine spoke. "Of course."

If God wanted Paige's attention, He'd gotten it. Now she intended to spend the night begging Him to work some kind of miracle in the next twenty-four hours—a miracle that wouldn't require her returning to her personal lion's den.

TWENTY-SEVEN

They should have found another way. There must have been someone else who could do it. In the midst of his desperation to find a solution for the tour, Josh had completely forgotten Paige wasn't a fan of flying. Which had clearly been the world's biggest understatement.

Sitting next to him in the plane, Paige's face was whiter than a soft serve ice cream, and drawn tighter than a freshly made hospital bed. Her eyes were clamped shut, and her knuckles stuck out like a mountain range as she gripped the arms of her seat.

Every flight to the next tour location had been like this. Sydney to Auckland, she'd spent most of the time breathing into a paper bag. Auckland to Wellington, she'd worn the mask of someone fighting the urge to scream. Now, Wellington to Christchurch, turbulence rocked the plane and it pitched and rolled, trying to gain elevation over the Cook Strait. Josh was beginning to wonder if it was possible for someone to stroke out from stress and fear.

Everyone in the band had offered her every

travel remedy they had, but she'd turned them all down. It turned out she'd rather give herself an aneurysm than risk having an adverse reaction again.

And every time, Paige got off the flight and did her job perfectly, which made him feel like even more of a world-class jerk for the way he'd first treated her in Sydney.

Flying had been a normal part of his life for ages. Even before *Harvest* had flourished and the band taken off, his family had traveled a lot. The closest he'd come to being afraid of flying had been on a trip to Russia. Even then it wasn't the flying itself that scared him. It was the entire trip—planes that creaked, shuddered, and groaned like they were one loose screw away from disintegrating, corrupt officials with large guns, road rules that seemed to revolve entirely around the size of the vehicle you were in. It had done wonders for his prayer life.

Prayer. He should pray. He closed his eyes and tried to conjure up something eloquent but all he could think was *God, help her.* Over and over, he repeated the plea as the turbulence increased and the A320 bounced its way between islands. Across the aisle, even some of the band's most seasoned travelers started to take on a bit of a green tinge.

Tears leaked from the corner of the eye he could see, running a trail down the side of her cheek and neck, and pooling at her collarbone.

His heart was about to collapse in on itself. Every atom in him screamed to reach over, pull her into his lap, and cradle her against his chest. Instead he settled for placing his hand over hers, tucking his fingers between hers. It didn't matter if anyone saw, or what they might read into it. He was done pretending he didn't care.

Josh thought she was terrified of flying. Which she was. How ironic. Terrified of flying, yet desperate for this flight to take forever. What was at the other end was more terrifying than being trapped in a death can. For once.

Paige had lost track of time with her eyes clenched shut, only able to measure it by the bounces and lurches of the plane, which all seemed to last forever.

Why had she agreed to come? Why hadn't she told them they'd have to find someone else? She should have. At this moment, that was blindingly obvious. But she'd been afraid if she opened that door and let anyone in, told them why she couldn't go, she might lose all the progress she'd made. That, once again, everyone in her life would see her as an object of pity. So she'd decided to soldier on, still harboring her secret. Not even her family knew where she was going.

She'd stuffed her guilt and regret so deep, she was about to shatter into a thousand pieces. Of course, of all the flights, this would be the one where Josh was sitting next to her, no doubt right now wondering if she would need some kind of mental health intervention when they landed.

Fingers curled around hers, warmth spreading up her arm. Unpeeling her eyes, Paige looked down at her armrest, at the long masculine fingers that were wrapped around hers. Her gaze traveled up the sleeves of the red hoodie, over the familiar rugged jawline and sculpted cheeks. Her chest stilled as she tilted her head and stared up into the gray eyes that caused her to lose her senses.

"I'm sorry." His whispered words nearly got swallowed by the engines.

"Why?"

"That we made you come. We should have found another option."

"You didn't know."

He shook his head. "I did. You told me." His fingers tightened around hers. "I didn't realize we were asking something that was too big for anyone to ask of you."

His eyes darkened like storm clouds. For the first time since it happened, Paige found herself overwhelmed by the urge to tell someone the whole ugly story. How her whole life had been broken in the city they were about to land in. How it was her fault her family would never be complete again.

"I . . ." Her voice cracked. "My—" She couldn't even get out the word *brother* before the wheezing started, her breaths coming faster and faster.

A paper bag was in front of her face. "It's okay, just breathe. In and out. In and out." *God, please help me.* She followed Josh's instructions, focusing all her energies on expanding and deflating the white paper balloon in front of her.

It wasn't until the wheels hit the tarmac that she realized, at some point, the arm rest had vanished, Josh had his arm wrapped around her, and she was curled into his side like she'd always had a place carved out between his arm and his chest.

TWENTY-EIGHT

Christchurch looked completely different. It had been over six years since the last major earthquake, yet for some reason, Paige had expected it would be the same devastated city she'd fled on a sunny March day in 2011. That she would walk into the airport and be confronted with the ghost of her brother from that morning, when she'd arrived disoriented from her twenty-hour journey but bursting with excitement.

She'd expected to feel Ethan around every corner, down every road. But most of the corners and roads that had held her brother's voice, his laughter, his attempt at playing tour guide were gone. Or didn't look anything like they used to. Only the drive down Memorial Avenue into the city and the loop around Hagley Park had sent searing memories through her shattered psyche.

Instead, the rebuild was in full swing—new shops, hotels, office buildings, and apartments, all rising from the remains of a broken city. Everywhere, beauty was rising from devastation, everything new. The city was starting afresh, moving on. Meanwhile, she still felt like time was frozen, as if she was the same hollow shell she'd been when she left. Intending never to return.

The day had passed in a blur running between the venue and the hotel, unraveling mixed up bookings, getting bags to the right rooms, and feeding and watering the band. No time for self-indulgent trips down tragedy lane. Once she'd passed a building from that morning and the memory of that moment ripped through her so powerfully, it was almost like she'd been ricocheted back in time. The voices of locals and tourists enjoying a beautiful summer day, even though it was now winter. The sun on her back. Ethan striding beside her. No one able to see the dark shadow of disaster looming on the horizon. The ghost of her present self wanting to scream at people not to cross that road, not to go into that shop, to be anywhere but here.

Paige sucked in a breath, forcing herself back to the present. She'd survived the day by focusing on doing her job. She'd come too far to lose it now with less than twelve hours until they left.

"Here's the receipt for the post-show pizza." One of the backstage guys handed her a long white piece of paper. She glanced at the figure at the bottom then pocketed the invoice to add to her pile of paperwork back at the hotel.

It was the final thing she'd been waiting for. Her job for tonight was done. Tomorrow she would settle up the hotel bills and make sure everyone was in the right shuttle at the right time to catch the right plane.

On the stage, the band had started the final set. The haunting sound of her strings arrangement rippled across the auditorium. The lingering notes drew her in, called her name. Made her yearn to feel the taut strings against her fingers. Kat was right. She may never be able to play like she used to but she was still here. Could still play. Which was a minor miracle it and of itself, all things considered.

Her gaze wandered to Josh—guitar hanging across his torso, his voice rippling across the theatre proclaiming truth, his arms raised in worship. He was born to do this. Live this life.

He had anchored her in this city where she had lost everything. She didn't know how. They hadn't even had a proper conversation since this morning's flight. But there was something about his strong, stable presence that made her feel like maybe, somehow, God would find a way to put all the broken pieces back together. That maybe, one day, she would be able to think about Ethan without the weight of guilt that pounded as relentlessly as a jackhammer, be able to think about this city without her arm throbbing, reminding her of the dreams this place had stolen.

All she wanted to do was to bury herself in Josh's arms, close her eyes, and hear him whisper her name and tell her that she'd get through this.

His tenor rippled across her and to her toes. *When everything is broken, still I will trust in You. When there are no words to be spoken, still I will trust in You.*

The tears streamed down her face. When was the last time she had trusted God, really trusted Him, thrown herself at Him without reservations, without a backup plan or a safety net?

Her fingers gripped the edge of one of the stage curtains. Her heart and mind wanted to stay in this safe place, with Josh close by, but her soul pushed her forward, insisting there was somewhere else she needed to be.

If she was going to do it, she had to go now. This set would last another half hour. It was close by. No one would even know she'd gone.

As she stepped back into the depths of the wings, Paige closed her eyes and let the end of the song roll over her like a wave on Bondi Beach. Then she moved toward the closest exit, gathered her coat around her and stepped into the night.

Each step of her boots echoed in the dark alley as she headed toward the streetlights that heralded Gloucester Street. Looking both ways, she crossed the road, skipping over the tram tracks that crisscrossed the central city.

She cut through another alley, this one well lit and throbbing with sounds coming from a nearby club, and entered Cathedral Square. Her steps slowed as the once majestic Christchurch Cathedral loomed up in front of her.

A black fence surrounded the Cathedral's crumbled remains. Behind the barrier, steel poles rose, propping up the remains of the stone façade.

She approached a metal gate set into the fence. Curled her fingers around the cold metal and pressed her face up against it. "I'm so sorry, Ethan."

On February 22, 2011, this had been the site of a miracle. The Cathedral was always packed with tourists, climbing the steeple for its views across the city. And when the earthquake had struck, it had collapsed—the steeple, roof, walls. Tons of stone and masonry crushed whatever lay in their path. People in the square when the earth unleashed its fury spoke of how they had seen people in the steeple as it crumbled underneath them. Others ran into the building in some misguided search for safety, only for the building to collapse.

When the search and rescue teams went in, there was no one. When the heavy machinery lifted tons of rubble in the search for bodies, no one. After days and weeks of searching for what eyewitnesses said they would find, nothing. The busiest tourist site in the city had been empty. Not a single person died in the Cathedral.

It was where she and her brother were supposed

to be. If they'd been there, everything would be different. But they weren't. And it was all her fault.

She turned from the spot where miracles had happened for others and cut diagonally across the square. What she was about to do would either undo her completely or help her begin making peace with the events that had buried her under the weight of surviving.

Either way, she was done with just existing.

Applause still ringing in his ears, Josh walked off stage and handed his guitar to one of the crew. Adrenaline streamed through his body from two hours of leading a thousand people, arms raised and voices united in worship. Everything else that came with touring could sometimes get old, but never that.

"Great set, bro." Connor walked up behind him and gave him a slap on the back.

"Thanks." Josh looked around. "Let's get everyone together for final prayer."

The next morning the band would be splitting up, with half heading home and the rest heading to the US to meet up with a fresh crew for the next round of gigs.

Connor let out his trademark piercing whistle, calling everyone together.

A few minutes later, the stage curtains were closed and the space was crowded with everyone from the musicians to the tech guys to the merchandise crew.

Kellie gave him a thumbs-up from across the crowd. Tucked in behind her, he could just glimpse hints of the colorful blooms they'd bought Paige. Not that she'd get to enjoy them for long, but hopefully she'd appreciate the gesture.

Josh looked around at the group. They were a tight team, as they had to be when they spent weeks a year on the road together. He cleared his throat. "Thanks for your hard work this week. I know it's a tough gig crossing the ditch to visit our seventh state . . ." He paused for the collective groan from the Kiwi contingent. "But I think we can all be proud." He never tired of the sight of venues packed with people worshipping. "Now, before I close us off in prayer, there's one other item of business."

He looked around, trying to catch a glimpse of the familiar ponytail. Nothing. No doubt she was trying to hide in the background. He searched again, checking each face. Still not there.

His breath seized. Something didn't feel right. In Auckland and Wellington, once they'd gotten on the ground, Paige had been her usual bossy, sassy, detail-obsessed self. Here, in Christchurch, she hadn't. She'd done her job as well as always, but it was like part of her had been absent. She was a mere shadow of the feisty American they all knew.

The growing silence brought him back to the present. "As many of you know, we've had a newbie with us on this tour. She got thrown in at the last moment and, I think we all agree, has done an amazing job. In fact, these ten days wouldn't have been possible without her." Out of the corner of his eye, he saw Kellie moving forward with the flowers. "So let's all give Paige a hand."

The stage burst into applause with the odd whistle. But there was no ripple of movement of anyone moving forward, no familiar blonde gliding through the ranks.

After a couple of seconds, the applause started dying out and people looked around. Anxiety clawed at his chest.

"Has anyone seen Paige?" Kellie, now at his side with the arrangement balanced on one arm, saved him from having to ask the question.

There was silence for a few seconds, then a voice called from the back. "I saw her step out the stage door during the final set. Thought she was just taking a breather."

Josh caught Connor's eye, raised an eyebrow, and had an entire conversation in two seconds. Josh moved into the wings, the clawing in his chest unleashing to something more crushing, as he heard Connor's voice asking people to bow their heads.

At the back of the stage, Josh pushed open the door that led out into a pitch-black alley. A distant streetlight at the end cast a flicker of light in his direction.

His eyes searched the space as well as they could. No Paige. He closed the door behind him, and walked toward the entrance of the alley, footsteps echoing around him. Surely she wouldn't have gone wandering in a strange city at night. Would she?

A shiver crept up his spine. Christchurch didn't rate at all compared to some of the dodgy cities he'd played in, but there wasn't any city in the world where he'd be happy with a woman being out alone late at night.

Jogging to the front of the alley, he turned left and found himself in front of the venue staring at a promotional poster for Due North. Through the doors, he could see the merchandise tables being packed up, and cleaners at work.

Had she gone to the bathroom? Tugging the door open, Josh strode through the lobby and ran into a cleaner exiting the ladies' restroom.

"Excuse me. Is there anyone in there?"

She shook her dark head. "No, sorry."

His feet took him back through the front doors and onto the street. Where should he even start looking?

His phone buzzed in his pocket. Of course! Stupid, stupid. The incoming text message was a reminder of a pending bill payment. Tapping the screen, he pulled up her details.

"C'mon, pick up, pick up." With every ring, his stomach twisted and wound around itself. "Please, God, please, let her pick up."

Voicemail. "Paige, it's me. Where are you? Please call me."

A hand landed on his shoulder. "No luck?" It was Connor.

Josh shook his head. "I . . . She . . ." He couldn't even get the words out, didn't even know what they would be.

"We'll find her. Don't worry. You go right, I'll go left, and if we haven't found her in ten minutes we'll pull more guys in to search. Kellie and a couple of others are headed back to the hotel to see if she's there."

His brother-in-law's calm suggestion helped focus his mind. "Okay."

Turning left, Josh started jogging. "Paige!" He hollered her name.

Cutting down a lane, he hit Cathedral Square, where the remains of the mighty Christchurch Cathedral still dominated the landmark, even from behind a fence.

Pausing, he scanned the rest of the area. A couple wandered through, hand in hand. A group of teenagers congregated near a tall metal sculpture. Some homeless people huddled up on benches.

Running diagonally across the square, he hit Colombo Street. He glanced at his watch. Six minutes.

He was choking on his own fear, his throat tightening with every second. If something happened to her . . . He couldn't even finish the thought.

Please God, please let her be okay.

Jogging past the bank on the corner and crossing an intersection, he hit Cashel Street Mall. Should he keep going straight or turn?

There were a thousand possibilities.

God, please, show me.

He paused, looked straight down Colombo, then turned in a full three-sixty. Looking, searching, for any clue. Something tugged him to the right. He took a couple of steps down the pedestrian mall. It had been decimated by the earthquakes, but signs of rebuilding were evident everywhere. His walk increased to a jog.

Was that . . .

A small figure jumped out at him, caught in the glow of a street lamp, hunched over on a wooden bench. Probably just another homeless person but . . . he took one step forward, then another.

The head turned, to show light reflecting off long blonde hair.

Thank you, God.

He pulled out his phone and called Connor, not even waiting for him to say hello. "I've found her."

He hung up and shoved his phone back in his pocket.

His relief that he had found her churned with something else. What did she think she was doing? Did she not know what could have happened to her? Just taking off like that. A few more minutes and they would have had the whole team out looking for her. Connor would have been calling the police.

He needed to calm down. Hear her out.

Sucking in a couple of deep breaths, he approached Paige from the side. Ten meters, then five. She didn't give any indication that she'd heard him. At three meters, the tears streaking her cheeks pierced him.

He stood frozen. She didn't look physically hurt. Thank God. But the look of torment on her face had every atom in him screaming to do something. Whatever it took to make everything okay.

She turned, and he found himself caught by her gaze. She just looked at him, blankly, almost as if she was looking through him. He looked over his shoulder. Nothing except a construction site.

Josh crept forward, his movements slow and cautious. He kept his voice soft as he ventured the question. "Paige? Are you all right?"

"What are you doing here?" It wasn't said in a *gosh, what a nice surprise,* kind of tone.

"What?" Shouldn't he be the one asking that question? "You just left before the end of the show. We were worried."

"Sorry. You can tell them all I'm fine. I'll see you in the morning." Her breath misted in the air and she tugged her jacket more tightly around her.

What kind of man did she think he was? "You cannot think I'm going to leave you here alone. It's the middle of the night." He took a seat on the opposite end of the bench she was sitting on.

Her head turned toward him but most of her face was shrouded in shadow. "Josh, it's okay. Go get some sleep. You've got a long flight tomorrow. I won't be long, and the hotel isn't far."

His jaw tensed. "I'm not leaving you here alone. I don't care if you're going to be another five minutes or five hours. I'll sit here for as long as it takes. But I'm walking you back to the hotel when you're ready. End of story."

"Fine." Paige's tone was neutral and he couldn't see her face clearly enough to tell if she was annoyed or accepting.

Burrowing himself into his jacket Josh alternated between watching Paige and keeping an eye on passing late-night revelers. He felt sick to his stomach. They were flying out in the morning. Had they pushed her beyond what she could handle? Had she had some kind of breakdown? He pulled his phone out and opened the messages. Amanda would still be awake in Sydney. She'd be able to give him some advice.

"It used to be a bakery." Paige's voice broke the silence as she pushed herself to her feet and took a couple of steps.

Josh shoved his phone back in his pocket as he stood. "I'm sorry?"

"Behind you. It used to be a bakery." Her voice was flat, like she was reciting facts from a guide book.

How did she know that? Another couple of steps and he was beside her. Even in the dim light, he could see her eyes were red rimmed and puffy. "Do you need me to call someone for you?" What was her cousin's name? It started with a K.

Paige looked around, stepping to the side so she could see past him.

"There was a sushi shop beside it. A clothing store on the other side."

He turned around, trying to see what she was describing. All that stared back at him were construction sites and temporary shops made of shipping containers.

"You think it's going to be the same, you know. Even though you know that it won't be. You see the pictures on the news, but seared into your memory is how it looked those last few moments before . . ." Her voice faltered. Tears slid down her cheeks.

He looked around. Slabs of new pavers under his feet, modern landscaping, lush green trees highlighting a rebuilt mall bordered by construction sites and new buildings. The defiant new life had sprung up from the ashes of the—Oh, no.

"You were here?" Everything in him ached to pick her up, cradle her to his chest, and whisper comfort into her hurt. But something tugged him back, keeping him planted to his spot.

She looked up at the outline of the buildings and pushed her hair back, biting her lip. Another tear slid down her face, dropping off her jaw and onto her jacket. "This is where my brother died."

This is where my brother died. Ethan. Her number one fan. Who had always watched out for his little sister, even when it wasn't cool. Her protector. Right until the end.

Paige stepped forward and strode toward the fence where the building used to be, pressing her palm against the metal frames.

"We weren't even supposed to be here. We weren't—" A sob cut off the rest of her sentence.

This was the third place they'd visited. They'd already been in a sushi shop and a café before walking into the bakery that used to stand here. She was jetlagged and hungry and couldn't make the simplest of decisions, including what to have for lunch. Ethan had tolerated her indecision with his usual good humor. They'd almost walked out of here too, but then she decided she needed something to drink. An extra two minutes. A stupid bottle of soda had cost her everything.

"As we walked back out, there was a rumble and then the world started shifting." For a second she'd thought it was a big truck driving by. Then the ground became a stormy ocean. She'd frozen like Lot's wife and watched the building across the mall start crumbling, collapsing, bricks hurtling down on people. A woman had run, fallen, thrown her body over the toddler holding her hand.

"Then things started raining down on me. Bricks and tiles. I heard Ethan scream at me to move. The next thing I knew, I felt his hands around my waist, picking me up off my feet and throwing me forward."

The roar. Years later, it still echoed in her head. Invaded her dreams. It was like nothing she'd ever heard, as if the earth had woken up and was yelling in fury. Above that, she could hear people screaming. "And when I lifted my head and looked back, there was half a building where I'd been standing."

The moment was etched in her memory until time ended—being sprawled on the ground looking for her brother through the dust in the air, the particles clouding her vision, choking her airways. Being certain she would see him lying nearby. But he wasn't. She'd scrambled around on her stomach in the rubble, screaming his name, her cries swallowed by the screams of those around her. And then she'd seen, poking out from under the rubble, the tip of his Chucks.

"I was screaming and trying to move the bricks off him but I couldn't. There were chunks of building. They were too big. Too big." She hadn't even realized she'd been trying to do it with one arm, that her left arm dangled at her side. Useless.

"There were people everywhere, crying and bleeding and screaming." There'd been a man a few feet away, his eyes open but unseeing, his head matted with blood. The two coffees he'd been carrying sat beside his body on the ground, upright and unspilled. "I kept crying for people to help me, and I kept screaming at Ethan that we were going to get him out."

"These two guys came out of nowhere. Their suits were shredded and they were scratched and bleeding. I was hysterical and screaming 'My brother's under there! My brother's under there!'"

One of them had tried to tell her it was too late but Ethan's foot had moved and they'd shifted huge pieces of concrete like it was nothing. "They managed to clear a whole lot of the stuff around him but he was pinned by two huge slabs right across his body, and I knew he wasn't going to make it. There was blood coming out of his mouth and I was beside him, pleading with God to please not let him die, to let me take his place."

God, if you save him, I'll do anything. I'll never ask for anything ever again.

Then his eyes had flickered and he'd looked straight at her, his gaze clear. And for a second, she thought God had answered her prayer. He tried to say something, but she was too far away to hear him above all the screaming and the sirens and the masonry still falling around them.

"Then I got down and wedged myself in next to him and stroked his head." Her fingers had been sticky with her blood and his. "I told him it was going to be okay, that we were going to get him out. He looked at me and his eyes were so clear, and he half-laughed, told me I had always been a terrible liar and to tell everyone he loved them. Then he was gone." His eyelids had flickered and he'd died with a smile on his lips, like she'd told a great joke.

There'd been something else too, the moment she had never told anyone about. The person who knew her best in the world had locked his gaze with hers as he lay dying under slabs of concrete and told her, *Paige, keep living. Promise me.*

She didn't even know what had made him say it. Until that moment, she'd lived life fearless, chasing her dreams. Did he have a divine glimpse of the future? Or somehow see her arm hanging at her side and know her dreams were finished before she did?

He hadn't even blinked until she'd promised him. And then she'd spent the next six years breaking that promise, stuck in a dead-end relationship and a job she hated, convinced she deserved nothing more. He would have been so mad.

How long had she stayed there, curled up beside her dead brother? Minutes? Hours? She'd tried to wipe the blood and grime off his face. Like it would make a difference. She'd clung to his broken body, begging God to let them swap places. At some point, she'd looked at her arm and realized she was seeing her own radius. Fought against people trying to help her. Eventually, she'd had to be sedated by medics before she would release her grip on his body.

Paige's sobs echoed in the dark empty mall. Arms were around her, gathering her in, holding her up. She wasn't even sure if they were human or divine.

I came back, Ethan. I'm sorry it took me so long. And I'm sorry I broke my promise. I'm so scared of moving on. But I'm going to do my best to make you proud.

Paige didn't even know when she suddenly became conscious that the embrace she was in was very human. Josh's arms were wrapped around her. Solid like branches. They made her feel protected, safe. She hadn't felt that in years.

Pushing herself off his broad chest, she took a second to reorient herself. Even in the dim light, she could see that she'd soaked his shirt with her snot, makeup, and tears. How humiliating.

"Sorry."

"What for?" His voice was low and gravelly.

She gestured at his T-shirt. "I've probably ruined your shirt."

Josh didn't even glance down at the damage. "I consider it an honor."

She looked up at him. His profile was even more rugged in the moonlight. Her breath caught. A surge of warmth flooded over her.

Josh had found her. In the moment when she thought she needed to be alone, God not only knew she didn't, but knew who to send.

She stared up at him. He gazed back, then lifted a hand to tuck a piece of hair behind her ear, his finger grazing a trail of fire down her neck on its way back down.

"Paige." His fingers settled on the back of her neck.

She couldn't breathe.

He blinked. A frown flickered on his forehead. His hand fell away.

"Yes?" She knew the moment was gone, but grasped desperately to bring it back.

"Um . . ." He pressed his lips together and took a step back. Cold air rushed in the space left between them. "I'm really sorry about what happened to your brother."

She stared at him. That was it? That was the best he could come up with?

But there was nothing he could have said that would have made the moment okay when every cell in her body ached for him to kiss her.

She swallowed the suffocating feeling of disappointment. He didn't get it. Josh Tyler wouldn't know anything about regret so deep you felt you were drowning in it. He was perfect, with his perfect family and perfect faith and perfect life.

The idea of a *them* was so wrong in so many ways. She didn't want this. Him. He was uber-Christian Josh Tyler. She hadn't been joking the day at the food court that she'd told him his life was her worst nightmare. Scrutiny. A life on the road. Constant change. So many expectations.

She yearned for order and stability. Predictability and a white picket fence.

So why had she almost given into the overwhelming desire to wrap her fingers across his neck and kiss him senseless?

Space. She needed space.

She turned and walked away, her footsteps echoing across the pavement. She was so stupid. Why did she let her guard down? Things had been so much easier when she'd thought he was an arrogant jerk.

She blew a breath out, watching it mist in front of her face and then waft away.

"Are you okay?"

She could feel him behind her, only feet away. She turned, focusing on the top of a building over his left shoulder. "Fine. Just give me a couple of minutes. Then we should head back."

Stepping around him, she returned to the spot where Ethan had given up his life for hers. Crouching down, she fanned her fingers across the stones and closed her eyes.

Big brother, I miss you. Every second of every day. But I can't keep living like this anymore. I want to keep my promise.

Josh had given her space until he couldn't bear it anymore, until the magnitude of her loss left him feeling as though he couldn't breathe.

He'd tucked her into the crook of his shoulder and stroked her hair as she cried. All he wanted to do was protect her, forever. The realization had struck him to his core. Somewhere in the middle of clashing against each other like mismatched cymbals and growing a friendship, he had fallen hard.

And now he'd ruined it.

Their short walk back to the hotel was silent. Both had their hands stuffed in their pockets, and a mountain of unspoken words between them.

He'd wanted so badly to kiss her. But the sane part of him prevailed. What kind of guy laid one on a girl when she'd just confessed the world's most traumatic experience? A girl he wasn't even dating?

It would have been the most selfish action imaginable, taking advantage of Paige when she was emotionally stripped bare.

Still, he'd failed. He may not have kissed her, but he had been useless at providing any sort of comfort. *I'm sorry about your brother.* What was that? Her brother had been crushed to death in front of her and the best Josh had managed to come up with was a stiff platitude like her cat had died?

No wonder steam had almost emanated off her as she stalked away.

They reached the hotel, the door sliding open and welcoming them into the warm lobby. Paige turned, her hands still jammed in her jacket. "Thanks for coming to find me. I'm sorry if people were worried."

"Paige, I'm really sorry." He tried to tell her with his eyes he wasn't talking about her brother this time.

She studied him, her head tilted, then uttered a sigh. "It's okay. Really it is." She dropped a self-deprecating laugh. "I mean look at you. You're Josh Tyler. The Perfect Man of God. I doubt you've done anything worth losing sleep over since the last millennium."

That was what she thought? That he'd never stuffed up so big his whole world had been broken?

"Thanks for walking me back. I'll see you in the morning." She turned and walked away. Everything in him ached to run after her and tell her how wrong she was. But instead, he stood there like a statue, watching the clock in the lobby tick off the minutes until he could pull himself together enough to find his own room.

A few minutes later, his door clicked shut behind him. The alarm clock on a bedside table flashed single digits into the dark room.

Josh ran his fingers though his hair as he sagged against the wall. Well, he'd certainly done an outstanding job of making a monstrous mess out of that.

"Don't try to be quiet for my sake." Connor's voice cut through the darkness, followed by a lamp clicking on.

His brother-in-law propped himself on his elbow in the bed closest to the balcony, his hair messy but his eyes wide awake and alert. "Everything okay?"

Josh slipped his jacket off and let it land on the end of his bed. Sitting down, he used his toes to wrench his feet from his shoes, not even bothering with laces.

"She's fine. Well not fine, but . . ." His words drifted into an abyss.

Connor sat up. He wore a tattered T-shirt from a tour in 2007. "Don't feel like you have to tell me anything. As long as you're both okay, I don't need to know unless it's on the list."

His brother-in-law was referring to the things they'd asked each other to hold them accountable for.

"No, nothing there." The silence stretched for a few seconds. Josh knew if he told Connor he couldn't talk about it, that would be the end of the matter. But he trusted his brother-in-law. He knew whatever he said would never be repeated. "Paige's brother died in the earthquake."

Connor let out a low whistle. "That's awful. No wonder she hasn't been herself."

"She'd gone to where he died. His name was Ethan. He was killed by a collapsing building in the Cashel Street Mall." Tears burned behind his eyes just thinking about the guilt on her face as she surveyed the spot.

"I remember seeing the pictures. It was like a war zone."

Josh opened his mouth to tell Connor that Paige had been here as well. That Ethan had died saving her life, but something held him back, a prodding in his spirit saying it wasn't his story to tell. Time for a redirect.

"I was completely useless, man. She was

292

broken and I couldn't come up with a single thing to say that wasn't lame." He stared down at his feet, his big toe poking through his left sock. "She let me off the hook, told me it was fine, that she couldn't expect uber-Christian Josh Tyler to know what living with regret felt like."

He dug his fingers into his hair. She couldn't be more wrong. If he was Jonah, regret was his whale that had swallowed him whole.

"You really like her, huh."

He looked up to find Connor studying him with intensity. "She's a great girl, a good friend."

"Josh." Connor's tone made it clear Josh wasn't fooling him.

His hands clenched. "It would never work. We're too different. My life is her worst nightmare. But this is what I do, Con. This is who I am. I can't change that. Not even for her."

He tried to ignore the fact that right now all he wanted to do was disregard number two on the accountability list, find her room and wrap his arms around her until the sun came up.

"I'm assuming you haven't told her about Narelle or Hannah."

"I don't talk to anyone about Narelle and Hannah." His chest caught just saying Hannah's name.

"Then I suspect your big obstacle to something with Paige isn't your life, it's that you've got the

Mount Everest of relationship baggage weighing you down."

You probably haven't done anything worth losing a night's sleep over since last millennium. Her words wore tracks around his mind and tied up his heart. She had no idea.

"I've gotta tell her, don't I?" His mind couldn't even form the words he would have to say to tell of his greatest regret. His biggest mistake.

"As far as I can see, you two don't even have a real friendship if you're happy to leave her thinking you're some super Man of God. Let alone the chance at something more." His brother-in-law drilled him with his eyes. "If the only thing stopping you is your pride then, yeah, you've gotta tell her."

"I leave for the US today. For two weeks." Two weeks without seeing her every day. He hadn't thought about it until that moment. Some space was probably a good thing.

Connor shuffled back down in his bed and switched off the lamp. "Guess you'd better do it soon then."

TWENTY-NINE

Paige snuggled down in her hotel bed and flipped open her leather Bible. Numbers. Not the most comforting book. But Numbers was what her reading plan for the day listed, and she refused to cheat and go in search of a Psalm to find a nice verse waiting to soothe her battered soul.

She wasn't a cherry picker. If God was going to talk to her through her reading today, then He was big enough to find a way to do it between the lines of men begetting more men and living to be six hundred and fifty-nine.

Kellie had left five minutes earlier on an early morning run with two of the other girls. Paige had the room to herself for the next hour or so.

She squinted, trying to focus on the words of Numbers six in front of her. The priest was waving something around as an offering. She closed her eyes and drew a deep breath. *God, I can't do this anymore. I really need something today.*

She opened her eyes, and looked back down at the page. Her breath caught as her gaze landed on the next set of verses.

The Lord bless you and keep you;
The Lord make His face shine upon you,
And be gracious to you;
The Lord lift up His countenance upon
      you,
And give you peace.

She repeated the verses a couple of times, rolling them around in her head.

Peace. She hadn't had peace since the day an earthquake ripped apart the very city she was now in. Since the day she'd started living like the best half of her had died with Ethan.

If there was anything she needed, it was peace. Peace about what she was going to do when her contract was up in six weeks. Peace about moving on. Peace about Josh.

She'd survived three flights in the last couple of weeks. It hadn't been pretty, but she'd done it. Her shrink called it post-traumatic stress dis-order generalization. She couldn't live her life terrified a building was going to collapse on top of her, so her brain had transferred that fear to a different trigger: flying. The first time she'd had a severe panic attack was when she saw Ethan's coffin being loaded onto the plane to be flown home.

She didn't want to live afraid anymore. She wanted to be the girl she used to be, the one who loved new places and new experiences. But it would take being sedated with divine peace before flying would be drama free again.

A knock at the door jolted her from her thoughts. This would be the third time Kellie had forgotten her room key when she'd gone for a run. Paige flipped her flannel pajama-clad legs out of bed, and padded across the soft carpet to the door.

Thank goodness they'd only ended up being roommates in Christchurch. Sharing quarters with the girl who was a superior match for the guy you had an inconvenient crush on was the definition of uncomfortable. At least Kellie had been asleep when Paige had crept in, saving them both from an awkward conversation.

"Really Kel, ag—" The words curled up and shriveled in her throat as the door swung open and it wasn't a petite brunette.

"Hi." Josh wore jeans, a black leather jacket, and a gray sweater that highlighted his eyes.

Paige modeled a matched set of flannel pajamas. With green turtles. Oh dear—her arms flew to cross her chest. At least she wasn't well endowed.

Josh looked down and shuffled his feet. Too late, she realized she hadn't even responded to his greeting.

He looked back up again, capturing her gaze with his. "You said some things last night."

She'd said a lot of things last night. In most

instances, she wasn't even sure which were in her head and which were out loud, what he knew and what he didn't. "Can you be a bit more specific?"

"About me having no idea what real regret feels like."

"Oh." Where was this going? Why was he here? And why for the love of all that was good, why hadn't she at least managed to run a comb through her hair this morning?

"I was hoping we could go somewhere and talk. There's something I need to tell you."

Now? They were about to have the awkward conversation where he told her that they could never be anything more than friends.

"Can I have a few minutes to get changed?"

If she was going to get dumped by a guy she wasn't even dating, the least he could do was grant her the chance to be wearing something besides turtle pajamas when it happened.

His eyes widened, as if it was news to him that she wasn't dressed. "Of course, sure. I'll meet you in the lobby whenever you're ready."

He tripped over the words, which made her feel a little better. "See you soon."

Paige let him stew for a good half hour, since that was how long it took to take a shower, dry her hair, do her makeup, and pick out an outfit that looked good but not like she was trying.

She recited the verses back to herself as she waited for the elevator and donned her mental armor. She had never done or said anything that explicitly suggested she might be tempted to something more than friendship.

Plausible deniability. That was what she had. Whatever he thought he'd seen or heard, he'd misinterpreted her. They could laugh about it. She could even tease him about being big headed and thinking every girl in Christendom was after him, and things could go back to how they were.

Better, even. Her part in organizing the tour was over. He was off to the States and she was heading back to *Grace*. They would have no reason to cross paths except for the occasional professional conversation.

He was all wrong for her and the physical attraction was inconvenient. That was all. She was not going to make the same mistake again. Stable. Secure. An ordinary nice guy. That was what she needed. Not some jet-setting superstar who gave her palpitations. Even if their time together on the road and seeing firsthand the way he cared for his team and put everyone else first had only added to the attraction.

She stepped into the lobby and squared her shoulders.

Josh was waiting by the front door. He smiled and lifted a hand when he saw her.

"All good?" he asked as she approached.

Paige conjured up what she hoped was a cool smile. "All good."

"Our taxi is just outside."

A taxi? Where were they going? Her questions obviously wrote themselves across her face.

"You'll see." He placed his hand in the small of her back and nudged her through the sliding doors.

He ushered her into the cab, then got in the other side. The car pulled away from the curb, the driver obviously apprised of their destination.

She glanced over at Josh. He bit his bottom lip, looking more stressed than she would have expected.

"Do you trust me?"

She wasn't good with trust. "Is that a trick question?"

He smiled. "It's only about fifteen minutes away."

The cab driver was strangely silent. She was used to drivers in New Zealand who chatted away like they were charging by the word.

She turned toward the window, watching as they left the central city and moved through suburbs and headed back in the direction of the airport. Every now and then, there was a sign of earthquake damage, but clearly this section of the city hadn't been hit as hard as others.

Eventually the cab slowed, then turned into a driveway.

She recoiled as she saw the sign and turned toward Josh.

Her mouth opened but no words came out.

He stared at her, his eyes pleading for her to trust him. "I know." His voice was a whisper. "Just give it a few minutes. If you hate it, we can leave."

This had better be good. She didn't even bother to wait for him, just threw open the car door and stalked up to the entrance. She couldn't wait to hear why he would think a cemetery was a good place to take her.

Josh's palms slipped on the door handle as he closed it. How had he ever thought this was a good idea?

Background noise suddenly registered as the taxi driver talking.

"Sorry, what was that?"

"Did you lose someone?"

"She lost her brother."

Compassion etched on the driver's face. "Want me to wait for you?"

Josh looked at Paige's ramrod back as she stalked away.

"I have no idea how long we're going to be." Probably about three minutes. That should be enough time for her call him every variation of presumptuous and insensitive, and demand to leave.

The driver shrugged. "It's slow this time of the morning. Doubt I'll get called away."

"That would be great, thanks." Depending on how long this took he might need to go straight to the airport. Connor had agreed to bring his bag if he didn't make it back to the hotel in time.

Josh leaned down to the passenger floorboard and picked up the bunch of flowers the hotel concierge had somehow conjured for him.

His feet crunched on loose gravel as he walked toward Paige. She stood, arms crossed, her face set in an emotionless mask. She didn't utter a word as he ushered her up the path toward their destination.

There was still a chill in the air, despite the morning sun. Josh looked around him. If it wasn't for the gravestones on their right, it would have been easy to mistake the manicured gardens echoing with the sounds of native wildlife for a park.

Within a few minutes, they'd reached the entrance to their destination. The cement path was flanked with two pillars. *22 February 2011* was engraved on a plaque on the left pillar.

Paige slowed, then stopped, her arms wrapped around herself. She looked to the left and the right, taking in the hedge and flowers that formed an outer circle, framing the memorial.

"This is—"

"The Avonhead Memorial and the place where they buried the unidentified victims." She cut him off with a whisper. Tears leaked from the corners of her eyes. "Mom and Dad and Sophie came here for the first anniversary. They told me about this. Ethan has a plaque somewhere."

He stayed back as she walked up the path toward the square stone monument sitting in the center of the garden, a second hedge running around it to create an inner circle dedicated to the four victims whose remains were never found.

Three small steps lead up to the monument. Paige climbed them slowly, pausing on every one. Even years later, multiple bouquets of fresh flowers sat at the monument's base.

He couldn't see the plaque on the stone pillar from where he stood, but his overnight research had enshrined it in his mind. He repeated it to himself as Paige stopped and ran her fingers over the words. *Etched in our City's memory, never to be forgotten. The City of Christchurch.*

Paige brought her fingers to her lips, then pressed them against the metal. After a few seconds, she stood and backed away from the monument, only turning when she was beyond the inner circle. She stepped across the dew-drenched grass, and walked around the slabs of stone that enclosed the inner circle and held memorial plaques to victims, stopping at each one for a few seconds.

She eventually came to one that caused her to drop to her knees and run a hand over the plaque, pressing a kiss onto its surface. Her lips moved but he couldn't hear what she said as she wiped away tears.

For about fifteen minutes, she just sat, silent and peaceful. Covering the distance between them, he rested fingertips on her shoulder and handed her the bunch of pastel flowers when she looked up.

Smiling through her mascara-streaked face, she curled her delicate fingers around the stems and brought them to her nose, inhaling the fragrance. She plucked a stem out and then placed the bouquet on the grass below her brother's memorial. *In memory of Ethan Roger McAllister 1980-2011. Beloved son, brother, and friend. The adventure continues.*

"Thank you."

They were the first words she'd spoken in the more than thirty minutes since they'd arrived. Josh's whole body sagged with relief.

She held up the remaining flower in her hand. "Just going to place this at the main memorial."

She rose to her feet, stepped back across the path and returned to the pillar, pausing a few seconds in front of it before resting the flower on top of the other bouquets.

Staying back, Josh settled himself on one of the wooden benches that surrounded the memorial.

Closing his eyes, he prayed Paige would find some kind of comfort.

The balance of the bench shifted underneath

him and he looked over into brown eyes flecked with gold.

Her lips curved upwards, full, rosy—*Get a grip, Tyler!* This was not the time.

"This was just what I needed. Thank you." Paige turned her face forward. "It gives you perspective, you know. I've often thought about the families who weren't left with anything of their loved ones." Her fingers danced across the wooden bench slats between them. "We got Ethan back. Whole. Recognizable. So many families didn't get that." She said the last sentence softly, as if more to herself.

"What was Ethan like?"

Paige closed her eyes for a second, as if conjuring him up in her mind. "He was an adventurer. His whole life all he'd wanted to do was travel the world. Meet people, experience different cultures. Before New Zealand he'd lived in England and Brazil. He only worked anywhere long enough to save up enough money to go on the next trip. He had a degree in aeronautical engineering. My dad joked he wanted a refund on the tuition fees he'd spent for Ethan to be the world's most overqualified bartender. He had the kind of infectious uncontained laugh where when he laughed you couldn't help laughing too. Even if you didn't know what was so funny. You would have liked him."

"I'm sure I would've." He knew it just from the

way her face softened and eyes danced when she spoke about him.

Paige gazed up at the sky, watching some leaves dancing on the wind. "I was supposed to be here for three weeks. He adored it here. Was talking about staying permanently. So I came to see the country he'd told me so much about. I didn't know when I'd have another opportunity."

"Why's that?"

"I was due to start with the Chicago Symphony that March. Ever since I first picked up a violin when I was five, all I had ever wanted to do was play. When I was seven, my dad took me to my first symphony. And I knew from the moment the curtains opened and the conductor picked up his baton that was my destiny. Ethan saved my life but my arm was a mess. Six surgeries, twenty-seven pins, three years of rehab." She said it factually. "My insurance gave me access to the best care anyone could ask for. But, at the end of the day, it wasn't enough. I'll never be able to play like I could. The specialists say it's a miracle I've gotten back as much function as I have. That I can play at all."

He couldn't even imagine the depth of her loss. He couldn't imagine his life if he couldn't play anymore. And he was no symphony contender. Not even close. *I'm sorry* didn't even begin to express his feelings. Instead, he wrapped his fingers around hers. "You still have an amazing gift. I've lost count of how many people have gotten teary when they've heard the *Almighty* demo."

"Really?" Paige looked at him with wide, hope-filled eyes that overwhelmed him with the desire to bury his hands in her hair and lose himself. But he couldn't. Not when Connor was right. She needed to know.

"Really." He pondered what to say next. Unlike him, her dream had been unjustly ripped away from her. Out of the two of them, he was the one who'd deserved to lose everything, yet hadn't. All he knew was that the girl he'd seen play had more musical talent in her left pinkie than he had in his entire body. "You need to play, Paige. People need to hear you."

She was silent for a few seconds, staring ahead. "I will. I just need to work out how it fits with my life." The breeze lifted her hair, swirling pieces that weren't captured by the loose braid around her face.

Tucking them behind her ear, she turned back to him. "Thank you for bringing me here. I know I was rude last night, I'm s—"

"Shush." Josh pressed a finger against her lips. "Don't even think about apologizing. Not for last night. I'm the one who's sorry."

"For what?"

"For not kissing you." The words were out of his mouth before they even hit his brain.

Paige's eyes widened and her jaw sagged.

What had he done? He groaned, burying his head in his hands.

Fingers curled around his bicep. "Josh."

"I'm sorry. I know I've just ruined everything." If there was one line he'd never crossed, it was making a move on another guy's girl.

"How?"

"You can tell your boyfriend I'll be in Chicago on Thursday if he'd like to beat me up in person."

The silence festered for a moment before she broke it. "I don't have a boyfriend."

He cast a look over his shoulder. Was she pulling his leg? But no, her gaze was clear and honest with a side of confused.

"But what about the guy I saw you at the airport with? The one who sends you forests worth of flowers?"

"Oh." Her face smoothed out. "Nate's not my boyfriend. Just a good friend. He'd like to be more, but he's not. It's a bit of a long story."

"So you're—" Words suddenly failed him as what she was saying almost spliced his heart in two. "You're not seeing anyone?"

She shook her head in slow motion, a glimmer of a smile on her lips. "I am not."

He sat back up, lost in the moment. He wanted to kiss her more then he could remember wanting anything. But he was going to do things right this time. And the day he got on a plane to go away for two weeks was not the right time.

He clasped his hands to stop himself from running his fingers through her hair.

"Okay then."

She tilted her head. "Okay then."

"So when I get back, we should talk." Too late he realized that he had no idea if she was even interested. "I mean, we don't have to. I'm not assuming you'd . . . It's just . . . And I need to tell you about . . ." His vocabulary failed him. Another few seconds and he'd be reduced to miming.

She tilted her head, studied his face. "I'd like that."

"You would?"

"I think so. It's just . . . I mean . . . You are . . ." Now it seemed to be her turn to flounder for words. She locked eyes with him, the gold that flecked them seeming to stand out even more in the morning light.

He was completely unable to resist the moment. Lifting his hand, he ran his thumb across her cheek. "Paige—" His phone buzzed in his pocket, the alarm he'd set for when he needed to be heading to the airport for his flight.

Paige peered at her own watch then gave him a push. "You need to go."

"I do." Every atom in his being resisted, but he stood, and she rose beside him.

"I'm going to stay for a bit longer. My flight isn't for another few hours."

"You're sure?"

She nodded. "I'd like to spend some more time here."

"I'll be back on the twenty-sixth."

"I know."

He wanted to promise to call, to write. But the truth was, between the brutal schedule and the time difference, he didn't know if that would be a promise he'd be able to keep.

She poked him in the chest. "Go. I'll never be allowed to help with a tour again if you miss your plane because of me."

Before he'd even had time to think about it, he'd looped his arm around her waist and tugged her close.

She gazed up from under long lashes and one hand settled on the arm that held her while the other fell on his waist.

He had to go. Now. If he didn't, there was a strong possibility he might not leave. At all.

His breath caught as he tumbled into her warm brown eyes. From the past, he could hear her saying that his life was her worst nightmare but he shoved the memory away.

A palm on his chest gave him a slight push. "Seriously, you need to go."

She was right. If this was meant to be, distance would only confirm it. And if it wasn't, well, he needed to leave before he did anything he might regret. He unhooked his arm and stepped back. "You'll be okay to get a cab back to the hotel?"

She held up her phone. "Google. It's a wonderful thing."

"Okay, then." Josh stepped back, but his feet were slow to turn him away. "I'll see you in two weeks."

She smiled, pointed toward the exit. "Go!"

He was walking toward the exit, feet like they were walking on air when he remembered. He hadn't told her about Narelle or Hannah. Hadn't even breathed a word about the truth that might ruin anything they could have before it had even started.

THIRTY

Well, this had been one of the most unexpected mornings of her life. Paige settled back into her seat and turned toward the window, attempting to hide the grin she couldn't hold back.

Kellie settled into the seat beside Paige. Nearby, the eight other band members returning to Australia also found their seats for the final leg of this trip.

She glanced at her watch. Josh would be in transit in Auckland right now, about to board his flight to Los Angeles. Talk about bad timing.

When Josh had groaned about ruining everything, she'd been certain he was about to blurt out that he had pledged himself to a life of celibacy. Or was one of those guys who didn't even hold hands until he got married.

He was sorry he hadn't kissed her. She rolled the words around in her mind, then closed her eyes and relived the tender look on his face as he'd said it. He'd looked at her like nothing else mattered, but with a hint of surprise on his face, as if he hadn't been expecting the words to come out of his mouth. But he hadn't tried to pretend he hadn't said them.

She allowed herself to embrace the truth: she liked Josh Tyler. She *liked* Josh Tyler. A lot. Her internal thermostat kicked up a notch as her mind turned to her chemistry with Josh and she fanned herself with her magazine.

"You okay?" Kellie asked the question from the seat over, a welcome distraction to Paige's chain of ill-advised thought.

"Fine. Why?" Beyond fine. Deliriously happy over the guy Kellie also had her heart set on. Her stomach twisted at the thought. Kellie was a nice girl who'd been nothing but good to her.

Outside the plane, the engines started up, the steady hum filling the cabin. The knots in Paige's stomach multiplied and she sucked in a deep breath. She'd made it through three flights in the last ten days. She could manage one more.

"You've been quiet today." Kellie rotated so she was facing her full-on. "Where did you disappear to this morning?"

Paige hesitated for a second. She'd had enough of pretending. "I went to visit the memorial garden. My brother died in the 2011 earthquake." She waited for the familiar feeling of guilt to lock her chest but it was absent. For the first time in six years.

Kellie's eyes widened. "I'm so sorry. I didn't know."

"It's okay. You couldn't have known. It's not something I talk about often."

A bump and the plane pushed back from the gate. Paige rolled the paper bag in her hand between her fingers.

"Was Josh with you?" Kellie asked the question quietly.

Paige turned in her seat. Fear filled Kellie's eyes. She didn't want to hurt her but she couldn't lie. "He was."

Kellie leaked out a breath and blinked quickly a few times. "Are the two of you together?"

"No." Something like relief started to cross Kellie's face and Paige knew it wasn't fair to leave it there. "Not yet. But we sort of talked about it."

"Okay. Thanks for telling me." Kellie's fingers twisted in her lap.

"I'm sorry." There was no point pretending she didn't know how Kellie felt about him. It was written across her every move and word every time she was near him.

Kellie shook her head. "Don't be sorry. I'm the one who should have done something ages ago. It was just that after everything with Hannah . . ."

Hannah. The name etched across his shoulder blade. Janine's comments about Josh being paranoid when it came to women. Sarah alluding to him not dating in years. It all made sense. He'd had his heart broken. Badly.

"It's been a long time." The engines kicked up a notch and the plane started trundling toward the runway. Paige gripped her paper bag in her fist.

"You're right. It has. I guess I had just hoped . . ." Kellie trailed off and ran a hand through her hair. "Well, he must trust you to tell you about his daughter. And he deserves all the happiness he can find. If that's you, then I'm glad for you both."

Paige opened her mouth, tried to respond, but no words could get past the boulder that had suddenly lodged in her chest. His *daughter?*

THIRTY-ONE

The September air blew a refreshing breeze as Paige closed her car door. She still couldn't wrap her head around September being spring. Though, going by her mother's detailed narrative the night before on Skype, she figured it was preferable to the ongoing heat wave in Chicago.

She pulled open the door to The Coffee Club, and stepped inside to the sound of conversations and the grind of the coffee machine. Where was Kat? She unwrapped her scarf, and slung it across the top of her purse while scanning the room for her cousin.

Even though she'd been back from New Zealand for a couple days, she hadn't seen her cousin yet. They'd conversed via text messages and Post-it Notes stuck to the coffeemaker. Which wasn't a great medium to describe how she'd turned into an emotional yo-yo. One second giddy that Josh had feelings for her, the next in a state of disbelief that he had a daughter. Was he divorced? Widowed? What had Kellie meant when she said 'after everything that had happened'?

She needed her cousin's perspective. Otherwise she was going to go crazy waiting for him to come home. Meanwhile, she needed coffee. She joined the line that snaked past a counter crammed with luscious-looking baked goods, and scanned the coffee menu.

"Just realized I forgot my purse, so hope you're buying."

Paige caught a glimpse of her cousin's bright top out of the corner of her eye before the rest of her came into view.

She turned to face Kat as the back of her shoe snagged on something, pinning her in place.

Twisting down, she got a glimpse of a black dress shoe planted squarely on the heel of her flat. "Excuse me." She tugged her shoe loose, then glanced over her shoulder for her apology.

Nothing. The suit was so engrossed in his smartphone, he didn't even look up. Jerk.

She turned back to her cousin. "So what can I get you?"

"Regular skinny flat white please. I would say thanks, but it's the least you can do since you're earning such big bucks at Harvest and all." Kat tossed her a teasing wink. The girl charged more for one day of her makeup skills than Paige made in a week.

"That's me. Big dollars central. Just like everyone else working there." The truth was she had about twenty bucks to her name. Thank goodness tomorrow was payday.

"Any chance you can get me an invite to the next yacht party?"

After a morning staring at spreadsheets until her eyes crossed as she tried to make the *Grace* budget work, it felt good to joke. "Sure. The new one is due to arrive any day now. Janine is so excited. This one has a customized spa suite."

They reached the counter as the conversation passed from the comedic to the ridiculous. Janine was renowned for hating spas, as she found enforced relaxation stressful. Crazy woman.

Placing their coffee orders, Paige also parted with some of her last remaining dollars for a gooey chocolate macaroon.

"That way." Kat pointed toward a comfy-looking couch that had just been vacated.

Settling back, Paige relaxed her shoulders into the soft leather.

"So who is it?" Her cousin was studying her over the rim of her cup.

"I'm sorry. What?"

"Is it Rich?" Green eyes beamed into hers. "Hmmm. He recently broke up with Helene. But then again, they didn't date long and his heart didn't really seem in it toward the end."

"Not Rich." Not that the bass player wasn't a nice guy, but no.

"Hmmm. Geoff? Bit more of the strong silent type . . ."

They would be here all afternoon if Kat went through every single guy in the crew. It was a big group.

"It's Josh." Paige tried to pick up her mocha, but her hand shook so much it sloshed over the sides into her saucer, forcing her to put it back down.

She hadn't heard from him since they'd parted in Christchurch. Of course, she of all people knew how crazy his schedule was, but that hadn't stopped her from over-analyzing the lack of contact.

Kat's brow wrinkled. "Is that the new drummer?"

Paige opened her mouth but then her cousin grinned.

"I'm kidding, obviously. A blind man could have seen that one coming." Her cousin settled back into the corner of the couch and studied her. "Why do you look like you're in mourning? You like Josh. He's a great guy. This is not a bad thing."

"I just. It just. He's . . ." Paige groaned. "Josh Tyler. How can I have fallen for Josh Tyler? I don't even like Josh Tyler."

"You know it's weird calling him by his full name like that, right?"

"I know. But Kat . . ." She waved her hands in the air. "It's *Josh Tyler.*"

Kat pursed her lips for a second. "I know who he is, Paige. And I'm pretty sure he puts his pants on one leg at a time, just like the rest of us."

Bad, bad illustration. Just the thought of Josh putting his pants on sent a tsunami of heat shooting up her face.

"I know. But I can't ignore what he is." Paige picked up the macaroon and took a bite, its chocolate center oozing onto her fingertips.

Kat shifted forward. "Of course you can't. But the most important thing is who he is, not what. Josh has plenty of people who are all about the what. Plenty of girls who are all about the image and the fame and perceived glamor. What he needs is someone who is all about the who. And not giving him a chance because of all that other stuff? That's as bad as all those girls who are after him because of it."

Her cousin was right. As always.

"So here's my question to you. Do you like Josh Tyler the guy? Not the musician. Not the profile. Not the son of Greg and Janine. The guy."

Considering how much Paige missed talking to him after only three days, not to mention the way her toes curled as she remembered the smoldering look he'd given her in the garden, she couldn't deny it. "Yes." She picked up her drink again and took a cautious sip.

"And he likes you?"

"Yes. Well, I'm pretty sure."

"Then start from there. Assuming you're at least open to working the rest of it out."

Easy for Kat to say. She wasn't the one whose stomach curdled just at the thought of everything that Josh Tyler came with. If only it were as simple as Kat thought. But Josh wasn't an ordinary guy. And her gut told her that trying to pretend he was would put her on the fast track to heartbreak.

But Kat was right about one thing: Paige's issues with megachurches and his family and profile weren't his. They were all hers. She needed to either deal with them or walk away now because from being with him on tour she knew one thing: he was born for it. And whoever ended up with him needed to be one hundred percent onboard with that.

She pulled in a breath. "I feel completely unequipped to be part of his life. And my visa expires in seven months. But it's not that. Kat . . ." She looked around them to make sure no one was close enough to overhear their conversation. "Josh has a daughter."

Kat put her cup down. "Had. He had a daughter. She died."

"Oh, my gosh." Paige's mug slipped in her hands and she almost dropped it. "What happened?"

Kat leaned back into the pillows. "I don't know.

I'd forgotten about it until right now. It was long before I started at Harvest. I only know anything because I heard Janine mention a granddaughter once, and Connor and Amanda only have boys."

Paige swallowed. The chocolate macaroon that had looked so tempting a few minutes ago now felt like sand in her mouth.

"Don't lead him on, Paige. If you're sure the life that he leads is not the one for you then get out now. Whatever the story is, Josh has already had enough heartbreak for one lifetime."

THIRTY-TWO

"That's the best you can do?" Paige tried to channel her incredulity through the phone.

"Yes, ma'am. That's as low as we can go."

"You heard me, right? You understand I'm talking about fifty thousand bottles of water, not fifty?" Maybe the magnitude of her order was getting lost in translation.

"That's right, ma'am. And one seventy-two plus GST is what we can offer."

She couldn't believe this. Back home, she would have had companies falling over themselves to provide product at cost to get the exposure *Grace* could provide. That was if they didn't give it to them and write it off as a marketing expense.

Yet here, Paige was reduced to haggling over every cent. There was no way she was paying more than a buck for a bottle of water. She was supposed to be getting them for seventy cents. But then her original supplier had called that morning to say they'd suffered a major equipment malfunction at their bottling plant and couldn't guarantee it would be fixed before *Grace*.

"Well then, thank you for your time, but we'll be looking elsewhere." She'd heard of vendors doubling prices the minute someone mentioned a w-e-d-d-i-n-g, but she'd thought getting a good deal for a church would be easier.

"Okay, thanks for calling." The man at the other end didn't sound the slightest bit bothered. "Please keep Wellspring Water in mind for any future refreshment needs you may have."

She breathed deeply, trying to channel something gracious and Christ like. The best she could manage was a neutral farewell as she returned the phone to its cradle. She leaned forward, to cross Wellspring off her list of potential suppliers.

Pushing her chair back, she stood up and stretched her arms toward the ceiling, her wrist aching from hours holding her phone. She grabbed the bottle off her desk and headed down the corridor toward the water cooler.

Three somber gentlemen in suits sat in reception. Briefcases by their sides, two of them scanned their surroundings as if taking in every little detail, while the third tapped away on his phone.

"Gentlemen." Geoff, the church's Chief Financial Officer, entered reception and gestured back toward the door he'd just entered through. "If you'd like to come with me."

They stood, not one of them cracking their stoic expression as they followed Geoff toward the other end of the floor where all the larger meeting rooms were.

"Who were they?"

Chloe glanced up from reception with a wrinkled brow. "A.T.O."

"Who?"

"Australian Tax Office."

"Oh." Paige leaned over the fill her bottle from the cooler. "Is that bad?"

Chloe nibbled at her bottom lip. "It's unexpected. They were here yesterday, too."

Oh. She was guessing a surprise visit from the A.T.O. was about as wonderful as having the I.R.S. show up on your doorstep.

"Why would they do that?"

Phoebe shrugged. "Who knows? Usually it's because someone has complained, like making accusations the church is doing something dodgy with money."

"Like you could, even if you wanted to." Paige had never worked in an organization that was more meticulous about documenting and approving expenditure. Not to mention checking and counterchecking before any invoices were paid. It was a wonder any money was spent, considering all the hoops involved with accessing it.

Chloe shook her head. "I've lost count of how many times we've been audited. They've never found anything. In fact, every time they've found we could have claimed more write-offs than we did and they owed *us* money. Greg makes sure that's the case because of the beating we'd get in the media if there was ever a hint that we might be evading tax. They'd crucify Greg and Janine."

Paige took a sip of her water, watching as Janine walked back from the direction of the meeting room and turned toward the reception desk. "Chloe, can you make us some coffee, please, for our close friends from the tax office?" Her trademark smile was absent.

"Is everything okay?"

Janine blew some air out from between her teeth. "They think we're hiding a yacht." Throwing her hands up in the air, she directed her next sentence to the ceiling. "With some kind of custom spa! What on earth would we do with a yacht with a spa? Seriously! Who makes up this kind of stuff?"

The words bounced around Paige's brain like a ball on the roulette wheel. A yacht. With a spa. A yacht, with a spa. Coffee. Kat forgetting her purse. Jokes about Paige earning the big bucks.

Janine tugged the cuffs of her white shirt down and tugged a stray hair into her chignon. "Pray for us ladies, because for some reason it seems there is nothing Geoff can say, or show them, that will convince them we haven't lost our minds and ordered up some floating palace with church money." Turning around, she strode back toward the meeting room like a woman prepared to do battle.

Paige froze, remembering the suit behind them who'd been standing on her shoe. Who'd looked like the same make and model as the tax clones now in Geoff's office.

This could not be happening. It felt like she was trying to breathe through a straw. Her knees gave out, water sloshing out of the top of her bottle as she managed to catch herself on a spare chair. What had she done?

Five minutes later, Paige forced herself to walk the plank to Janine's office. Her knock echoed against the open door. She had to do this now. Before she lost her nerve. Before it was too late.

Janine looked up from her laptop screen, her face creasing into a smile that would soon be erased. "Paige, come on in."

Stepping through the door, Paige closed it behind herself with a click.

"Is everything okay?" The concern etched in her boss's voice caused a few renegade tears to start forming. *Don't cry. You cannot cry.*

Janine stepped out from her desk. Her feet were bare, a stark contrast to the suit she was wearing. One look at her neglected toenails would have told the tax guys all they needed to know about Janine and spas.

"Here, let's sit." She gestured toward the

couches a few steps away. "Can I get you something to drink?"

"No, no. I'm fine." Paige's knees gave way as she dropped onto the couch.

Janine took the spot next to her.

"I . . . It's all . . ." Paige would have to resign. It was the only honorable thing to do.

"Take your time. I have plenty of it."

Paige stifled an ironic laugh. Anyone who saw Janine's calendar knew time was one thing she did not have. Drawing in a shaky breath, her fingers plucked at non-existent lint on her pants. "About the tax guys out there."

"Oh, honey. I'm sorry. I should have thought to let you know this was going on sooner. I promise you it's nothing unusual. We've been audited many times by the A.T.O. because of a malicious rumor. Though they will deny that until kingdom come. They've never found anything untoward. I can show you the previous reports if you like." Janine stood. "Just give me a couple of—"

"No!" The word burst out. "The rumor's because of me. I need to go talk to them and then resign." She snuck a look up and caught a glimpse of Janine's mouth dropping. "This tax audit. Investigation. It's all my fault. I'm so sorry." The words started tumbling out and over themselves. "Kat and I were joking. I had no idea anyone would think that we were serious." The renegade tears started to breach.

"Whoa, whoa, slow down. Can you tell me what happened?"

"Kat and I were out for coffee. She forgot her purse and made a joke about how I could pay since I was earning the big bucks here. She was kidding. She knew how broke I was until payday. And I made a comment about getting her access to the new yacht. With the custom spa."

Janine leaned back against the couch, closed her eyes, and blew some wispy bits of blonde hair off her face. "I was wondering where the yacht part came from."

"I can clear my desk out today—"

She was interrupted by a burst of laughter as Janine's eyes flew open. "Do you know how we got landed with our first big tax audit?"

"No?"

"I made a joke at a conference about the church paying for me to have a tummy tuck. Sarah was a baby. I'd gained a lot of weight during the pregnancy, hadn't been able to shed it as fast as I had with the other two, and was feeling self-conscious about it. Next thing I know, we have a bevy of auditors in here trying to find the secret cosmetic surgery account."

She shook her head, a wry smile on her lips. "Greg got us landed with one once too. Can't for the life of me remember why that was. Then media accusations have set off at least a couple, though the A.T.O. will deny that until the cows come home. Then a disgruntled employee landed us with another."

"But if I hadn't . . ."

Janine shrugged. "Then it probably would have been someone, or something, else. We're high profile. We take in a lot of money. A lot of people are convinced there must be something dodgy going on, because it's happened in so many churches. Some people flat out don't like the tax breaks we get for being classed as a charitable entity. It's been a few years since the last one, so we were probably already on the list."

"Could I go and tell them—"

Janine shook her head. "You could, but it wouldn't make a blind bit of difference. Once they start an audit, they're bound to see it through. And since it would be almost impossible to steal so much as a communion wafer in this place, they won't find anything. Again. It'll just be a few weeks of admin pain and a few caustic headlines if the media get wind of it, and it'll be done."

"There must be something I can do?"

Janine shook her head. "Look, if I thought it would help, I'd tell my GP to release two decades of medical files that show I suffer from insane sea sickness and am pretty much the last person on earth to buy a boat. But once things like this are out, the truth doesn't matter. It has to run its course. There has never been and never will be a yacht, and we know the A.T.O. will vindicate us. In the meantime, we hold on and ride it out."

"How do you do it? All of it?"

"Because I know it's what God has called us to do. That's the only way we can do it. If there was any doubt . . ." Janine shook her head. "It wouldn't be possible."

There was a knock at the door, and Greg stuck his head in. "Sorry, can I interrupt for a second?"

Janine flashed him a smile. "Perfect timing, honey. I've got great news. We've found the missing yacht!"

Paige wished she found it as funny as her boss did.

THIRTY-THREE

His plane hit earth with a hard bump and then seemed to bounce back up into the air.

There was no need for Josh to assume the brace position, since he was sure the entire plane would have to come apart before he'd be released from the economy seat confines he'd been jammed into for the last fourteen-plus hours.

Never again would he pass up an upgrade in an attempt to show solidarity with the band. At least Paige wouldn't be able to mock him for not having appreciation for how the less fortunate traveled.

A smile snuck up on him at the thought. They hadn't had much contact in the past two weeks, and he'd found himself counting down the days like a lovesick teen. The lack of contact wasn't because he was trying to play it cool. It was more that he didn't want to pass two weeks in semi-flirtatious electronic banter when there were bigger issues they needed to address.

How on earth was he going to tell Paige about Narelle and Hannah? Even now, eight years later, just thinking their names churned him up inside. He didn't even know how he was going to get through telling her the whole ugly, horrible story. He couldn't even bring himself to decline Narelle's Facebook friend request. From two years ago.

Even if Paige was still open to something once he told her about them, he still didn't know her plans for her future or the status of her visa. And before anything progressed, he wanted to talk to his parents and get their thoughts. He wanted—needed—to do this right.

The sun rose through the windows, casting a pink hue across the airport. He checked his watch. Just after six. The seatbelt sign clicked off, starting a mad stampede as everyone escaped from their seats and accessed their bags, as if cramming a couple of hundred people into the narrow aisles would get them off the plane any faster.

The queue started shuffling forward, allowing him a bit of space to lever himself out, his back cracking with the effort.

Two hours later, he cleared the final biosecurity hurdle and walked, blinking into the fluorescent lights of the arrivals hall.

"Did we arrange a shuttle or something?" he asked Connor, who was navigating another equipment-laden trolley behind him.

His brother-in-law checked his watch. "Yeah, but our flight was early, so it's probably still another fifteen minutes away."

Perfect. Josh was going to need to set up an IV of espresso to make it through today. "What can I get you?"

Connor put his hand over his mouth to stifle a yawn. "Something strong."

"Anyone else?" Josh looked around, and saw that pretty much the rest of his crew were being greeted by family. Small children wound themselves around their fathers' legs and there were a few passionate embraces that were borderline inappropriate for public display.

"When was the last time anyone suffered the M5 for us?"

Connor looked at the chaos reigning around them, shrugging his broad shoulders. "Probably last millennium. When it didn't cost a fortune in tolls."

For a second, a vision flickered in his mind of walking through the glass arrival door to find Paige waiting for him after a long flight. He shook it away before it could take root. Even if they were dating, which they weren't, Connor was right. The tolls to the airport cost a fortune.

Far better for her to be waiting at home, cooking a nice dinner—enough. This was ridiculous. She probably couldn't even cook. And heaven help him if his mother ever heard he was expecting someone waiting at home ready to serve him dinner. He'd be out on the street before he knew it. Coffee. He needed coffee. Good strong coffee.

There. Hudsons'. He pulled his wallet out of his pocket and started digging through it for some Australian dollars among the sea of US green.

"Two flat whites, extra shot in both please."

He glanced down at the newspaper on the counter. What the? His mother looked up at him from the front page. An old photo, judging by the haircut. The headline seared his eyeballs: *A.T.O. investigates Harvest purchase of luxury yacht.*

A yacht? Seriously? He scanned the article only long enough to gather that some lunatic thought his mother had ordered a luxury launch, and the A.T.O. would once again be tearing the place apart trying to find it. Just like the cosmetic surgery she never had.

He flicked the paper over the counter. "And this, please."

Whoever had landed them in this better be watching their back. He was finished with watching his parents get done over in the court of public opinion without anyone fighting their corner.

After dropping off Connor, Josh bypassed home and headed straight for church, the newspaper clasped so tightly between his fingers, he could see the ink rubbing off the pages.

Why, God? All his parents wanted to do was serve Him. It was what they'd spent their entire life doing. And because they happened to end up with a large church and an influential ministry, this was what they got—derision and suspicion. Heaven forbid the media should ever report the great things they were involved in, like supporting single mothers, funding clean water projects in Africa, raising money for scholarships for underprivileged kids.

No, all anyone seemed to care about was that his parents lived in a nice house and his dad drove a nice car. Never mind his mum's decade old clunker. Or that they crisscrossed the world most months and worked 340-odd days a year. So much for a worker being worth their wages.

And don't even get him started on how even the most hack journalist could have worked out his mother hadn't set foot on a boat in about thirty years.

The shuttle pulled up in front of the main entrance, and Josh opened the door before it had even stopped. He jumped out of the van, and counted out the fare while the driver unloaded his bag and guitar.

Great. Media in front of the building. He kept his eyes to the ground, blocked out the insulting questions shouted his way, and got inside as fast as he could. Stashing his gear in a nearby coatroom he took the stairs to the offices two at a time, his feet pounding against the wooden boards.

He passed reception, and headed down the hall leading to the staff offices.

Both his parents' doors were closed, so he turned around, pulling out his phone to text them and let them know he was back.

Where to now?

A flash of golden hair caught the corner of his eye. *Paige.* It had slipped to the back of his mind that she'd be here in all the turmoil since seeing the paper.

He stilled. The blinds to her office were open. She sat in her chair, her hair pulled into a messy bun on top of her head. Her brow furrowed, bottom lip pinned by top teeth, she looked like the textbook definition of a stressed logistics coordinator as she stared at the Gantt charts on the wall.

Even her clothing—a T-shirt and old jeans—looked like she'd pulled them on straight off the floor.

His heart thundered, but his mind fought to restrain him from striding into her office, closing her blinds, and sweeping her off her chair and into his arms.

Get a grip, Tyler. You haven't even been on a date yet.

He paused. Gathered his scattered emotions. Drew in one deep breath, followed by another. Then he crossed the short distance to her open doorway.

"Hi." It was more of a croak than a word. So much for cool and collected.

She didn't even move, still staring at the wall like it was playing a riveting movie.

"Paige?" His words cracked through the room, and she jolted, her head jerking in his direction.

"Josh?" A collision of emotions crossed her face.

"Is everything okay?"

She tried to smile, but her trembling lips gave her away. "Fine. Just, you know, busy. When did you get back?"

He stepped into her office, pushing the door shut with his foot. "Few hours ago." He glanced around. Her couch was way too small for his frame but he folded himself into it anyway. It beat towering over her when she was obviously upset.

This was not how he imagined their reunion. He'd planned for smiles and a conversation where he asked her if she wanted to have lunch, dinner, clean the building's toilets, anything to get to spend time with her.

Instead she was broken up about something, and he had no idea whether to push or back away.

She sucked in a shuddering breath and twisted a stray piece of hair around her finger. "I'm sorry. It's been a tough couple of days." This time she summoned a genuine smile. "I'm glad you're home. I missed you."

He locked eyes with her chocolate gaze. Leaning forward, he set his elbows on his knees.

"Me too." He eyed the open blinds. "Feel like taking a walk? Getting some coffee?"

She heaved out a breath so large it was like she'd been holding the world's air supply. "Yes, please."

Grabbing her gray jacket off the back of her chair, she tunneled her arms down the sleeves then slung her purse over her shoulder. Like there was any chance he would let her pay for anything.

"Ready?"

"Yeah."

He opened the door, allowing her to step in front of him, her hands plunged into her pockets. He tried not to think about how perfectly her hand had fit in his on the plane, but to no avail.

Easy, Tyler. Don't get ahead of yourself.

Cutting down the back stairs, they exited through a side door and into the brisk, early spring air. Brisk for Sydney, anyway.

A few struggling bursts of sunshine managed to fight their way through the cloud cover, but a cool wind sent leaves tumbling across the campus and people hurrying from building to building. Australians weren't good at dealing with temperatures under 20°C.

Josh hadn't thought this through. The café on campus would have them being scrutinized by half the staff, but his car wasn't here. He was sure he couldn't fold himself into her tiny machine. Even if he could, there was no chance he was letting her drive. Not because his manly pride couldn't handle it, but because he'd seen her drive and he wasn't giving her any reason to get behind the wheel more than necessary.

He shoved his hands in his pockets, curling them into fists to warm them up. After two weeks of late American summer, it was going to take a few days to readjust. Paige was silent beside him. He liked that about her. Unlike some girls, she didn't seem to need to fill every silence with words. Not that she held back when she had something to say.

"Want to walk for a bit?" He slowed his stride to match hers.

"Sure."

They settled into a comfortable silence as their feet found a path that meandered around the campus.

His mind buzzed with all the words he wanted to say, but didn't know how: he'd missed her, he'd thought about her before every concert, he'd kept turning around expecting she would be there. Malcolm, their US logistics manager, was more than competent but he wasn't Paige.

"Thanks for everything on the tour. You did a great job." Josh winced. He finally saw the woman he hadn't stopped thinking about in weeks and *that* was the best he could come up with?

"Thanks. How was the States? Everything go okay?"

"Fine. Busy. Those new hotels you booked for us were great."

"I'm glad." Paige hadn't so much as glanced at him during the awkward pleasantries. They lapsed back into a silence straining with things unsaid.

What he wanted was to be was the average guy who got to ask the woman he liked out for dinner and a movie. Straightforward. Simple. Except even that would potentially expose Paige to a level of scrutiny she might not be prepared for.

A gaggle of six girls in their early twenties approached. "Hey, Josh. Welcome back." One he vaguely recognized but couldn't place gave him a friendly smile. Her gaze flicked between him and Paige.

"Thanks." He offered a smile but didn't slow his stride as they passed.

Was it fair to ask her to think about giving up so much, when he spent months of the year on the road? Could she reconcile herself to the world he and his family lived in? The profile, the expectations? The days like today, when the people you loved were being defamed on the front page of the newspaper and there was nothing you could do?

It made no sense. None whatsoever. And then, when he looked down at his side, every fiber in his being told him he would spend the rest of his life regretting it if he didn't at least try and find out.

He realized she'd paused at a fork in the path. Her brown eyes peered up at him, her cheeks flushed. She pinched her bottom lip between her top teeth, then released it. "I missed you."

"I missed you too." He couldn't stop the smile stampeding across the face if he wanted to.

She returned it with one of her own. "Okay, then."

"Okay." He stood there staring at her. He hadn't been in this place in years. Had no moves, no smooth spiels for situations like this.

"What are you thinking?" The wind blew some loose strands of her hair across her face and she captured them, tucking them behind her ear.

About kissing you. Picking you up and spinning you around and making you laugh. For the rest of my life. What came out was, "I need to talk to you about something."

The expectation on her face deflated like an old balloon. "I need to talk to you about something too."

He gulped at the turn in the conversation, his mouth suddenly drier than the Sturt Stony Desert in February. "Let's sit down."

He gestured toward a bench set about twenty meters away, surrounded by bushes on three sides. It wasn't right out in the open and would ensure they could have this conversation in private without anyone creeping up on them.

Their feet plodded through the grass. They sat, a more-than-appropriate distance between them. Next to him, Paige's gaze was steady and expectant. He was tempted to let her go first. Just in case she wanted to say she'd thought about it and wasn't interested in him, his life, after all. But that would be taking the easy way out. She'd told him about Ethan. He needed to tell her he wasn't even close to the guy she thought he was.

"I can go first." Paige offered the words in a small voice. As if she knew this conversation could change everything.

"No. It's okay. I should." He wanted to hold the moment, before he shattered all her remaining illusions. He didn't know what she thought might be coming, but he could guarantee it wouldn't be this.

Josh leaned forward, elbows on his knees. "You made a comment in Christchurch about me having no regrets."

Behind him, she stayed silent. He bit his lip. He looked back at her over his shoulder, capturing her gold-flecked gaze. "I need to tell you some-thing."

"Okay." She settled back, waiting for him to speak.

"A long time ago, I dated a girl called Narelle.

More than dated." Eight years later, even just hearing her name aloud sent stabs though him. None of them good. All the great stuff they'd shared had been washed away in the tsunami of devastation that destroyed them.

He steeled himself. "We'd been together a couple of years. Were going to get married. Or so I thought. But I kept putting off proposing. The band was just taking off and I was spending a lot of time on the road. I wanted things to be a bit more settled, more certain."

He'd been twenty-four. Had the world at his feet. Thought he was invincible. Chosen.

"We—" He paused. "No, strike that. I let us make some bad choices. Narelle got pregnant." He tried to keep his tone neutral. The buck stopped with him.

Paige's eyes widened and a whoosh of air escaped her lips, but she didn't respond.

He sat back, clasping his hands so tightly his knuckles turned white. They'd done the same the day he'd sat in their lounge and told his parents. He'd seen the devastation and disappointment written across their faces.

"It tore my parents up. I let them, Narelle, myself, everyone down so badly. I was going to step down from the band, marry her. Try to make it right. As right as I could. The rumors had already started. My parents had speaking engagements cancelled. And a book deal. Then . . ."

He sucked in a breath. "Narelle went into labor at twenty-three weeks. It was one of those unexplained things. The baby lived for only a few minutes. A little girl. Hannah." His throat clogged. He swallowed, trying to clear it.

"I'm so sorry."

"I got to the hospital too late to be there, but I got to hold her for a few minutes. She was tiny. Perfect. All she needed was time—" He couldn't go on. His words choked him.

He swallowed hard. "We tried to carry on. Tried to fix our relationship. But it was broken. The truth was that every time I looked at her, I couldn't get beyond the fact I'd taken something from her that wasn't mine to take.

"Then I found out my life insurance provided coverage for the death of a child. Not much, but enough to pay for the plot Narelle's family bought, cover the expenses. To make a claim, I needed her birth and death certificates.

"Narelle got all angsty about the birth certificate. Cagey. First she said she kept forgetting to get me a copy, then she couldn't find it, then she said she didn't want to make the claim. Eventually she told me why. I wasn't listed as Hannah's father." He took a deep breath, then swallowed. "Where my name should have been, it said *Father Unknown.*"

There was a sharp intake of breath beside him but he barreled on, couldn't let himself stop to

345

see what Paige's reaction was to his great big ugly shame.

"It turned out that while I'd been busy, consumed with the album and the band and the tour and being the great up-and-coming Josh Tyler, she'd been feeling neglected. Fallen back in with some old high school friends. The kind who thought the defining characteristic of a good weekend was being unable to remember most of it."

"When I was away, she'd go out with them. Drink too much. Then one night she went home with some nameless guy."

Josh sucked in some air. "It wasn't until after I got back from that tour that we . . . slept together." His stomach still curdled at the memory. Him coming off a great tour, high on playing night after night in front of crowds of thousands, convinced he was God's gift to the world. Her, wrapping herself around him, telling him how much she'd missed him, that they were going to get married anyway, so what did it matter?

Unlike her, he didn't even have the excuse of large amounts of alcohol that dulled his senses and numbed his reasoning. But he'd been drunk all right—punch drunk on his own pride and ego.

"We had the mother of all fights when I found out. She said there was no way she could tell me, that I would have discarded her without a second thought if she had. And the truth is, I would have. I was the great Josh Tyler. Worship leader extraordinaire. I was arrogant and blinded by my own ego. Josh Tyler with used goods? Never going to happen. The only chance she had was to make me the same."

Narelle had lost as much as him. More. She'd saved herself for twenty-four years, only to lose it all in a hazy blur with a guy she couldn't even name, then resorted to luring him to bed to cover up what she was afraid may have resulted.

For every recrimination he'd heaped on Narelle's head in his anger and pain, he'd never doubted that she loved him, that what they'd shared had been real, even if the ending was steeped in mixed motives and deception. In desperation, she'd done the unthinkable, but it didn't wipe out the two years they'd had before that.

He kept his gaze down, focusing on the lush grass at his feet unable to handle seeing the disappointment, or worse, in Paige's eyes. "To this day I have no idea if Hannah was my biological daughter or his. I choose to believe that she was, is, mine. That she at least got to be the product of something real, not some drunken mistake with someone unknown."

That was one of the only things he was proud of from that time. Even after he'd found out, he'd still wanted Hannah to be his daughter, begged

Narelle to change the birth certificate. He'd argued that she deserved better than to have her father listed as *Unknown*. Beyond his family, until now, he'd never breathed that Hannah might not be his to anyone.

"So please know, I know what it feels to live with regret so bad that it shadows you every second of every day. To wake up every morning wishing you could have a do-over and make things different.

"I promised myself I would never ever let my family down again. Let the people I love down. My parents' work, the band, it's so much more now. The platform, the impact, all of it. And Christians, I've discovered, are often not the most gracious or forgiving when a high profile someone doesn't meet their expectations. I will never risk everything my parents have worked for ever again."

He lifted his head and turned toward Paige, offering a half-smile. "And just for a record, despite the rumors. I pretty much haven't dated anyone since. Not seriously. Never even wanted to."

Josh paused, holding her gaze, and tugged a piece of stray hair back behind her ear. "Until I met you."

Until I met you. The words echoed in his own ears, whipped up by the wind.

Paige's eyes widened and her lips parted.

His chest contracted, either from terror or anticipation.

He hadn't intended to put those words out there. Not yet. But he had. And he wasn't going to take them back, because it was true. This American with her sassy wit and hidden depths had his mind going places it hadn't gone for a long time, and his heart wishing for things it had no business desiring.

Paige pulled her jacket tighter around her. "I'm so sorry for your loss." She blew out a breath. "I had heard about Hannah."

His jaw dropped. What? How?

"None of the details. It wasn't until after you'd left Christchurch and all I knew was that you had a daughter who had died. I wanted you to tell me in your own time. But now I've—" She cut herself off with a shake of her head. "There's something I need to tell you."

"Okay." She'd changed her mind. She'd realized what dating him would mean and it was a thanks-but-no-thanks. He couldn't blame her.

Paige twisted her hands, her fingers tumbling over each other. "The tax investigation. The yacht."

"There's no yacht." It was the most ridiculous claim yet.

"I know." She looked at him, lines etched into her forehead. "It was just a joke."

"I don't understand." He sat back. The slats of the bench pressing into his back.

"It's all my fault. This whole thing. Kat and I were out for coffee. I made a joke about the church buying a yacht. There was a tax guy behind me. He thought I was serious. That's how this whole thing started."

It was like someone had just cut off his air supply. The weeks, if not months, of auditing his parents and the church would go through. The media prowling around out front like dingoes circling a carcass. The fact that even when they were cleared, their name would still be tarnished. Again. It was all because of her?

She was saying something about wanting to tell the media, offering to resign, but he couldn't process any of it. All he could hear was the voice in his head telling him that it could never work. No matter how much he had fallen for her, how much he'd missed her. If she didn't understand by now that you couldn't go around making stupid jokes about his parents in public, she never would.

"So my parents know."

Paige ran her hand through her hair, her fingers snagging on the now lopsided bun. "I told your mom straight away. She keeps trying to convince me it's not a big deal."

Of course she was. His mother was one of the kindest people on the planet. She wouldn't dream of giving so much as a hint to Paige about the stress this would be causing behind the scenes. The fear that even with all the financial controls in place and rigorous auditing that went on that something could have been missed somehow, somewhere.

"I see." His family had already paid too much for his mistakes before. He couldn't take a chance that it could happen again. No matter how much he wanted to. The one woman he'd seriously dated since Narelle had ended up selling them out to the tabloids. Paige could do just as much damage by being careless.

He was a Tyler, for better, for worse. The big picture was paramount, not his individual happiness. If that meant he had to spend his life single, or marry someone who didn't capture his heart but would never let the family down, that was what he had to do.

Paige was just sitting at the end of the bench, worrying her lips, twisting her hands. He should've listened to his head weeks ago and not let her get close.

"Paige, I . . ." His voice trailed off. He re-gathered himself and tried again, ignoring everything in him screaming that there had to be another way. "Paige, we can't do this. I think you're incredible but it's not going to work. This stupid thing with the yacht is more proof. I can't change who I am or the life I lead." He could barely get the words out. "I'm sorry if you feel like I've led you on. That wasn't my intention. But I think we should just be honest with each other now, before anyone gets hurt."

Too late for that.

He sat there, watching a world of emotions cross her face, half expecting the well-deserved sting of her palm against his face. He waited for her to tell him her stupid throwaway comment was nothing compared to his past mistakes, or worse, to make an argument for him to reconsider. But she wouldn't beg. That he could already tell from her ramrod straight back and the set of her shoulders.

Instead she sat there in silence, studied his face for a few agonizing seconds, then let out a small sigh. "I understand." She stood, her boots digging into the soft ground underneath the bench. Her gaze was direct. "I'm not going to say that I don't wish it could be different, but I get it. You have a big calling on your life and you need the right girl beside you. And she isn't me." She walked a couple of steps, then turned back around, her coat flying around her in the wind.

"You know what though?"

"What?"

"The right girl. The one who is perfect for your life, who loves you and only wants what's best for you? Who is always watching out for you? She's been here this whole time."

"What are you talking about?"

"Kellie, Josh. It's Kellie." She gave him the kind of wistful smile that wrenched his heart in two. "Bye, Josh." This time when she walked away, she never looked back.

He ground his heels in the mud to stop himself from leaping up and running after her, telling her he was wrong, that she was the right girl, the only girl, he wanted beside him.

He'd made the right decision. Done the right thing. His calling required sacrifices. This was just one of them.

Paige should have known she'd lose him the minute she'd told him about the investigation.

After all, this was the man who had fifty pages of rules just to be a member of his band. Sure enough, she'd seen the shutters go over his eyes, then his heart as soon as he realized what she'd done.

One minute, she was throwing caution to the wind and putting herself out there. Ready to tell him that she had counted down the days while he'd been gone. That she was willing to be all in even though it scared her. The next, it was all in pieces. The damp grass sank beneath her feet as she trudged back to the office.

He was right, though. That was what hurt the most. They'd both been fooling themselves, trying to imagine a place for each other that just wasn't meant to be. Wasn't possible. The songs were wrong. Love didn't conquer all. Not that what they'd had could even be defined as love.

She didn't belong here, in this country where they drove on the wrong side of the road and spelled things weird and made up fake bears to mess with people. She'd been so busy trying to jam herself somewhere she didn't fit, she couldn't recognize the obvious.

She'd gone and done it all again. She'd wasted almost seven years on Alex and then what? Josh showed up with his sexy Australian drawl and brooding gaze and zings of chemistry and the ability to make her feel like the only girl in the world. And she went and lost her mind over another guy who was never going to be right.

What was wrong with her? She was thirty-one years old. Why couldn't she just go for the guy who was right and stable and a good match, not the ones who set her world on fire, then left her with the ashes?

What was wrong with him? Why on earth didn't he just put everyone out of their misery and marry Kellie? They were perfect for each other. Kellie would never bring the tax office down on his family's head. Never need a paper bag on an airplane. They'd produce cute musical little VBS-attending children. It'd be like the modern Christian Von Trapp family.

"Argh!" She directed her frustration toward the

now-gray rolling clouds in the sky. A drop of rain hit her square in the eye. Perfect. Even the world was spitting in her face.

She needed to pull herself together. She'd be unemployed in a matter of weeks, a reality she'd been denying as she was consumed with trying to imagine whether she could embrace the life Josh had. Now she needed to start sending her resume out. She'd been blown off course but she'd taken this job for one reason—to give her the experience she needed to go home and land one of her dream jobs.

It was time to get her life back on track.

THIRTY-FOUR

"Excuse me?"

Josh looked up to find someone waiting just inside the front doors of the main building. A vaguely familiar guy approached, holding a bouquet of flowers.

"Can you tell me how I find the main reception?"

"Sure. It's just up here." He gestured toward the stairs. "I'm heading there myself."

"Thanks."

Josh turned to him as they headed up the stairs. "What brings you here?"

"Actually, you might be able to help. I'm looking for Paige McAllister."

Big surprise. Not. Josh always managed to be right there whenever flowers were being delivered for Paige. Josh looked the guy full in the face. It was him. Chicago airport guy. Mr. It's Complicated.

They reached the landing and Josh willed his feet to continue across the walkway to the office. "Sure, I know Paige. Follow me." They'd given each other a wide berth in the three weeks since their conversation, but he was about to be in a meeting that included her so there was no point delaying the inevitable.

He cut through reception, and stuck his head into Paige's office. She sat with her back to him, typing.

He tapped against the doorframe.

It was good this guy was here. Josh and Paige were over. Not that there had even been anything to be over. So why did everything in him want to sag under the weight of disappointment?

She spun around, a look of confusion creasing her face when she saw him. "Hey." She tilted her head, as if trying to decipher the mystery behind his visit.

"Hey." He kept his voice cool. "There's someone here to see you."

She stood, her brow wrinkled. "Who?"

A strong sense of déjà vu overtook him. An almost identical scene had played out like this before over another bunch of flowers. The main difference being this time the sender had crossed the world to deliver them himself.

Josh turned and beckoned to the guy, who had a sheen across his forehead and was grasping the stems like they might leap out of his hands and make a run for it.

Josh stepped back from the doorway as Mr. It's Complicated navigated around him.

"Um, surprise."

Over the guy's shoulder Josh watched as Paige grabbed the back of her chair, face bleaching to white. "Nate? What are you doing here?"

Then he turned and walked away.

Nate was here. Nate was here. Nate was *here*. Standing in the doorway to her office bearing another enormous bunch of flowers.

"Come in, come in." She stepped back and almost fell over her chair.

He stepped into the room and proffered the flowers with a hesitant smile. "For you."

"Thank you." He looked good. She took the colorful bouquet and placed it down on her desk. Hug. She should give him a hug. She lurched forward, every movement feeling robotic. "It's good to see you." He wrapped his arms around her and she breathed in the familiar scent of his sandalwood cologne.

Nate looked around her office, his gaze taking in everything from the Gantt charts on her walls to the photo of her family on her desk. "I'm sorry to just barge in like this. The—"

Her computer dinged, interrupting him with a zero-minute meeting reminder popping up. With less than two weeks to go until *Grace*, the planning meeting was compulsory. "Oh my gosh, I have to go. To a meeting. I'm sorry. I can't miss it. Have a seat. Stay here. I won't be long." She grabbed her papers and bolted down the hall, slipping into her seat as Janine introduced the first item on the agenda.

Paige's mind whirled like an out-of-control Ferris wheel as she tried to focus on the meeting.

"What do you think, Paige?" Josh's eyes probed hers. "Should we release tickets to the upper tier even though we know the acoustics aren't as good? Not to mention the view."

It was like a B-grade movie stuck on replay. Hadn't they had this exact conversation the last time flowers showed up from Nate? Except that time it was about the tour instead of *Grace*.

What was Josh thinking right now? She ground her teeth together at the urge to tell him the guy sitting in her office wasn't her boyfriend, that nothing had changed in that regard since their conversation in Christchurch. Nothing. And everything.

Josh wasn't even supposed to be in this meeting. Kellie was the *Grace* worship liaison. Why wasn't she at the now-daily whole-of-team meeting Janine convened?

She forced her thoughts to get in line. "My view is the same as the tour. Only if they're at a discount and we disclose the quality issue."

What was Nate doing here? What did she think he was doing here? Someone didn't fly halfway around the world and show up with half a florist's worth of flowers to go out for coffee.

"Agreed." Janine leaned back in her chair.

"The last thing we want is people feeling ripped off. Now where are we with all the speakers' itineraries? Everything confirmed?"

Paige checked her notes. "Everyone except Nicole. Her P.A. emailed today saying she was going to need to switch to a later flight. Her new flight has her landing only a few hours before her first session." Her stomach clenched. What if there was some sort of delay? What if they ended up with a session about to start and no speaker? No. No panicking. This was what she did. She had contingencies for contingencies.

"Plan B if something goes wrong and she doesn't make it in time?"

"We swap your afternoon session with her late morning one. That will give us an extra four hours. If it's a longer delay than that, Nicole has said she's happy to do a prerecord and send it to us for emergency use."

"Hmmm." Janine's brow furrowed. "It'll have to do. Let's pray it doesn't come to that." She moved to the next item on the agenda and turned to the styling team lead. "Design all good?"

Paige tuned out as Carrie outlined a few minor changes they'd had to make to the aesthetics. Two weeks and *Grace* would be over. Three weeks and her contract would be up. Even if she wanted to stay, her visa didn't allow her to work for one organization for more than six months.

She'd already started sending her resume out to

recruitment firms back home. Surely with *Grace* and the tour added to her experience it would only be a matter of time before something came up.

"Anyone got anything else?" Janine looked around, but the only sound in the room was people shuffling papers and repacking folders. "Great. See you same time tomorrow."

Paige looked up from gathering her papers to find Josh gazing at her, his expression inscrutable. Why did she even care what he thought? They'd both agreed they were wrong for each other.

"Josh, can I grab you for a second?" Janine's words filled her both with relief and trepidation. She could avoid an awkward moment with Josh, but it also meant she couldn't delay facing what waited for her down the hall.

"I'll see you guys later." Paige picked up her folder and headed for the door. She should be thrilled that one of her best friends was here. She was. Really. She sucked in a deep breath, trying to stop her insides from rolling around like they were inside a pinball machine.

Nate looked up from his phone as she stepped into her office. The flowers he'd brought her were arranged in a vase on her desk. "Hope you don't mind. One of your admin people helped me find one."

"No, of course not. They're gorgeous." She

walked across the room and leaned in to get a whiff of the fresh fragrance.

She glanced at the clock. Almost midday. She grabbed her purse from beside her desk. "Want to go for some lunch?" Thankfully her afternoon was free of meetings.

Nate unwound himself from his seat, gathered his black leather jacket, and pulled it on. "That would be great."

They bumped into each other as they both headed for the door, and laughed.

What was she so nervous about? She had known him for years. He'd stuck by her during the absolute worst days of her life. He had all the characteristics she wanted in the person she'd spend her life with. And now this—the kind of grand gesture most girls dreamed about a great guy making.

Paige stepped out the door and barreled straight into a familiar chest. She bounced off, saved from a graceless tumble only by Nate standing behind her.

"You okay?" Both men spoke at once.

"Fine. Thanks."

Josh stuck his hand out. "Josh Tyler."

Nate shook it. "Nate Andrews."

"So what brings you all this way?"

If Paige could have killed him with her laser eyes, she would have. What was he doing?

Nate shuffled a bit, glancing at her. "Um, Paige."

The two guys locked gazes. For crying out loud, what was this? The OK Corral?

Then Josh smiled. "She's a great girl. We'll miss her."

Nate slipped an arm around her waist, a little too possessively for her liking. "We miss her back home. A lot."

Josh captured her gaze, stormy eyes locked on her face. "She's very missable."

Her breath caught, air stalled in her lungs.

Josh shifted his gaze over. "Nice to meet you, Nate. Hope you enjoy your time here."

He was gone before Nate even had a chance to answer.

She wanted to run after him, tackle him, and demand he return the piece of her heart he'd taken. *She's very missable.* After weeks of nothing, three words were it all took to turn her inside out.

Instead, she pasted on a smile and turned to the man beside her. "Right, shall we go?" Not waiting for his response, she strode through the office and down the stairs, leaving Nate to follow. The day was warm and clear as they stepped outside. "Want me to show you around a little?"

Nate gave a slight shrug of his shoulders. "Sure."

She chose the path leading in the opposite direction from the route she and Josh had walked the morning of their ill-fated conversation.

They walked for a few minutes, Paige babbling to fill the silence, naming birds, trees, wildlife, making up a few things just to have something to say.

"You probably know why I'm here." Nate cut across her awful tour guide spiel.

What was she supposed to say to that? *Yes* sounded like she'd expected him to fly halfway around the world to put everything on the line. Playing dumb would demean them and their friendship.

She sucked in a breath. "I think so."

"Are you going to tell me not to say it again?" There was a slight hitch to his voice.

She turned, looked straight into the blue eyes of the guy who had patiently loved her for years. Who deserved the best. She shook her head. "No."

A glimmer of hope flickered in his gaze. He reached out, took one of her hands, and shifted on his feet. For a split second, she thought he was about to get down on one knee. No, please, no.

He took a deep breath, then a look of horror crossed his face. He passed his other hand across his buzz cut. "I had a big speech planned. Now I can't remember a single word."

This was excruciating. She wanted to put him out of his misery, but how? She didn't even know her answer to the question she knew was coming. "It's okay. Take your time."

She needed as much of it as she could get to sort through her ricocheting feelings. Could she do this? Throw her heart into giving whatever they might have a chance? It would mean going back to Chicago as soon as she was finished here, but was that a bad thing? She'd come halfway around the world for what? To fall for the one, the *one,* guy she couldn't have because he came with a life that was her definition of a personal nightmare.

Nate was familiar. Nate was safe. Nate was home. Her family loved him. Her friends loved him. He'd been there through everything after Ethan died. He'd never asked anything more of her than she could give. What was wrong with her? Why wasn't she telling him he didn't need a speech and throwing herself into his arms?

"So." Nate took his hand back, shoving it in his pocket. "You've probably guessed from the airport and the flowers and everything that I'm crazy about you."

"They were a good hint." She smiled, trying to cut through the nervous tension buzzing between them.

"I know things haven't been easy for you for a long time. What happened in New Jersey, Ethan, things with Alex, your job, all of it. And I knew the right thing was to give you space, let you work it out, however you needed to. But Paige, I fell for you the first time I met you and the last six months have been some of the most miserable of my life. Not knowing if you'd come back or not. Afraid to open my email in case I discovered I'd missed my chance and that you were dating someone new. Wondering if there was a possibility that having so much distance between us might have made you think differently about what we have."

There been times in the last few months when the thought had crossed her mind. Could Nate be the one? Could the whole Josh thing have just been a crazy detour to get her to where she was meant be?

"So I'm here because I need to be put out of my misery. To know if there's a chance you could see me as more than just your friend Nate, or if I need to go home and try and let you go. For good." He finally lifted his head, looked her straight in the eyes. "Because this whole friends thing is killing me."

It was possibly the best declaration a girl could ever dream of. If life was a movie, this would be the point where she'd have a magical epiphany and throw herself into his arms, kissing him passionately while he swept her up and spun her around. Slow motion, wide frame.

Instead her heart was being torn in two. One half wanted to give herself to the person that made the most sense. The other half was still with the one who didn't.

Paige tried to gather her thoughts. "So this is pretty much the nicest thing anyone has ever done for me." Barring her brother giving up his life, but that would ruin the moment. "I can't believe you flew all the way here to do this. And yes, since I've been here, I have appreciated more how amazing you are and how great what we have is." Wow, could she get any lamer? This was like something from a straight-to-DVD chick flick. "But I need time to think. Not long, just overnight. This has been a big surprise. I can't just give you an answer. I need to be sure."

He nodded. "Okay."

Okay. So what now? "Do you still want to go get some lunch?"

He looked at her, then shook his head. "No thanks. I've said what I've come here to say, so I'll give you space to think about it."

Wow. She didn't know this Nate. This determined can't-just-be-friends guy.

He pulled a card out of his pocket, held it out to her. "This is where I'm staying. I'm in room 817."

She took it and looked at it. It was a hotel not far away. "Okay. I'll call you."

"What's the best way to get a cab from here?"

Paige reached into her pocket. It was empty. She must have left her phone back on her desk. "If you just head back to reception, Phoebe will call one for you."

"Thanks." He paused, then stepped forward and pulled her into a brief hug, "I've missed you." He whispered the words against her hair, then released her and walked away without a backward glance.

She watched his retreating back get smaller and smaller as he took the path back to the main office. She had a huge decision to make. One way or another, everything between them was going to change.

THIRTY-FIVE

"Wow." Kat let out a low whistle from the opposite couch. This time the tables had turned. She was the one sipping a soda, while Paige sat surrounded by empty chocolate wrappers, destroying a container of fudge brownie ice cream for lunch.

"That about sums it up." Paige dug her spoon down, extracting a big chunk of brownie.

"I have a few other words for it too. Romantic. Gutsy. Bold. Expensive. Want me to go on?"

"Not really."

"Inspiring. Breathtaking." Kat took a sip of her drink.

Page swallowed her mouthful. Loaded her spoon up again. "Not helping." At this rate, she'd be a whole new dress size by morning.

"You don't need any help."

"Come again?" Another spoonful of creamy deliciousness down the hatch.

"You already know the answer."

"I do?"

"Yes, and that's why you're here, eating your way through a bucket of ice cream, rather than

369

taking some cruise around the harbor staring into Nate's eyes."

"Bit more complicated than that." Paige peered into the carton. Oh, wow. It was half empty. Time to put the spoon down.

Kat kicked her feet up on the glass coffee table between them. "Okay, I'm going to humor you. But only because I love you. Because if I didn't, I'd want to wring your neck about now for being so obtuse." Her cousin took a sip of her drink. "What was that show we used to watch when we were kids? The one with the girl that Tom Cruise jumped on Oprah's couch for, and the guy with the floppy hair?"

"Dawson's Creek." Although her cousin already knew the answer. Those were the days, hunkered down on a Friday night, eating ice cream and loving to hate Jen for swooping in and stealing Dawson away. Not only had they spent their teen years following the Creek, between them they owned the entire DVD collection. Kat could still quote chunks of episodes.

"And who was in the eternal love triangle?"

Another scoop of ice cream. "Joey and Dawson and Pacey."

"And which one is Nate?"

"Dawson." Paige mumbled the words. Nate was one hundred percent Dawson. Stable. Loyal. Predictable. Transparent as a piece of cling film.

Kat held a hand to her ear. "Louder! I can't hear youuuu."

"Dawson."

"And who was the right guy for Joey?"

Paige sighed. "Pacey."

"Exactly."

"Except I'm not Joey, Nate isn't Dawson, and there is no Pacey."

"You're being a real pain. You know that, right?"

Yes, she knew. But only because before Kat waded in, her gut had already told her the right answer. She wanted Kat and her gut to be wrong.

"Nate is a great guy. He's generous and kind. He's stable and loves God and is crazy about you. And I know people say that marriage isn't all about fireworks and candlelit dinners and romance. But it's also a whole lot more than taking the trash out and who will remember to pick the kids up on time from Little League. I know you're still hurting from the way things unfolded with Josh, but choosing Nate because you're disappointed and disillusioned and think you're better off playing it safe is wrong. All wrong."

Paige bit her lip to stop herself from pointing out that Kat was hardly qualified as an expert on marriage, given her tendency to sabotage even the most promising relationships.

Besides, as much as Paige hated to admit it, Kat

371

was right. She stirred her spoon through the now-melted ice cream goop. "You think I deserve better than the guy who checks all the boxes but doesn't set my world on fire?"

"I think *Nate* deserves better."

Ouch. Her mouth opened, but no words came out.

"He's a great guy and he deserves to be with someone who is crazy about him. And that girl. *Is. Not. You.*" Heavy emphasis on the last three words. "So you need to give him up. Let him find the girl who is."

"What if I give him up, then realize he was the one after all?"

Kat rolled her eyes. "Seriously? Like that's gonna happen. After what, seven years? This is not a TV show where the writers take six seasons to draw out what everyone has known all along."

"To be fair, I've only been single for nine months, and I've been here for six."

"Yup. But if Nate was the one, you would've either A, worked it out ages ago and given Alex the axe long before you did or B, be with Nate right now, not working your way through a tub of Baskin-Robbins' finest."

Paige huffed and shoved the ice cream container onto the coffee table. Kat was right. She was being a pain. She wanted slap herself right now.

What she needed to do was clear. It was time

to gather all her mettle, as her grandmother would say, and do the deed. She leaned back and extracted the hotel card from her pocket. Might as well put them both out of their misery.

The large tiles of the hotel lobby blurred under Paige's pacing feet. Maybe she should have written what she wanted to say on cue cards. She was probably going to start crying and mess this horrible thing up, forcing poor Nate to interpret from her tears and flailing hands.

Her heart thundered like the *Endeavor* launching. Nate had been nothing but good to her and she was about to hurt him. Again.

Outside, the spring sun commenced its drop beneath the horizon, gray creeping over the landscape of gum trees and intersections.

She had to let him go. Let him move on. Find someone. Trying to keep things as they were was pure selfishness. She'd been that for long enough, had taken up the space in his life that should have been for someone else. Why? Because she'd found some sort of pathetic self-worth in knowing he was there, waiting for her to look his way?

She didn't care to analyze it more. Not wanting, quite yet, to confront what other ugly parts of her character she might find lurking under the surface.

"Hey." Nate's black Chucks landed in front of her.

She looked up.

"Hi." Her lip started to wobble. *Stop it, Paige. Get a grip!*

"I . . . I . . . I'm sorry." It was all she managed to get out before she choked, the tears starting. Dang it. All she had to do was hold it together for ten minutes. Couldn't she have at least done him the decency of not turning into some pathetic weeper when she was the one telling him he'd come all this way for rejection?

"Shush, it's okay." Nate pulled her into his arms, ushering her to some couches nearby.

She flapped her hands, tried to fan away the tears as she gulped in some air.

"Here, sit." He gestured at the floral-patterned couch beside them.

"I just . . ." Again, cue cards would have been excellent. She struggled for the right words. "You are so amazing, so great. You deserve someone who is crazy about you. And I am. Just not like that."

He nodded. "I know."

"You know?"

"I knew this afternoon when you told me you needed to think about it. If you needed to think about it, the answer was kind of obvious."

"Oh." Paige didn't know what else to say.

"I'm already booked on a flight out in the morning."

"Okay."

He looked resigned, but not devastated. In fact, he looked almost eager to be packing himself back into a cramped flying tube. "I've liked you for so long, it's been impossible to see around you to anyone else. I was eighty percent sure when I got on the plane this would be how it was. But I had to know for sure. Had to know that I had given it everything I had, put it all on the line. And I'm glad I did. Now I can move on, no regrets, no wondering."

"Is there someone else? Back home?" The words bypassed her brain and came straight out of her mouth.

A glimmer of a smile. "I don't know. Maybe."

She wobbled a smile. "Good. That's great. I'm glad."

He ducked his head. "We'll see. Nothing has happened. I had to do this first. Had to be fair to her."

Wow. She hadn't seen that coming. "Well, I'm sure she's amazing. She must be to have caught your eye. I hope it works out."

"Thanks. What about you?"

She shook her head. "No one."

"Not that guy I met in the office?"

Her heart constricted. "I'm not the right girl for him."

"I'm sorry."

"It's okay. It's for the best."

He shuffled, staring at the carpet for a second.

"I should go. Early wake-up call and all that." He looked up. "You get why I probably won't be in touch for a while?"

She blinked back more tears. "I get it. I'll miss you, though."

He smiled. "I'll miss you too."

They stood and he pulled her into a quick hug. "Take care of yourself." Then he turned to walk away.

"Nate?" He paused. "I'll be praying it works out with whoever she is."

He turned back for a second. "Faith. Her name is Faith."

Four hours later, Paige pushed open the front door, her shoulder straining under the weight of her laptop and the few trees worth of paper filling her satchel. It was going to be a late night making up the hours she'd lost with the Nate situation.

Faith. She rolled the name around in her head. Nate and Faith. It had a meant-to-be ring about it.

She turned to disarm the alarm but it was already off. Kat's job must have finished early. "Kat?"

Paige walked into the living area. Kat sat at the breakfast bar. "How was your afternoon?"

"Fine." Kat's voice was flat and she didn't so much as glance Paige's way. Odd. She waited for her cousin to ask how things had gone with Nate but there was silence. Even stranger.

Paige dropped her purse and laptop satchel on the love seat as she made her way across the room.

Her cousin's fingers played with the stem of a wine glass standing in front of her. An open bottle of chardonnay sat on the counter. Jeepers. Her cousin wasn't a teetotaler but this was new.

"What's wrong?"

Kat glanced at her with red-rimmed eyes then looked away. "Nothing. Allergies."

What allergies? Paige was pretty sure she would have noticed those in the last thirty-odd years. "Is it Dan? Has your father done something?" She took a couple of stabs in the dark. Kat had been remarkably tight lipped about her break up. She'd described it as "difficult but necessary" and that was all the information that Paige had managed to get out of her.

Of course it hadn't helped that between her working long hours on the tour and *Grace* and Kat bouncing between the four corners of the earth they had hardly seen each other the last month. Grabbing a soda from the fridge, she rounded the counter and perched on the stool next to Kat.

"My father is fine. As far as I know." Kat ran a hand through her hair.

"Are you missing Dan? You're allowed to. You guys were together awhile."

Her cousin slumped on her bar stool. "I don't

miss Dan at all. That's the problem. I miss Caleb."

Caleb? Who the heck was Caleb? Paige scanned her memory banks trying to place the name in connection to Kat.

"Not every day, obviously. That would be beyond pathetic. But every now and then it just hits me. Out of nowhere." Kat picked up her glass and drained the last of her wine.

Paige's memory bank finally came up with a match but it couldn't be right. There was no way her independent kick-butt cousin was pining for a guy from a decade ago. There had to be a more recent Caleb she'd forgotten about. Or hadn't known about at all.

"There was a guy on set today who looked so like him I almost thought it was." Kat gave a deprecating smile. "Which was crazy. What would a farmer be doing on a soap set in urban Sydney? But for a second I imagined him turning around and seeing me . . ." She buried her face in her hands. "I even checked out his left hand."

Holy moly. Kat *was* talking about Caleb Murphy. Everything suddenly clicked into place. Her cousin's inability to make the jump from like to love. Her seeming preference for long distance relationships. The Kevlar strength emotional wall she put up when it came to men.

Kat had never gotten over her first love.

Paige wrapped an arm around her cousin's

shoulder and Kat collapsed into her. With her other she grabbed the side of her stool to prevent the unexpected weight from toppling her over.

Paige leaned into her cousin and stroked her hair. All this time she'd thought Kat's relationship issues were the remnants of her parents' bitter divorce and her father's stand over tactics when it was the guy who long ago broke her heart.

"This is so ridiculous. He's probably married with a passel of kids by now."

Paige didn't know what to say. She'd never even met the guy. It had been ten years. Maybe more. Kat was probably right. "Want me to Google? I can Google stalk with the best of them."

Kat pulled in a breath. "Why not? Let's put an end to this insanity. I should have done it ages ago. Try Caleb Murphy Toowoomba."

"Too-what?"

"T-o-o-w-o-o-m-b-a."

Paige's fingers flew over her phone as she input the words and then scrolled through the results. The first page were links to farming articles. Then, in the middle of the second page, she paused, her stomach cinched.

"What is it?" Kat straightened up, bracing herself for the bad news.

"Are you sure you want to know?"

"Not really. But we're too far in for me to say no now."

"It's an engagement announcement. From a few years ago." Paige clicked on the link. Caleb still looked like the photos Kat had sent. Sandy blond hair, tall, weathered features. He had one of those please-just-take-the-photo looks going. Next to him a petite brunette beamed. "What do you want to know?"

"Does she look nice?"

Paige studied the brunette's open face and wide smile. "She does."

"Do they look happy?"

"Yeah." Paige put her phone down on the counter. "I'm really sorry."

Kat swiped a hand across her nose. "Me too. The stupid thing is he was right. It wouldn't have worked. I was never meant to be a farmer's wife."

Paige could no more imagine Kat milking cows and mucking out stables than she could imagine her deciding to take up dirt bike racing as a career. "You'd make anyone a great wife."

"We both would." Kat heaved a sigh as she leaned forward and screwed the cap back on the wine bottle. "Josh and Caleb's loss, I guess."

The breath left Paige's lungs. She couldn't be like her cousin. Spending years holding to a guy who had walked away. She'd wasted enough of her life as it was.

Her visa was valid for another six months. She could find another job here easily enough. But if she stayed here she knew that part of her would be hoping that Josh with his infuriating *she's very missable* might change his mind.

It was time to book her flights home.

THIRTY-SIX

"Hey." Kellie caught Josh as he was walking out of the main auditorium. They'd just had a new sound desk delivered that week—a Soundcraft Vi6. Such a beauty. He'd spent hours losing himself in playing with every button, every dial, every mix combination. He needed the distraction. Their next live album would be an acoustic extravaganza with this baby in the house.

"How's she going?" Kellie smiled up at him. She was one of the few people who appreciated the difference the between an adequate and an amazing sound desk. Not that their previous one hadn't been great, but the Vi6 was like driving a Porsche after a lifetime thinking a Toyota was sufficient.

"It's like . . ." He tailed off, unable to find the words.

She laughed. "You're hopeless."

"How's the choir coming?" He matched her shorter stride as they walked down the hallway.

"Fine. Just can't believe it's October and we're already rehearsing for Christmas."

"I know." He shoved his hands in his pockets.

Paige would be gone by Christmas. The thought struck from nowhere, catching him unguarded.

Then he realized Kellie had stopped walking. "You all right?"

She looked up at him, something in her eyes that he couldn't decipher. "Can we talk for a sec?"

"Of course. Always." He stood, waiting for her to start.

She looked around, then pointed at the door to the nearby mother's room. "Let's go in there."

Odd. But before he could process any further, she'd opened the door and was flicking on the lights.

Letting the door slide shut behind him, he stood in the middle of the room, surrounded by couches, changing tables, and baby supplies.

In front of him, Kellie paced out small circles. Her boots left small indents in the plush carpet as she walked, her long shirt making a swooshing sound. Was she sick? She'd had a few days off with the flu last week. Was it something more than that? Something worse? "You're scaring me. What's wrong?"

She stopped, then walked until she stood a couple of feet away from him. Her head just came to his shoulders so she had to look up. She opened her mouth, closed it, opened it again.

His hands settled on her shoulders. "What is it, Kel? Whatever it is, you can tell me."

She took a deep breath. "We've been friends for a long time, Josh."

He nodded. "Yes."

"And I feel like I know you well and you know me too."

"That would be accurate."

"And we make a good team."

"We do."

He was being led somewhere, but didn't know where. Paige's voice suddenly hit replay in his mind. *The girl who is perfect for your life, who loves you and only wants what's best for you? Who is always watching out for you? She's been here this whole time.*

He'd thought about her words a couple of times but shoved them into the back of his mind.

His insides seared like the time he'd mistaken a jalapeño for a pickle. Kellie wasn't going to ask him out, was she? She was pacing, clearly nervous, having trouble making eye contact.

She was everything he wanted in a wife. So what if she didn't send his pulse racing? Or turn him into an emotional pretzel, the way Paige did? There were more important things. Like compatibility. Shared goals. The same values.

Maybe God just wanted him to take a step of faith and it would all just fall into place and be right. He opened his mouth to say yes. Or why not? Let's give it a shot. See what happens. Not exactly the most romantic way to start a relationship, but great partnerships had been born from less. What harm could one dinner do?

No matter how much he tried, he couldn't get the words out. They barricaded themselves in his throat and refused to move. Until two busted their way through. "I can't." They croaked out.

They were the right words. Regardless of anything else, it wouldn't be fair to even be thinking about anything with Kellie when there was a feisty blonde American whose voice he couldn't hear without his heart feeling like it had cracked wide open.

"Kel, I think you're an amazing woman. I know you're going to make some guy really lucky, but I don't think that guy is me." His fumbled words hit the room with all the grace of a dancing rhino.

She'd stopped pacing and was frowning at him. "What on earth are you talking about?"

The way she was looking at him made him feel like he'd taken a wrong turn without knowing it. "Um. You. Me. Us"

Her eyebrows skyrocketed. "Us? What us?"

He swallowed. "I'd heard you . . ."

She held her hand up. "Okay, let me stop you there before this gets excruciatingly awkward for both of us. I'm seeing someone."

"You are?" The surprise pitched his voice a little high, making him sound like a pubescent boy. He coughed, "I mean. That's great. Good for you."

Well, didn't he feel like a complete idiot.

Her face softened. "Look, I'm not going to pretend that there wasn't a time where if you had asked me out I wouldn't have said yes. But when we were in Christchurch and I saw the way you looked at Paige I knew it was never going to happen."

He stared at her. Had it been that obvious?

She took a step closer. "Do you want to tell me what happened? As a friend? Why aren't the two of you dating? Paige told me on the flight home you were talking about it."

Josh cleared his throat. "Honestly, not really." What was the point? He'd made his decision. Rehashing it didn't change anything.

He scrambled to change the topic. Recover some dignity. "So, what was it you wanted to talk about?"

Kellie leaned against the arm of one of the couches, crossed one ankle over the other. "Oh, yeah. You need to restructure the band. It's too much for you. You need a couple of 2ICs, and I think I should be one of them."

It was a good idea and she would be one of the most obvious contenders. "You're right. I have been thinking about a new structure. I'll be talking to the board about it in the next few months."

"Good. One more thing."

"Yeah?"

"Don't ever assume a girl is asking you out ever again. It makes you look like an absolute plonker."

"Yeah, I'm really sorry about that."

She grinned up at him. "You know what?"

"What?"

"Say it with a promotion and a raise."

What a day. Josh grabbed his bag from the passenger seat as he got out of his car. He'd made an absolute idiot of himself. Proving, once again, that his instincts when it came to women were complete and utter rubbish.

He should take a vow of celibacy and be done with it.

And that suited him fine, given that every time he was allowed near a woman, he made a monumental mess of everything.

He dropped his bag at the bottom of the stairs, and wandered into the kitchen in search of comfort food. This was the kind of moment he imagined a drinking guy would crack open a beer. Or something stronger.

But he didn't and so he would settle for . . . His eyes scanned the refrigerator shelves. Leftover pasta. That'd do. Into the microwave.

He popped a can of Pepsi open and leaned back against the bench, gulping down half the soft drink while waiting for his pasta to warm up.

The microwave dinged. He extracted the bowl,

picked up his can, and headed for the family room. Sport. He needed to lose himself in some sport and not surface for a good few hours.

He didn't know where anyone was, but the resounding silence indicated he had the house to himself. He rounded the corner and slammed to a stop.

Every single adult member of his family sat in the family room, looking at him. Dad, Mum, Connor, Amanda, Sarah. Creepy.

His eyes scanned the room. What was going on? None of the women were crying, so obviously no one had died.

"Hi." Silence greeted him. "What's up?"

"Come, sit." His father gestured to the lone remaining chair. "We want to talk to you."

Josh looked around the room. "What is this? Some kind of intervention?" He meant it as a joke, but no one even cracked a flicker of a smile.

He placed his pasta on the coffee table, holding on to his can as he perched on the edge of the recliner. This was worse than the time he'd been called into the principal's office.

"What's up?" His stomach was doing a routine from Dancing with the Stars. It had been a long time since they'd had this type of family conference.

His father leaned forward. "We're worried about you."

"About me? Why?"

His mother clasped his father's hand and spoke. "Because you haven't been yourself for the last month. You've been withdrawn, reserved, brooding. You've lost your joy when you lead worship."

"Kellie's seeing someone." The words burst out of him. They were met by a collective whoosh around the room.

He scanned their faces, waiting to see the disappointment on them. Amanda, thoughtful. Connor, pensive. Both his parents looked confused. Sarah—for some reason she looked annoyed.

"I feel like I've missed something. What does Kellie have to do with anything?" His father leaned back in his seat.

"She's the kind of girl I should date."

"Says who?" His dad was using the inquiring pastor look Josh hated.

"C'mon. You all think that I should. Why wouldn't you? She's godly and talented, in the band, and knows our family, and gets what it would take to be a Tyler. No one would have to worry about someone like her ever doing anything that would cause drama."

Sarah was taking him down with the evil eye.

"Spit it out, little sis."

"You are *such* an idiot." Sarah ground the words out through her clenched jaw.

"What's so stupid about me wanting to marry

someone who's a good fit for our family, our life?"

Sarah groaned. "Seriously? Even if she wasn't seeing someone, you don't even like her."

"What would you know about who I like?"

"YOU LIKE PAIGE!" He almost dropped his drink as every single member of his family yelled at him.

Sarah was perched at the edge of her seat, looking like she wanted to take a swing at him. His mother had her hands up in the air, like she was about to tear her hair out. Connor looked like he wanted to take him outside and fight it out. Even his normally unruffled older sister was giving him a scathing look.

The only person who wasn't worked up was his father, who had leaned back and seemed to be immensely enjoying the show.

"It doesn't matter how I feel about Paige. She's not right."

"Why not?" This from his mother.

"Well . . ." All the compelling reasons he'd constructed in his head suddenly didn't seem so bulletproof. "She hates flying. I can't be with someone who can't travel."

"Actually, I heard she did better on the flight back from Christchurch." Connor stretched his legs out in front of him.

"She hates megachurches."

"Can't blame her. Most of the time I'd much

prefer to be pastoring a nice, medium-sized church." His father stretched out his legs as if he was talking about nothing more controversial than favorite pancake toppings.

"Have you even asked her why?" His mother again.

His stomach twisted even tighter. "No."

His mother muttered something under her breath that he couldn't entirely decipher, but what he could make out involved her casting aspersions on her own parenting.

"She brought the tax office down on our head, your heads." He pointed at his parents.

"So have both of us. Actually." Mum turned to Dad. "I was trying to remember how you did it, hon. What was it again?"

"Actually, I've done it twice. First time I made a joke about flying around in a private jet." He frowned. "Can't even remember what the second one was for."

"So your father and I have three between us. Would you like to evict us from the family?"

"I have a big calling on my life. I just don't think she's the right girl for it." Now he was getting terse back.

Sarah was almost apoplectic, her face turning fuchsia. "Dude, would you listen to yourself? What have you been doing? Snorting your own press pack?"

She was right. He sounded sanctimonious and

more than a little arrogant. He didn't mean it like that. Right now, he wasn't entirely sure what he'd meant.

"Son, none of us can live this life in our own strength. You're right. It's not easy, and it's public, and a lot of responsibility rests on our shoulders. The only way any of us can do this is in God's strength. That's it. The moment we start relying on ourselves, we need to get out, because it will end badly. And I hate to break it to you, but we don't need you to watch over us. That's God's job."

Ouch. "I'm like the last guy on the planet she'd want to be with."

"That's why she's perfect for you! Because she likes you despite all that stuff. She doesn't like you because you're Josh Tyler, worship leader extraordinaire, or any of the stupid hyped-up PR. She doesn't drink from the Tyler groupie Kool Aid. She hates all that stuff, and still she likes *you*. Well, she did. Until you screwed it up."

Thank you, Sarah.

"Can you at least admit you like her?" Connor ventured the question.

"I'm crazy about her." Josh ran his fingers through his hair. "I'm flat-out nuts about her. Every second of every day, I wish things could be different."

"So what's the problem?"

"The last girl I was this crazy about was Narelle."

The room stilled at the name that came with so much baggage.

"See? We all know how I messed that up. I don't trust myself not to do it again."

"You were twenty-four. You thought you were invincible. You made some dumb decisions, didn't set the right boundaries. It's all true. But you aren't that person anymore."

"After everything with Narelle, I don't deserve someone who makes me feel like Paige does."

There it was. Out.

His father sighed. "Josh, I fly loops around the world teaching about grace. But clearly I've failed if my own son doesn't get it." He waved his hands around. "None of us deserve any of this. What we deserve is eternal separation from God. What we got is reconciliation, redemption. If you don't get that, maybe you need to think about what you're doing on stage, leading people in worship."

"If you don't want to do this, then don't. The band will continue. We're not short of musicians." Connor spoke up.

Not do this? He loved what he did. Didn't ever want to do anything else.

His father leaned forward. "If you want to go be a plumber, or a mechanic, or an accountant, go forth. This isn't the family business. We're not doing this to build some sort of Tyler family empire. We're building the Church."

His father's words cut him deep in his spirit. He was a hypocrite. The worst kind. The kind that got up in front of thousands of people and sang the words, but didn't believe them, live them. Not for himself, anyway.

"What if it's too late?"

"What if it's not?" Sarah asked.

"What if she's moved on?"

"What if she hasn't?"

"What if she's with the American guy?"

"She's not." His mother butted in.

"She's not?" His heart started tap dancing.

She shook her head. "Definitely not."

"What if we all get raptured tomorrow? Or a giant comet falls from the sky and lands on our house and we all burn up in a fiery blaze of glory?" Sarah was on her feet. "Seriously, what are you still doing here?"

His father motioned to his sister to calm down. "Buddy, you need to go settle some stuff with God before you do anything else. But make it quick, because from what I hear, Paige is getting on a plane as soon as *Grace* is over. Only you know the right thing to do, but don't you dare go making yourself some kind of martyr for our sakes."

THIRTY-SEVEN

It was four-thirty in the morning. Paige stood and spun a three sixty-degree turn in her sneakers. The arena sparkled, lights twinkling like stars dotting the ceiling. At the front, huge swaths of shimmery organza dropped down, interspersed with strings of fairy lights. *Glory in the Highest* hung in huge silver cursive lettering across the back of the stage.

On every one of the ten thousand seats sat a *Grace* gift bag, placed by a team of volunteers who had worked until after midnight.

Huge screens hung on either side of the stage, with another hanging from the middle of the ceiling for the women in the upper tiers.

Through the open doors, she caught glimpses of informal seating areas designed to match the soft pastel hues in the main auditorium. Merchandise areas were accessible but discreet so attendees didn't feel like they were having product shoved in their faces. It looked . . . *incredible.*

But it was more than just the design. There was a calm, hovering presence that filled her senses, giving her confidence that all the hours of prayer were about to come to fruition, that God would use these two days to change peoples' lives.

In four hours, thousands of women would be streaming through the doors, seeing what she saw right now for the first time, feeling what she felt.

"What do you think?" Carrie, the head designer, had crept up beside her, clad in a similar outfit as Paige—sneakers, athletic pants, and an old T-shirt. Her hair was half in, half out of her ponytail, showing the effects of hours up and down ladders, driving the team nuts with her insistence on things being *just so*. It had all been worth it.

"It's . . ." Paige had to pause for a second to gather herself. "Amazing. I can't believe we made it."

"I know." Carrie offered a watery smile. "I've been doing this for years, but it still gets me every time."

Paige was wearing old clothes. Her hair was in two braids over her shoulders, wavy wisps escaping all over the place.

Josh stood in the wings of the stage and watched as Paige directed people, calm, smiling, arms full with a clipboard and a huge stack of precariously balanced papers. Pausing for a second, she attempted to blow some hair out of her face, laughing as it fell back down into her eyes.

He loved this girl. The truth hit him square in the chest with a fierceness that almost knocked him over. He'd spent the last two days wrestling with God, with his past, with his own fears and doubts and insecurities. Not wanting to do anything, take a single step, until he was sure.

He hadn't seen her until this moment. She'd been carried away by the rolling tsunami of getting *Grace* set up in the twenty-four hours from when they took possession of the arena to when the doors opened this morning. His mother had crept into the house after two this morning, dusty and disheveled like she'd been personally crawling up in the rafters hanging banners. If he had to hazard a guess, he'd say Paige hadn't slept at all.

He'd pulled into last-minute rehearsals to find musicians having creative meltdowns, and trying to navigate his relationship with Kellie. Not that she had been anything short of professional, but there had been an undercurrent that had left him unbalanced, uncertain of everything he did or said around her.

Now he stood, watching the girl he loved, the ache inside him getting so big that he had to hold himself back from leaping off the stage. He didn't want to wait another second to tell her that of all the mistakes he'd made in his life, walking away from her was his biggest. And then he'd beg for a second chance.

But he couldn't. This was her moment, not his. *Grace* needed all her attention. Doing anything to throw off her equilibrium, especially when he had no idea what her response would be, would be selfish. Besides, his mother would kill him if he stuffed it up again.

He would wait. For as long as it took.

It was halfway through day two and everything ached. Paige slipped off her flats, flexed her toes, then stretched out her feet.

The first day had been an unmitigated success, with the exception of a couple of blocked toilets. Fortunately, she was well versed in the art of plunging, and had brought multiple changes of clothes with her, prepared for any and all messy incidents that might occur.

She leaned back in the folding chair she'd placed near the offstage exit, closed her eyes, and allowed her body to relax, just for a second, as she listened to the hum of voices traveling across her headset and around the building. A vehicle blocking a fire exit needed to be moved, a restock of merchandise was being arranged, someone was on the hunt for a misplaced cell phone. The ordinary background chatter of a big event. All was well.

Behind the buzz, she could hear the rise and fall of the team leading worship, Kellie's gorgeous voice bringing people together. After this, they had another session, afternoon tea, one final session, and the conference would be done. For the ten thousand people who got to leave.

Once they were gone, the crew had six hours to strip everything back and return the arena to the empty shell it had been when they arrived.

The band moved into a new song, Josh's husky voice taking the lead. Paige opened her eyes, her gaze shifting right, through the wings and out onto the stage, where he stood, shining under the blinding stage lights. The back of his T-shirt stuck to him, the powerful lights cooking the musicians like they were turkeys in a Thanksgiving oven.

She shoved down the ache that rose within her at the sight of him and allowed the song to roll over her. In a week, her contract at Harvest would be finished. In two weeks she'd be on a plane back home. She wanted to savor every moment of this event. Even the moments that made her wish for something more.

Especially those moments.

God, please bless him. Help him find the woman who's right for his life. She managed to coble the words together in her head and force them out over the strident objections of every neuron in her brain. She couldn't say she meant them. Not yet. But she was trying.

She had plenty to be grateful for. Being able to play the violin again without being overtaken by loss. Finding some measure of peace in

Christchurch. Flying without needing to breathe into a paper bag the whole time.

She breathed out, imagining the tendrils unraveling around her soul. She'd gained a lot in the last six months. Josh wasn't the one, but someone would be. Kat was right. She just needed to trust in a master plan that went beyond the guy in front of her.

"Paige, are you there?" Her headset crackled with the sound of her food and beverage guy.

She pressed the button on the radio pack to give her access to the airwaves. "I'm here, Gerry. What's up?"

A pause. "We seem to have a bit of a water issue."

"What kind?"

"We seem to be short about three—" The line crackled then broke up. ". . . bottles for the afternoon tea."

"Sorry, you broke up, did you say three hundred?" She did the calculations in her head. That would still give them just over six thousand bottles. That should be fine. On average, they went through two bottles per woman per day, and some women accessed the water coolers around the arena to refill bottles rather than grab a new one.

"Three thousand."

Three thousand? She shoved her feet back in her shoes, stumbling to stand. That only left them with four thousand bottles. That wouldn't be near enough. They'd be at least a thousand short, probably more.

"Have we misplaced them? Or have we never had them? Have we checked everywhere? Every storeroom?" Stupid bottled water had been the bane of her life this entire job. They had to be somewhere. They had been so meticulous when taking deliveries. She couldn't believe someone wouldn't have picked up that only 37,000 bottles arrived when 40,000 had been ordered.

"Just trying to work that out. Have people looking everywhere, nothing yet."

"Where are you?"

"Catering B."

"All right, I'm on my way." She glanced at her watch. The new session was about to start. They had an hour to find them.

Josh walked off the stage as fast as he could. He was going to melt if he had to spend another second under those lights. When he met Shadrach, Meshach, and Abednego in heaven, he was going to tell them they didn't know how good they had it. At least when they were thrown into the fiery furnace, no one had expected them to perform.

He placed his guitar on the stand waiting for him just off stage, and moved to follow the rest of the band through the door into the green room.

Then he stopped, distracted by a flicker of familiar blonde hair slipping through the door leading to the bowels of the arena. He followed.

He'd spent the last day and a half watching Paige, waiting, desperate to talk to her. Instead of lyrics running through his head, it had been the incessant chant of *I love Paige, I love Paige.* He was lucky he hadn't blurted that out half-way through a song. On the flipside, whether accidentally or on purpose, she had yet to come within about fifty feet of him.

He grabbed the edge of the door as it was about to shut and bolted after her. The conference had gone flawlessly, a perfectly oiled machine. If he had to wait any longer, his heart might give out under the strain.

She was about twenty feet away and moving fast. "Paige!"

His voice bounced off the sterile white walls of the tunnel.

She stopped, then slowly turned. "What?"

Her voice echoed back at him, tired, yet sassy.

He took a couple of steps. Her hair had half fallen out of the bun it had been in this morning and now haloed around her face. Her white shirt was rumpled and streaked, and half the hem of the left side of her navy pants had unraveled.

"What, Josh?"

"Do you have a moment?"

She looked at him and tugged a piece of hair

behind the black band of her headset. "Do you know where my missing three thousand bottles of water are?"

What? "No."

"Then no, I don't have a moment. You find me a storeroom with a hundred and fifty boxes of water, and then we can talk." She rotated and kept walking.

"Wait." Wow, that didn't sound desperate. Not at all.

She stopped, spun around, and marched right back up to him. "What? What do you want from me?" She punctuated her words with a finger stabbing the middle of his chest. "What can we possibly have left to talk about?"

His mouth opened, but nothing came out. He was struck dumb by the sheen of tears that brimmed in her eyes.

She threw her arms up. "Exactly. Nothing!" She spun back around, started to storm away.

"I love you." The words spilled out of him. Worst timing in the world, throwing them out when she was in a crisis. But he couldn't— wouldn't—take them back.

She slammed to a stop, but didn't turn.

A door opened a few meters up the corridor, and someone stuck their head through. "Paige, there you are. We found the bottles."

"Great, good work." The guy disappeared as quickly as he'd shown up, but Paige didn't move. She just stood there with her back to him.

"Paige McAllister. I. Love. You." The words fell out in jagged spurts and echoed back to him. Why, of all places, had he chosen this sterile echoing tunnel?

She turned and stood there, looking at him, tears spilling down her cheeks.

"I'm sorry. I know I've been a jerk. And stupid. And pigheaded." He took a step toward her.

"Arrogant."

Okay, so she was going to make him work for it. He nodded, took another step. "Unbelievably arrogant." He had maybe two more steps until he would be close enough to touch her. "And a sanctimonious hypocrite."

She gazed at him, the flicker of a smile on her lips, fanning the hope welling inside him. Then she was looking over his shoulder, expression frozen in . . . horror?

He turned and found himself staring at his mother. His mother?

What was she doing? She was supposed to be teaching this session, as evidenced by the headset mic perched on her coiffure.

She stepped toward them, a strange Mona Lisa smile on her face. He widened his eyes, trying to send her the message, *Go, go away. Now!*

"Honey, I know I told you to make some kind of grand gesture, but—" Her mouth wobbled, as if she was trying to maintain control. She motioned toward him. "Your mic's still on."

He bit his lip to stop himself from spraying an expletive into the ears of thousands of women and wrenched his battery pack from his belt. He stared down at the flashing green light. How was his mic still on? He was always double micced for events like his, but they had the power to kill it at the sound desk. Why hadn't they?

"They tried to kill it at the desk, but either the distance or this—" His mum gestured to the concrete around them. "Meant they couldn't."

Oh.

"So I'm supposed to be teaching right now, but I'm being outshone by the fact that there are ten thousand women out there who haven't swooned so much since Patrick Swayze said, *No one puts Baby in a corner.*"

A roar suddenly rolled across them, whistling, clapping, foot stomping. Josh could barely unscramble his horrified thoughts above the din.

"So we have two options. Either we turn that thing off, or we mic up Paige and you two can have my session, since I'm pretty sure no one cares what I have to say right now."

The roar hit new heights. The concrete under his feet trembled from the vibrations coming from the main arena.

He'd lost her. This would be her worse nightmare. He'd completely lost her.

He turned around, steeling himself for the rejection on her face.

Paige was shaking her head, crying, and *laughing*.

She was laughing so hard, she was clutching her stomach, her whole body shaking as the roar kept going and going and going.

Suddenly she straightened up and walked toward him, her gaze unwavering on his. She walked until she stood on the ends of his toes, then reached a hand up. Before he knew what she was doing, she'd unwrapped the mic from around his head and was holding it to her lips. She paused, looked up at him, and unleashed a smile that almost took him out at the knees. "Sorry, ladies. He's all mine."

The roof almost came off.

The sound was deafening. She almost couldn't think. But it didn't matter, because all she needed to know was in the gray eyes staring down at her.

She flicked the button, turning the light from green to red. Then, just to be sure, she pulled the headset out of the radio pack and chucked it on the cement floor.

Josh shoved the radio pack into his pocket, then tugged her closer, running his fingers down her back, sending sparks flying to her feet. "I can't believe you did that."

The next thing she knew he'd unplugged her

headset, untangled it from her hair and thrown it down to join his. He grinned at her. "Do you have somewhere you need to be? I don't want to distract you."

She ran her palms up his chest. "Not right now. Everything is under control."

If he kept running his fingers through her hair, she'd lose all sense of reason. She couldn't, not yet. She had one thing to clear up first.

"What about Kellie? Is there any chance . . ."

His fingers paused, and he moved one hand around to tilt her chin so their noses almost touched. "There's never been anything with Kellie. She's seeing someone. And how could I ever have anything with Kel when my heart is wrapped around you?" His words were husky, his breath warming her lips.

Her fingers curled around the top of his T-shirt. "Josh Tyler."

"Hmm?"

"You going to kiss me, or what?"

He unfurled a dangerous smile at her, tugging her closer until she was melded against his chest. "Demanding much?" One hand stayed in her hair, while the other ran down her back, up her side and along the side of her face. His nose touched hers. Her breath came in spurts.

He tilted her face and leaned in, millimeter by millimeter, then brushed his lips against hers. Softly. Slowly. Until she couldn't stand it and wrapped her arms around his neck, pulling him closer as her world shattered into a thousand pieces.

If he grinned any more, his face would hurt for a month. Time disappeared while they stood in the tunnel, talking, kissing. Mostly kissing. People walked by carrying on with *Grace* business, occasionally breaking into their world with a piercing wolf whistle.

Whatever had remained of Paige's hairdo had completely unraveled, and it tumbled around her face and over her shoulders in blonde waves.

"All right, you two lovebirds." It was Connor, clapping Josh on the back. "This is all very lovely, but we've still got one last worship set. You coming?"

Josh looked down at her. He'd rather stand in this cement tunnel for the rest of his life.

"Go. I have things to do and I'm certainly not being responsible for the worship leader missing the closing session." She gave him a shove.

He smiled at her, his heart overflowing. "No, you're just responsible for him derailing his mother's final teaching session." He let his fingers trail down her arm.

"Josh Tyler, if you're not careful you are going to get me into a whole lot of trouble."

"Don't worry, we're already scheduling chaperones." Connor cut through the moment.

Josh grabbed her hand as they walked back toward the stage door. Her fingers fit perfectly in his.

The other band members were already getting their gear on and starting to walk on stage. He was still in his sweaty T-shirt from the previous session, but there was no time to change. So he tugged Paige to him for a lingering kiss. "I'll see you soon."

She smiled up at him and gave him a push. "Go."

He grabbed his guitar off its stand, and slung the strap over his head as he walked toward his mic stand.

The arena was in full uproar. He plugged his guitar in. Thank goodness the final set was always joyful, lift-the-roof-off praise. He was incapable of singing anything contemplative or reserved right now.

He glanced down at the monitor in front of him, then behind him to make sure everyone was in place. Connor gave him a wink. Amanda was grinning at him.

He strummed the opening chord. The noise was insane. Suddenly a word materialized through it all. *Paige. Paige. Paige.* But it wasn't in his mind this time. It bounced from the top of the rafters to the front row.

His mother, *his mother,* was on her feet yelling it, along with the other guest speakers.

He turned, looking toward the wings to see if she'd heard it too. She stood just behind the curtain, laughing, shaking her head in a *don't you dare* kind of way.

"Don't y'all want to worship?"

"Paige, Paige, Paige." Feet were stomping. Whistles split the room. Rafters shook.

He grinned at her. She shook her head faster, her hair bouncing all over the place. "You want to meet the girl I love?"

The chants got louder.

He tilted his head at her. "Y'all know she was responsible for pulling this thing together?"

The response had his ears ringing. The Super Bowl had a quieter crowd than this.

Paige hated stuff like this. Hated the limelight. Josh smiled at her, gesturing her to come out of the wings with a tilt of his head. She would make the worst pastor's wife in the history of the world.

But all that mattered as she stepped out of the wings and into the spotlights were the strong, steady gray eyes of the man she loved. What she thought didn't matter.

Someone else was managing the logistics of this relationship and He had impeccable credentials.

ACKNOWLEDGEMENTS

After wrestling 85,000 words into submission you'd think it would be easy to spiel off a page of acknowledgements but this part seems to get harder with every book!

As always, none of this author life could happen without the "real" Josh. Thank you for the many (many) nights that we finally manage to settle the tribe only for you to lose me to my laptop. I'm sorry about all those things you tell me that I don't even register because I'm distracted pondering the woes of imaginary people while you're talking. I love you!

Living on a book deadline while chasing three small benevolent dictators isn't possible without many helping hands. Kylie Lincoln, Ann-Maree Beard, Fiona Conway, Anna Holmes, Elise Teves, Steph Mowat and Olivia Williams have all stored up extra treasure in heaven for watching my kids, feeding my family and generally being the best author cheerleaders in the Southern Hemisphere.

Thank you to my family and family-in-love for their unceasing support. Even when I forget to tell them important pieces of information like that I have another book coming out (sorry about that, Dad!). A special thanks to my father-in-law, Steve "Hard Sell" Isaac: Chief Book Buyer of Awesomeness and #1 Word of Mouth Marketing Machine.

Every book is a whole new adventure and one that isn't possible without an amazing team. A huge thank you to Halee Matthews who was a developmental editorial ninja and was right 95% of the time, even though I hated admitting it! I'm grateful to Iola Goulton for her copy editing prowess and being close friends with the Chicago Manual of Style so I don't have to be. And I am forever indebted to Elizabeth Norman, who proof read this baby when I couldn't face reading my own words yet again and entertained me with many a dramatic Facebook message.

Jenny Zemanek at Seedlings Design is not only responsible for the gorgeous cover but an absolute dream to work with when I had no idea what I wanted and the lovely Melissa Tagg answered many a random Facebook message of "Um, so what do I do next?"

All the love to my amazing readers—especially my wonderful Street Team—whose support and enthusiasm keep me going through loooong rewrites, weeks of untangling terrible plots, and the days when it feels there are too many wife/mum/author/day job balls to keep juggling.

If I could send you all amazing New Zealand chocolate, I would!

Finally, to the One with whom all things are possible. None of this is worth anything without you. Thank you.

ABOUT THE AUTHOR

Kara Isaac is a RITA® Award nominated author of *Close To You* and *Can't Help Falling*. She lives in Wellington, New Zealand, where she juggles a day job in the public service, with a husband in ministry and chasing three small benevolent dictators. She enjoys great books, romcoms from the nineties, Mexican food and Double Stuf Oreos. She loves connecting with readers at www.karaisaac.com, on Facebook at Kara Isaac – Author and on Twitter @KaraIsaac.

Books are produced in the United States using U.S.-based materials

Books are printed using a revolutionary new process called THINKtech™ that lowers energy usage by 70% and increases overall quality

Books are durable and flexible because of Smyth-sewing

Paper is sourced using environmentally responsible foresting methods and the paper is acid-free

Center Point Large Print
600 Brooks Road / PO Box 1
Thorndike, ME 04986-0001 USA

(207) 568-3717

US & Canada:
1 800 929-9108
www.centerpointlargeprint.com